CW00369492

The Body in the Bonfire

The Body in the Bonfire

Katherine Hall Page

ROBERT HALE · LONDON

© Katherine Hall Page 2002, 2008
First published in Great Britain 2008

ISBN 978-0-7090-8591-1

Robert Hale Limited
Clerkenwell House
Clerkenwell Green
London EC1R 0HT

www.halebooks.com

2 4 6 8 10 9 7 5 3 1

Typeset in 11/15pt Sabon.
Printed and bound in Great Britain by
Biddles Limited, King's Lynn

To booksellers
most especially
Charles and Mary Groark
Sundial Books, Lexington, Massachusetts
Kate Mattes
Kate's Mystery Books, Cambridge, Massachusetts
and
Pat Robinson
Bookland, Brunswick, Maine
who were there at the very beginning

About, about in reel and rout
The death fires danced at night.

—Samuel Taylor Coleridge,
The Rime of the Ancient Mariner

Acknowledgments

Long overdue thanks to Jeanne Bracken, reference librarian extraordinaire at the Lincoln Public Library, Lincoln, Massachusetts. My thanks also to Jim Samenfeld-Specht, my Aussie guide. Thank you to the following students: Diana Davis, Adam Globus-Hoenich, and Nicholas Hein for technical and other savvy advice. As always, thanks to my editor, Jennifer Sawyer Fisher, and my agent, Faith Hamlin.

Prologue

The noose was on his pillow, the dark rope starkly outlined against the crisp linen case. It was the first thing he saw when he opened his door. He whirled around, knowing the hall had been empty, but unable to suppress the thought that a mob of crazy white men might have suddenly sprung up from the carpeting like dragon's teeth sown in mythic soil. He closed the door quietly and walked over to his bed. He had a single room. Had never had a roommate. He doubted it had been with his comfort in mind.

It was neatly done, the rope coiled expertly, each slipknot, lacking its load at present, pulled tautly to the same size. He picked it up. It wasn't a snake, no fangs to pierce his skin, sending the venom through his body. Poison. Last week for his Western Civ class, he'd read Plato's description of Socrates' death. First his feet lost feeling, then his thighs, until the hemlock reached his heart and he died. Feet first.

The rope was rough. He passed his hand along the coarse surface. But it could not bite. Not bite, but snap, and his feet would be hanging, his whole body hanging from some tree, some lamppost, some flagpole. Feet first.

He opened his bottom desk drawer and dropped the noose on top of a folder filled with clippings. He'd gotten used to those. He switched on his computer, sat down, typed in a password, and opened a file. It was a kind of diary. He typed the date:

'January 15, 2001.' Then: 'Today I found a noose on my bed.' He stared at the words on the screen. A noose. Not the carefully clipped news items slipped under the door or inside his back-pack, detailing the latest execution of some poor brother for whatever crime in Texas or some poor sister arrested for you name it in Mississippi or Massachusetts. Not the 'Nigger, why don't you go back to Roxbury?' and worse E-mails. Go back to Roxbury?

He pushed his chair away from the desk and stretched his long legs out in front of him. Maybe he could have gone back in the beginning. But it was too late now. He saw it in the eyes of the kids he'd grown up with, the unspoken accusations – 'Tom,' 'Oreo.' His mother would say they were jealous, wanted the opportunities he had, would have. He knew it wasn't that. It wasn't envy; it was betrayal. A stone's throw away from fear – and hatred.

No, he had no one to hang with at home now. He almost laughed out loud at the thought: No one to hang with at home, and here they wanted to hang him.

He closed the file, shut down the computer, and made a phone call.

A noose on his pillow. Now I lay me down to sleep ...

Another room. Another boy.

Maybe there would be a snow day tomorrow. He looked hopefully out the window, but there were no flakes falling through the beam of the streetlight. It had been a very sucky winter so far. Not much snow at all, just cold. Cold when he got up in the morning. Cold when he walked to school. Cold at school. He wore his jacket all day. He didn't have time to go to his locker anyway. Why did they even give you lockers when there was no time to go to them between classes? He carried his books around with him in his backpack. It probably weighed a hundred pounds or more. And he was still late to English at least twice a week. There was no way he could make it to class on time when it came after phys ed. English. He hated his teacher. She was young, but she acted old. Always saying those stupid 'You can, but you may not-type things when anyone asked her to take a leak. Not that anyone said 'take a leak.' He'd like to do it just once, just to see her face. They were reading *Romeo and Juliet*, which in his opinion was the stupidest play ever written. It could all have ended after the friar married them in Act II. They knew their parents were going to freak out, so why did they stick around? They should have left Verona then. Or when Romeo was banished. They had plenty of time. And the stupid friar. Why didn't he stay with Juliet? He knew she was going to wake up with those dead people, but all he thought about was his own hide. Boring. The most boring play in the world.

He stared at his computer screen. 'The Use of Comic Relief in Shakespeare's Romeo and Juliet.' He could use some comic relief right now. Honors English. He hadn't wanted to sign up for it, but his mother had made him. He knew what she was thinking: Your brother and sister took honors courses. There's no reason why you can't, too. Not if you want to get into a good college. What she said was, 'I don't want you to sell yourself short.' She sounded like his English teacher. 'Sell yourself short.' What kind of dumb thing was that to say? Someday he would show them all. Show them what he could do. And it wouldn't be long. Not if he could help it – and he could.

His hand rested comfortably on the mouse. It was better than – no, make that as good as jerking off. He clicked rapidly and changed the font of the paper title, then the type size a few times. Juliet's nurse was supposed to be funny. When the teacher read some of her lines, she actually smiled, a thin-lipped, slight-turning-up-at-the-corners-of-the-mouth smile. He failed to find the humor in it all and didn't smile, but some of the kiss-asses in the class smiled, too, or gave little laughs. Little 'I'm so cool and smart' Shakespearean laughs. He picked up the book and flipped through the pages. The nurse. He typed, 'One example of the use of comic relief in Shakespeare's *Romeo and Juliet* is the nurse.' He hit command S, then changed the margins, put everything into Geneva, and double-spaced. He did a spell check. He looked at his watch. It wasn't late. He closed the window he'd been working in.

Soon he was at a Web site. Every once in a while, he scrolled up, then back, tapping the command keys. His fingers were hot-wired to his brain, his eyes riveted to the screen.

'Dinner's ready. Come down immediately. Everything's on the table. Do you hear me?'

His mother's voice invaded his concentration. It slipped under his closed door like a subpoena. 'Yeah, I hear you,' he yelled back.

Shit. Dinnertime. He left the site and went back to his paper. An hour had passed since he'd written the first sentence. It was due tomorrow. And he hadn't written up his lab for science. That was due, too. He pounded his fist on his desk. Where was the fucking snow when you needed it?

One

'You have got to be kidding! What on earth would I teach them?'

Faith Fairchild looked across the table at her friend Patsy Avery. They had met for lunch in Cambridge at the restaurant Upstairs at the Pudding. Patsy liked the braised lamb shanks and Faith liked everything.

'You've taught cooking classes before. This really wouldn't be very different.'

'Number one, they're teenagers, and number two, they're boys. And did I mention that they were teenagers?'

The waiter appeared to refill their water glasses and they halted their conversation. Not that there was anything either confidential or shocking in Patsy's request that Faith teach a basic cooking course – Cooking for Idiots – during Mansfield Academy's upcoming Winter Project Term. Not shocking, no. But definitely surprising – and puzzling. Why did Patsy – with no connection to the school, as far as Faith knew – want her to teach a course to a bunch of zit-faced preppies?

The restaurant occupied the top floor of Harvard's Hasty Pudding Club – the Pudding, as it has been affectionately known for over two hundred years. It staged various Harvard theatricals, most notably the annual Hasty Pudding show – musical comedies affording generations of Harvard undergraduates the opportunity to indulge their tastes for outrageous drag and outrageous puns. This spacious upstairs room with its high ceiling looked like a stage set itself. Strings of tiny lights hung in spun-sugar garlands over large stars suspended from the chandeliers, sending a warm glow over the rich green walls, trimmed in crimson, of course, and gold. Framed Pudding show posters adorned the walls, and a huge gilt mirror hung behind the dark wooden bar, creating the illusion of another interior. The tables with their pink cloths and the painted gold banquet chairs were doubled, along with their occupants: professors in suits, some of the men clinging proudly to their bow ties – no clip-ons, please; Cantabrigian ladies fresh from the latest art show at the Fogg, eager for food and gossip; couples – assignations and/or business; students with trust funds – the food wasn't cheap; bearded men in corduroys and women in long, shapeless dresses with chunky amber beads who were or weren't famous writers; and herself and Patsy. Faith ended her inventory where it had started.

The water was poured. They all agreed it was a shame winter now prevented eating outside on the lovely rooftop terrace, although the room was indeed charming. 'It always makes me feel as if the Sugar Plum Fairy is going to pirouette out from the kitchen with my order,' Patsy said whimsically. She was not a whimsical person. The waiter lingered, offering an attempt at a soft-shoe instead, and more bread, both of which were refused with further pleasantries all around. He left. Faith finished one of her Maine crab cakes with red pepper aioli, which was quite tasty (but not peeky-toe crab), and was about to ask her friend what was going on, when Patsy started talking first.

'I did it last year and had a great time with the kids. My course was called What Letter Would You Give the Law? And they were bright, articulate – plus, they kept me in stitches. Their ability to see through bullshit was truly amazing.'

Patsy had given Faith the opening she needed.

'Speaking of which, why don't you tell me why you want me to do this? It can't simply be for my own pleasure, a dubious one, as I've pointed out. I'd like to keep the knowledge of what awaits me as the parent of an adolescent until the night before each of the kids' thirteenth birthdays. Teenagers may be funny and smart. They're also terrifying. Now, you have no connection to the school that I know of, other than your course, so how come this sudden desire to recruit victims for them? And I mean both the kids and whoever runs this project thing.'

Patsy dipped her fork into the rosemary polenta that accompanied her lamb. 'It's not why I invited you to lunch. I really did think we were long overdue, but yes, there is an ulterior motive behind the cooking class thing.' She raised the fork to her mouth. Years in Boston had hardened but not destroyed her New Orleans accent, and her words still came out slowly, as if each had been chosen with care especially for the listener.

'I'm glad to hear it,' Faith responded. 'Ulterior motives are my favorite kind.'

Patsy laughed, finished the polenta, and continued.

'I'm assuming you know about Mansfield—'

Faith interrupted her. 'And you're assuming wrong, counselor. Even though I've lived in Aleford for what often seems like fifty years, I've never set foot on the Mansfield campus. It could be on another planet, although there are lots of things in town that also fall into that category. I know very little about the place, other than its being all male and grades nine through twelve.'

'Okay. There isn't much more you need to know – about the place, that is – but we'll get to the situation in a minute. Mansfield isn't one of the top schools; it isn't at the bottom. It's loosely associated with Cabot – you know, the all-female school on Byford Road, going away from town. Cabot's older than Mansfield. Anyway, Mansfield started its Project Term about ten years ago to give the kids a break between midyear exams and the next semester. You can't just flake off, though. You have to keep a log of what you're doing, but what you do can be anything from learning Sanskrit to building a canoe. Faculty and people from the community – basically, anyone the headmaster can ensnare – offer the courses. Seniors can design their own. The kids make suggestions, and that's where you come in.'

'Having been raised by liberated boomer parents, these guys now see cooking as an essential life skill so the little woman won't have to come home with the bacon and fry it up, too?'

'Wasn't that a commercial? But I digress. Yes, it's a life skill whether they get married or not, but the suggestion was made by a student who, with my prodding, is more interested in having you on campus to employ your superior snooping skills than to whip up a beef Wellington. Something pretty nasty is going on at Mansfield.'

'The situation!' Faith's face brightened. At last all would be clear – or clearer.

'Dessert, ladies?' the waiter asked, offering them the menus.

'Just coffee for me,' Faith said, glad that dining at the Pudding didn't require eating Hasty Pudding, that cornmeal and molasses concoction still unaccountably relished by New Englanders.

Patsy reached for the menu.

'Don't be absurd. We'll both have the white-chocolate bread pudding with plenty of ice cream. And I'll have coffee, too.'

He left, and Patsy said, 'Can't have too much bread pudding, as far as I'm concerned. Will doesn't like skinny women, thank goodness.'

Faith laughed. Will, Patsy's husband, was as thin as a rail himself, despite a voracious appetite, especially for the care packages both their southern families sent periodically.

Dessert arrived swiftly, and Faith was glad Patsy had ordered it, if only to prolong the afternoon. Ben Fairchild, now in first grade, was in school all day. Three-year-old Amy was going to a friend's house after preschool. The afternoon was a gift of time, a rare gift.

'All right, so there's a "situation" at Mansfield. Why don't you start at the beginning. Isn't that what you lawyers always say?' Faith asked.

'Fine. The very beginning was last year. One of the kids in my Project Term class was Daryl Martin. He's a junior now. Very smart – and big dark brown eyes painted with the same brush as his very smooth skin. He's tall, well built, and runs track, so he's in great shape. All this is relevant, aside from any purely aesthetic considerations on my part. Daryl's from Roxbury. His father drives a bus and his mother cleans houses. He's their only child. I haven't met them, but it's an old sweet story. Everything for Daryl, and when he got a scholarship to Mansfield starting his freshman year, they must have been overjoyed. Unfortunately, what he's also been getting this year are racist E-mails, truly sick newspaper clippings, and, the day before yesterday, a noose on his pillow.'

Faith choked on her coffee.

'A noose! Has the school been in touch with the police?'

'No, because nobody at the school knows. Or somebody does, but he's not talking. Daryl is adamant about solving this himself, although he did call me. I went right over after work. Saw the noose, too. Somebody was a Boy Scout, a sailor, or learned to tie knots from Grandpa.'

'Why won't he at least tell the headmaster? Daryl could be in real danger. First a noose, then a burning cross – possibly with Daryl as kindling. I don't mean to sound flippant,' Faith added, 'but I think he should be treating this as a death threat and notify the authorities.'

Patsy nodded. 'I agree with you, but that's not the way Daryl sees it. He called me as soon as he found it. We became friends during the Project Term course and have been in touch since then. He's been to dinner a few times. Will thinks as much of him as I do, and Lord knows, it's good for him to see a few more black folks out here – and for us, too. Needless to say, there aren't a whole lot of students of color at Mansfield. Anyway, I went to the school straight from work and we sat in my car, away from the main part of the campus, talking for over an hour.

He didn't want anyone to see us together. Didn't want anyone to get his guard up, he said.'

She could still feel the warm air inside the car. Daryl had suggested they walk down by the pond, but Patsy told him it was freezing out – and dark. Two very good reasons to stay inside the car with the heat on. He'd taken the noose from his backpack and the folder with the newspaper clippings and the E-mails he'd printed out. She'd looked through them in silence. He fiddled with the radio, the way kids do, surfing from one channel to the next, a few notes, a few words, disjointed connections.

Now, in the rarefied air of the restaurant, as Patsy listened to herself explaining to Faith what had happened, she went back into the dark interior of the car. Cars, especially moving ones, offer unique opportunities for conversations. Not merely because of physical proximity but also because of the sense that you're removed from everything else in the world, no interruptions – especially if you've remembered to turn your cell phone off, and she had.

'Stop screwing around with the radio, you're making me crazy.'

'No problem.' Daryl smiled his slow, easy smile.

'But we do have a problem. I can't let you put yourself in this kind of jeopardy.'

'Nothing's going to happen to me,' he said, his voice rich with the invulnerability of youth. 'We're not allowed to have locks on our doors. Don't exactly understand the thinking behind this, whether it's to keep us honest and so they can think we are. Or in case of a fire – that's what the housemaster said. I push the chest of drawers against the door at night. It's the only time I don't know what's going on every minute – and who's in my space.'

'But I thought you liked Dr Harcourt. Why can't you talk to him?'

'I *do* like him. He's a decent guy. That's part of the problem. I didn't think I'd have to explain it all to you.' He sounded disappointed.

'Well, maybe you don't. Start talking, and when I recognize the tune, I'll start singing.'

She'd started singing pretty soon.

And now she was doing a reprise for Faith.

'Daryl's afraid that the moment he tells Robert Harcourt, the headmaster, there'll be all this soul-searching and "opportunities for dialogues on race" – Daryl's words – and he'll never catch the SOB – not his exact words – who did it.'

'And you agree with him?' Faith asked.

'I do, although I wish I didn't. Being a black student at an elite private school like Mansfield is hard, the way it's hard at any traditionally all-white institution. You've got to start by understanding that as a private school, Mansfield is exclusionary by definition. Students apply for admission. The school doesn't have to take you. Yes, they accept a certain percentage of minority students, but those kids – black, Hispanic, Asian – don't know whether they're there so the school can pride itself on being inclusionary, so white kids can learn about differences, or whether it's because of their own merits.'

'And this uncertainty is on top of all the other normal teenage angst,' Faith commented.

'Exactly. Daryl's on full scholarship, but not all minority students are. Yet there's an automatic assumption that all of them must be and that the school's standards were relaxed to let them in. This isn't only Mansfield, of course. It's Aleford. It's America. Visible differences mean you're "the other", "not from here", "not one of us". A black friend of mine in town has a daughter at the high school. The first day of freshman year, the girl was sent by her counselor to a meeting for METCO students – you know, that's the program that brings minorities from inner-city schools to suburban schools, starting in elementary school. When the girl pointed out the mistake, the counselor didn't believe her until she went and looked up the student's address in her file. It's the little things, the everyday racism, that grind these kids down.'

Patsy thoroughly attacked the last morsels of bread pudding on her plate, scraping it clean.

'And by the way, Daryl's had several conversations with the other black students at Mansfield and is convinced he's the only one being targeted – at the moment. It may be because he stands out, not just because of race but in sports and academics. He's also the head of the Black Student Union.'

Faith was depressed. She'd grown up in Manhattan and took the diversity of the city for granted. It was what she missed most. She worried about bringing up her kids in a town where everybody knew your name – and everybody looked the same.

'I was glad Daryl called me,' Patsy said. 'But as we talked, I realized that there wasn't a single black teacher or administrator on campus he could turn to for help. I was the only black person he knew out here. The only black adults he ever sees at Mansfield are occasional speakers – or the maintenance and kitchen workers.'

Faith knew all this. Patsy and she had had their own 'dialogues on race', but hearing it again and in this context was profoundly depressing – and energizing.

'Okay. So what's the plan?' Faith wanted to drive straight to the campus and search every room for rope.

'We had to come up with someone who could be on campus and do some effective sleuthing. I'd only be invisible at the school if I put on a maid's uniform and cleaned the boys' rooms, but since they don't have maids – one of Mansfield's rules is that the kids have to clean their own rooms – that was out. Plus, my court calendar is packed for the next few weeks. And Daryl himself was out. The moment someone saw him entering or leaving another student's room, he was sure he'd be accused of something. There was really only one choice – you.'

Faith beamed. This was the kind of praise she rarely received. Her husband, the Reverend Thomas Fairchild, tended to look upon his wife's past involvement in a series of murder cases as hazardous to her health – and, his wife suspected with good reason, hazardous to his standing in the parish. Faith knew congregations inside and out as the daughter and granddaughter of men of the cloth. Her resolve to avoid the fabric had dissolved when she met and fell in love with Tom. Seven years and two children later, she was still in Aleford, far, far from the Big Apple, her native home and previous site of her catering business, Have Faith. She had no regrets, only cravings.

'It was Daryl who came up with the idea of using Project Term to get you on campus. It gives you a legitimate reason for being there, and the cooking class had actually been suggested. He's one of the student representatives on the committee that offers and approves projects.'

'Cooking for Idiots. If I can't teach a course like that, I should get out of the business.' What had seemed like a burden she didn't even want to think about assuming was quickly becoming an exciting challenge.

'Daryl will take the course, so you'll be able to stay in close touch. He told me he has a couple of ideas of who's behind this – and it may be more than one person. Apparently, there's a very popular history teacher who has a kind of cult following. A guy named Paul Boothe. Daryl's not sure how it ties in – Boothe's an old-fashioned liberal type – but there are vibes. When you go really far left and really far right, sometimes the circle meets. Then there's the whole drug thing. Kids with money can get what they want, and out of control is out of control. He had to leave for dinner before he could go into it. You'll be able to talk to him more.'

'Okay, but there's one thing I don't get.'

'What's that?'

'I'm no Bill Gates, but I have E-mail. When you send a

message, the recipient knows who's sent it from the return address. You did say he's been getting racist E-mails, right? So why hasn't he been able to figure it out from the address?'

Patsy nodded. 'I thought of that immediately, too, but Daryl said it's really very easy to conceal your identity on the Internet. You simply subscribe to one of the free services, like Hotmail, and use an alias.'

Faith frowned. She had to learn a whole lot more about this stuff before Ben surpassed her – and he was getting close. Tom was hopeless. He'd finally given in and was using a word processor to write his sermons, but for an adventuresome spirit, he was approaching the no-longer-new technology with trepidation. As was her father, who was still writing out his Sunday offerings in longhand, wiggling his fingers and saying, 'These are my computer.' Faith thought her father should simply admit he couldn't type, but she could excuse this small affectation in a man so otherwise without pretense. Unlike these two throwbacks to the scriptorium, her mother, Jane, a real estate lawyer, had her own Web site. Faith wrested her thoughts from the information highway back to the present track.

'When does Project Term start?'

'Next Wednesday. Everybody's knee-deep in exams now. The kids have until next Monday to sign up. Daryl thinks he can maneuver some of his suspects into taking your class. I'm not sure how, but if anyone can do it, he can.'

Faith was relieved. She'd thought Patsy would announce the first class was tomorrow. Now she'd have a week to prepare – for both her Mansfield jobs.

'Niki's away, but this is a slow time of year for me. I don't know why more people don't give parties in January and February to relieve the doldrums, but they don't.'

'Too depressed,' Patsy suggested. 'I might want to be invited to a soiree during these inhuman New England winters, but I sure as hell couldn't bestir myself to give one. It's a colossal effort these dark days just to turn up the thermostat. Anyway, where's Niki? I hope someplace warm.'

Niki Constantine was Faith's assistant, and she'd announced last summer that she would be hanging up her toque for a few weeks to go someplace she'd never been before and do things she'd never done. Faith had pointed out that Niki might have trouble with the latter category, but the former would present no problem. As Niki often complained, the farthest she'd ever been from Watertown, Massachusetts, where she'd been born and raised, was to a cousin's wedding in Cincinnati. Interesting, yet not the stuff of dreams.

'She's in Australia. It's summer there. We got her first post-cards from Sydney yesterday. Mine was an oversized one with a picture of a grinning crocodile, and Niki wrote, "Haven't seen the real thing, but happy to report *have* met a Crocodile Dundee, or should say, 'Dunme.' There is nothing not to like about this place". Then there was a line or two about her circadian rhythms being messed up, since it was six in the morning Australian time and three o'clock yesterday afternoon in Boston, and how she'd misplaced yesterday and hoped the biological clock thing wouldn't mean she'd get pregnant, only her mother would be glad – marriage first, of course. Niki gets a lot on a postcard. She'd done a spectacular harbor tour, saw Tom and Nicole's house – what a perfect couple, not the Hollywood norm! – plus had time to find the Rocks, actually a shopping center where she bought an *akubra* – a hat to us. Then she must have met her bloke, because she signed off with "Why don't we have pubs?" '

'I love that girl!' Patsy exclaimed. 'She is wasted in the kitchen. She should have her own TV show. Just Niki sitting in some big old easy chair talking. I would watch it all the time.'

'I agree, except for the "wasted in the kitchen" part. I don't know what I'd do without her. I told her to take off as much time as she wanted, and apparently she is. Tom's postcard was pithy. It featured a scantily clad Australian beauty and said, "Travel is broadening. May stay awhile". The kids' cards had native flora and fauna and mentioned kangaroos. I guess you don't really believe in them until you see one, or so Niki says.'

The waiter appeared with the bill. Patsy snatched it, despite Faith's protests, and for a minute or two they went through the typical woman thing, until Patsy said, 'Just say thank you,' which Faith did and it was all over.

Out on Holyoke Street, Faith asked, 'What happens next? Do I call Daryl or the school or what?'

'You don't do a thing. Someone will get in touch with you.'

Faith sighed as the enormity of what was going on hit her hard.

'I hope I'll be able to do something. It's so horrible. The E-mails and the clippings started last fall, you said. And the noose was Monday?' Faith wanted to be sure of the timing.

'Yes. January fifteenth.' Patsy paused. 'Martin Luther King, Jr's birthday.'

'What do you know about Mansfield Academy?' Faith lifted her head up from her husband's shoulder. They were sitting on the couch before a fire. The kids were asleep, even and especially Ben. Pix Miller, her closest Aleford friend and next-door neighbor, had once told Faith that she had never thought about the fact that at some point her kids would stay up later than she and her husband, Sam, did, until it happened. Pix, possibly with a thought to cushioning blows, frequently added items to this 'Things I Never Thought to Think About' list. Not being able to walk around in underwear or anything but opaque nightclothes until they all left for college was another. Faith was treasuring these nights with Tom and planned to keep putting Ben, and later Amy, to bed at 7:30 as long as she could get away with it – sixth grade, seventh grade?

Last year, the grown-up Fairchilds had found themselves in a downward spiral. Parish duties, Faith's work schedule, and the kids were claiming all their time. Then a tragedy threatened to pull Faith and Tom even further apart. When they had almost reached bottom, they found they were actually clinging to each other, and the relief was something Faith knew she would never take for granted. Hence the blazing hearth and this precious time alone. She knew they were working at their marriage – the phrase had such a utilitarian sound – and she knew she'd never give up on the job.

Tom had poured some cognac for them, and now he took a reflective sip of the Remy Martin before answering his wife. Questions like this, which seemed to come out of the blue, never came out of the blue where Faith was concerned. Something was up.

'Sumner Phelps graduated from Mansfield.'

Faith was not surprised. Sumner was a member of First Parish's vestry, and private school was written all over his Brooks Brothers wardrobe. He had a Massachusetts accent so broad, it suggested a parody. But it wasn't. Sumner was the real thing.

'He got me invited to do a chapel talk the first year I came here, and either I bombed or they stopped using the town's settled clergy' – Tom loved the archaic term – 'because that's the one and only time I've been there. Sumner filled me in on the school's history before I went. Mansfield itself is old, but the present school is relatively young. They celebrated their twenty-fifth anniversary last year. Remember, the kids marched in the Patriots' Day parade?'

'Yes. Proper navy blue blazers, gray flannels, and striped ties. They looked like they were dying in that heat. But what's with the two Mansfields? What happened to the first school?'

'It had never been one of the big-name schools – Sumner didn't tell me this, of course – no Choate or Exeter. It probably would have drifted along with an increasingly incompetent faculty – you know the whole private school thing, especially in those days, was that a teacher should be paying *them* for the privilege of being there – plus the enrollment was dwindling and tending toward misfits who'd been rejected by better schools. But there are a lot of schools out there like Mansfield used to be that are still surviving. No, Mansfield had the misfortune, or fortune, depending on who you are, to have a financial officer who managed to deplete the endowment in a very short period of time, acquiring a very nice château in Switzerland in the process. When it was discovered – and the miscreant out of reach – Sumner and some of the other alums realized the only thing to do was put the school on the market.'

'And Robert Harcourt bought it?'

'Robert Harcourt bought it, kept the name for historical or sentimental reasons—'

'Or because it was a condition of sale,' Faith remarked, interrupting him.

'That, too. Anyway, he immediately embarked on a vigorous campaign to attract staff, students, and fill the empty endowment coffers. He was amazingly successful, according to Sumner, and it's true that Mansfield has a decent reputation now. Harcourt was smart, young, and energetic. It was the seventies, so he used all the right buzzwords, but he made it clear there wasn't going to be any of that Summerhill nonsense. Teachers have great leeway in designing their own courses, yet they're still expected to cover all the basic, and rigorous, material little Chandler will need to get into Harvard, Princeton, or Yale. Now, are you going to tell me why this sudden interest in Mansfield? They take a few day students from town, but surely you're not planning to send Ben there?'

For a moment, the idea of Ben in high school obscured all rational thought. He'd have hair on his legs – and other places. She wouldn't be giving him baths anymore, so his body, which she now knew as well as her own – or Tom's – would become a sudden mystery, along with a lot of his thoughts. His voice would change. He'd have to use deodorant.

'So?' Tom kissed the top of his wife's head, nestled conveniently close. Her blond hair, just grazing her chin in its current cut, smelled like her shampoo, her perfume, and very faintly of the lemon chicken they'd had for dinner.

Faith leaned forward and poured Tom some more cognac.

'You might want this.'

'That bad?'

'That bad.'

By the time Faith had finished telling Tom about Daryl Martin and what she proposed doing, it was very late. The fire had burned down into smoldering embers that popped unexpectedly from time to time, but neither Tom nor Faith had put another log on, even when Tom had risen in anger, pacing about the room.

'You *have* to try to get him to go to Harcourt – or the police. You and Patsy can't be responsible for what might happen otherwise. And what about his parents? Don't you think they have a right to know what's been happening to their child?'

They had been over this several times.

'You *know* that was my first thought – and Patsy's – but Daryl is seventeen. He's not a child. It's his decision. Patsy said he was even more determined that his parents not know than that the authorities not be informed. He told her it would kill them to find out that Mansfield isn't the utopia they believe it to be. Patsy is pretty sure his parents, who, she pointed out, live in one of the most racist cities in the country, have no illusions about the school. But she had to admit that it would be a blow to them. Daryl even got a little angry and said he'd hire Patsy as his lawyer and then she'd have to keep quiet. That's how passionate he is about all this.'

'I can understand that,' Tom said. 'I'm just worried.'

'So am I, but the best solution at the moment seems to be the one Daryl has come up with, and I feel I have to go through with it. If I can't turn anything up, he tells Harcourt. That's the deal.

This has been going on for months, so a few more weeks won't matter that much.'

Tom pulled her close. 'I hope you're right.'

'So do I,' Faith said, wishing he hadn't said those particular words. She touched the wooden coffee table – surreptitiously. After all, she was a minister's wife.

As they were going up the stairs to bed, Faith stopped and said, 'I didn't tell you what finally convinced Patsy to do what Daryl wanted.' She repeated his words, which Patsy had quoted to her at lunch. ' "Mrs Avery, you know as well as I do if I go to the head-master or the police, everyone will say and do all the 'right' things, but it will still be my fault. It will still be, like, none of this would have happened if you hadn't been here in the first place, boy." '

Patsy and Daryl worked quickly. The next afternoon, Faith received a phone call from the headmaster himself.

'I can't tell you how delighted we are that you've agreed to be part of our Project Term. My wife and I were at the Davidson wedding you catered last summer and it was the best meal we had all year.'

'Thank you,' Faith said. It *had* been a great meal and a great wedding – a virtually unlimited budget for an only daughter. 'I'm looking forward to working with your students.' This sounded stilted, but she didn't know what else to say. She couldn't very well come out with 'Wild horses wouldn't drag me into a roomful of teenage boys, sharp cooking utensils, and a hot stove, except I have to investigate a hate crime on your campus.'

'I wonder if you and your husband might be free tomorrow evening for our weekly faculty sherry hour? I had the pleasure of meeting the Reverend Fairchild a number of years ago when he led one of our chapel services. The faculty and students take it in turn now under my supervision. If you could make it, it would give you a chance to meet all of us and learn a bit more about our Project Term and the idea behind it.'

'I would like nothing better,' Faith said sincerely, 'and if Tom is free, I'm sure he would be happy to attend also.' She was still sounding the way she had when she'd talked to her headmistress, lo these many years ago, at her own private school in Manhattan. She pictured herself in her uniform, standing before that large mahogany desk, head slightly lowered, explaining once again why she was perpetually tardy and Hope, her sister, one year younger and living in the same apartment, attending the same school, was not. The students at Mansfield wore uniforms, too; they'd donned them for the parade. The idea was to erase distinctions – or perhaps highlight them. There was no mistaking the class where they belonged.

Harcourt was apologizing for the measly honorarium given to Project Term leaders. Faith hadn't realized there was any money involved, but he was right. It was a 'mere token of appreciation'. She could kiss the Kate Spade bag she'd been eyeing in Spade's Newbury Street boutique good-bye – for the moment.

She found herself in the absurd position of saying words to the effect that money didn't matter. To bring enlightenment to a young mind was reward enough.

It was high school all over again, and she hoped she'd snap out of it fast.

'We'll look forward to seeing you tomorrow, then, about five o'clock? Or – I've just had a sudden thought – if you could come by earlier, my assistant, Ms Reed, could show you around a bit – where you'll be teaching. But this might not be convenient for your husband.'

'I'm sure if he can't get away, he wouldn't mind meeting me later, and I would like to get to know the campus better before I start next week.' Much better, she thought to herself.

'Excellent! Then why don't you meet Connie – Ms Reed, that is – at Sutton Hall, our main offices, at three-thirty. You can't miss it. It's a large white building with pillars at the end of the central drive on the right-hand side. The sherry hour is at my house, which is across campus. Perhaps you could meet your husband at Sutton – it's easier to locate – and then Connie will bring you both over.'

The micromanagement was starting to get to Faith. She felt more than competent to find both places, but she murmured a thank-you, then a good-bye, and hung up the phone. Now all she had to do was come up with some ideas for Cooking for Idiots. This wasn't going to be a coulibiac of salmon or warm chèvre and frisée crowd. But she was damned if she was going to teach them how to make pizza. They already knew how to use a phone.

Hearing a knock at her kitchen door the following morning, Faith looked out to see who it was. No one in Aleford used the front door unless delivering bad news or invited for dinner. It was Pix. Faith quickly got up from the table where she'd been going through her recipe notebooks and cookbook collection in preparation for next week's classes to let her in.

'I was just about to knock on *your* door,' she said. Talking to Pix about what to do with these teenagers had been paramount in her thoughts ever since she had agreed to the Mansfield gig. With Mark a senior in college, Samantha a sophomore, and Danny a high school freshman, Pix was a veteran. In any case, since Faith's arrival in Aleford, Pix had been her main source for advice about living in New England, raising children, and life in general.

'I thought you might like to go for a walk. It's beautiful out,' Pix said, stepping into the room, which Faith had remodeled before the kids were born, jettisoning the avocado fridge and range – daring in their day – for Sub-Zero and Viking. She also had added counter space and cabinets. From the paucity of both, she imagined previous tenants as subsisting on tea and toast, with the occasional casserole dropped off by one of the faithful. She'd been about to offer tea and toast – Darjeeling and cinnamon – when Pix had made her suggestion.

Faith had been enjoying the January sunshine as she worked, but the idea of actually going out into it had certainly not occurred to her. For one thing, it meant putting on many layers of clothing. For another, it meant cap hair. But there was a plaintive note in Pix's voice, quite unlike her usual positive timbre.

'Sure, just let me throw a few pounds of down on and I'll be ready. Where shall we go?'

'I don't care. Not the center, though. How about Miller's Woods?'

Not the center. As she got her things from the hall closet, Faith wondered about Pix's reason for avoiding downtown Aleford. It could simply mean that Pix wanted to enjoy the beauty of nature. Miller's Woods, once owned by some ancestor of Pix's husband, Sam, and now conservation land, was a lovely spot. But her pointed elimination of the center could also mean she didn't want to see anyone, and Pix, whose family had also been here forever, couldn't walk the block from the library to Aleford Photo without running into a dozen acquaintances, all of whom had to engage her in conversation, of course.

Whatever it is, I'll know soon, Faith reflected.

And she did. Pix turned the key in the ignition of her Land Rover and it was like popping a cork from a bottle.

'I'm very worried about Danny and have no idea what to do. I'm almost at my wit's end.'

Pix was coming to *her* for advice. As soon as the universe stopped whirling about, Faith sat up straight and gathered her own not-inconsiderable wits about her. 'Tell me about it,' she said.

'Sam isn't taking it seriously at all, of course.'

'Of course,' Faith murmured sympathetically. 'What do fathers know?' She was on sure ground here.

'Exactly. And I know Danny. I know something's wrong. He had a rocky start to the year, but all ninth graders do, although Mark and Samantha seemed to make the transition with no trouble. But it isn't fair to compare the three. They're so completely different.'

'Like all families.' Again the terra was firma. Faith continued: 'I remember that Danny missed his buddy from middle school. Brian?'

'Yes, and he still misses him. For some reason, Brian's parents sent him to Mansfield as a day student, and Danny hasn't found a friend or group of friends to make up for Brian. Why you'd pay the outrageous amount of money it costs to send a child to private school when we have such an excellent high school, I cannot fathom, but it's none of my business what the Perkins family does.'

'Only it would be a whole lot better for Danny if Brian went to Aleford High, too.'

Pix pulled into the Miller's Woods parking area with a decisive turn of the wheel and stopped the car. 'It most certainly would.'

They set off down the path and Faith tried to find out what exactly Danny was doing to upset Pix this way. Danny had inherited the post of Fairchild baby-sitter from his sister, Samantha, and he was a favorite at the parsonage.

'Has he been having trouble at school?'

Pix was taller than Faith and had a long, athletic stride. She'd uncharacteristically left the dogs at home, but she was still walking as if they were tugging at their leashes. Faith felt a bit like a puppy herself, quickening her pace to keep up and panting ever so slightly. She hoped her query would give pause, and it did. Pix stopped abruptly.

'School is hard for Danny. He has to push himself a little more than the other two did. It's not that he isn't bright, but he doesn't plan his time well and he sells himself short – doesn't seek out challenges.'

This sounded like a pretty tall order to Faith, but she kept her mouth shut. She had no idea how she was going to behave when it was her turn. She doubted she'd be able to turn to Ben and

Amy and say, 'Pumping gas is a fine occupation, so long as it's work you love.'

'I know you've always had to work with him on his home-work.'

'Oddly, that's less of a problem now. Mansfield has mandatory study hours for freshmen after the end of the class day, and Danny has been going over to see Brian, which means they sit and do homework together, then walk back home.'

'How else does Danny spend his time?' Faith was beginning to feel uneasy. An isolated, perhaps depressed kid. Did Pix suspect drugs or alcohol? Samantha and Mark *were* pretty hard acts to follow.

'He spends most of his time in his room, sitting at his computer. He told Sam he's teaching himself to program – and I did find a copy of *C for Dummies* on his desk – but I suspect he's playing games more than anything else. Stupid *Star Trek* games. So pointless and such a waste of time.'

A Yankee mortal sin. 'Thou shalt not waste time.' Why it wasn't the eleventh commandment had been a much-debated theological mystery since Cotton Mather stepped in for Moses.

'But isn't this typical teenage behavior? Wasting time, I mean. When I was his age, I used to talk on the phone endlessly, driving my mother crazy. This sounds like the equivalent.'

'I suppose you're right. He keeps telling me these games are educational. Something called Riven is supposed to develop logic and problem-solving skills. He read this to me from an article – from a computer magazine, of course. That's all he reads. And manuals.'

'At least he's reading.'

'But not real books. Anything I suggest, or that he has to read for English, is automatically boring. That's his favorite word, *boring.*'

Faith again recalled feeling like this at Danny's age, and later, but it was clear that Pix had been the Pix she was at forty-some-thing when she was in her teens, too.

Pix answered Faith's unspoken thought. Obviously, it had occurred to her, as well.

'I suppose I wasn't very normal.' Pix was shredding a dried-up milkweed pod with systematic intensity. 'I didn't fight with my parents, and the wildest thing I did was go to Crane Beach with Sam and some other kids after our senior prom. Somebody had a bottle of Kahlúa we passed around.' She laughed, and Faith felt relieved. She'd been on the point of telling her friend to lighten up. Whatever the other two Miller children had been up to in high school, they'd handled – and kept to – themselves. Danny was going to be another story. Maybe because he was the youngest, the only one at home, and the focus of all his mother's attention now. Maybe just because he was Danny.

Pix's smile faded with the reminiscence. 'But I haven't told you about last night. Why I'm behaving like this – and I'm sorry to be dumping it all on you.'

Faith gave her friend a hug. 'Don't be ridiculous. What happened last night?'

'I went into Danny's room to put away his clean laundry. The door was closed. It always is – and I respect his privacy, so I knocked. He mumbled something, so I went in and was putting his things away.'

Faith made a mental note to start training Ben now where to put his clothes, and then she swiftly tuned back in to what Pix was saying.

'I looked around the room as I was leaving and something seemed different about it. I was almost out the door when I realized his stereo system was missing. You know, the one Sam's parents gave him for Christmas. He'd been hinting for months and he was over the moon when he got it. Normally, he'd have had his headphones on, I realized. I asked him where it was and he didn't answer me, just kept on typing at the computer. I went over to him and demanded he tell me where it was. First, he said it was none of my business; then he started yelling that he'd loaned it to a kid he knew. I told him to get it back immediately. Said that it was an expensive gift and should stay in his room. He stopped yelling and said very quietly that it was his and he could do what he wanted with it. Then he said, "Please get out of my room and stay out".'

'Oh, Pix, scenes like that are horrible. I'm so sorry. But you know this is just typical teenage stuff and there must be a good explanation for the stereo.'

'That's not it. Why I'm upset is because of the way he looked at me when he told me to get out. He looked ...' She stopped and tears welled up in her eyes. 'He looked like he hated me.'

'Anger, not hate,' Faith said calmly. 'He was very, very angry. You'd found something out he didn't want you to know, and maybe he has done something stupid with the stereo, lost it in a bet or whatever. Which would make him even more angry at you, because he's mad at himself.' Danny was a human being, after all, and this was the way it usually worked.

Pix wiped her eyes with one of her big Eddie Bauer down mittens. 'He didn't say a word during supper. It was just the two of us. Sam had to meet with a client. When Danny finished clearing the table, he came up behind me while I was loading the dishwasher and gave me a hug. I hugged him back and started to say something about what had happened. He broke away and said, "I don't want to talk about it. Not now or ever". I should have kept my mouth shut.'

Faith agreed, but it was most women's tendency to want to make everything all right – right away. And Pix was most women.

'He hugged you,' she said. 'He loves you. That's a given and that's what you've got to focus on; nothing else matters.'

'You're right, of course.' Pix sent what was left of the milk-weed pod skidding across the icy surface of the small pond they had reached. It stood in the middle of the woods, the trees surrounding it bare, their branches sharply etched against the cold blue sky. The ground was frozen solid; sharp ridges bordered the ruts left by the previous spring's mud. It had been hard walking over them. Faith hadn't felt her toes for some time, but she followed Pix closer to the frozen water's edge. Ben and Amy liked to come here to feed the ducks. There were no ducks now. No sign of any living creatures, except the two human beings who peered at the cracks in the pond's surface, seeking patterns, augurs to fill their separate needs.

'I'll schedule an appointment with his guidance counselor. Danny likes him. Maybe he'll have some suggestions. Losing a best friend at school is hard. They'd been together since kindergarten. We may have been underestimating the effect on him. Brian Perkins is an only child. I wonder how he's feeling?'

'Probably like Danny – who's pretty much an only child himself now, with the others away. Since Danny's spending so much time at Mansfield, it doesn't sound as if Brian's replaced him, either.'

Pix nodded and straightened up. 'It smells like snow. You know, that peculiar empty-air smell just before a storm.'

Faith didn't know. This was apparently another regional genetic knack, but she nodded sagely and sniffed deeply. Her nose was a little stuffed from the cold. Maybe that was the point. If you *couldn't* smell, there would be snow.

'I've been pouring my heart out and never thought to ask why you were on your way over to see me and why you had all your recipes spread out on the table,' Pix said. 'Do we have a big job coming up?' Pix worked part-time for the catering firm – keeping the books, going over inventory, and anything else that did not involve her in any way with the actual preparation of food. She was notorious for her reliance on boxes with the word *Helper* on them and mysterious casseroles with an elbow macaroni base.

Faith began telling her about teaching the Mansfield Project Term course and then, with a thought to her friend's current stress level, hastily decided on an edited version that omitted

Daryl Martin. Pix knew all about the Project Term, which was no surprise to Faith. Pix knew a little something – or a lot – about everything in Aleford.

'Sam did one once on fly-fishing. Someone spilled the beans about his passion for fishing – and his ability to tie flies. They couldn't fish at that time of year, but they had a grand old time watching videos, practicing casting, and, of course, tying flies. He took the boys fishing on the Sudbury River later that spring. And Millicent usually does a course on local history, except I hear she's too busy finally distributing all the stuff she stockpiled for Y2K, then held on to in the vain hope that "something" would happen when the *real* millennium arrived this year.'

Faith had seen Millicent's preparations, and it would indeed take weeks to dole out and transport all the bottled water, unspeakable freeze-dried food, and batteries she'd amassed.

'It wasn't a computer glitch she was anticipating this time,' Pix explained, 'something more in the nature of the earth opening up selective maws, a Doomsday scenario. Not exactly a Congregationalist notion, but then, Millicent has always marched to a different drummer.'

'Yes.' Faith laughed. 'A fife and drummer.'

Millicent Revere McKinley, who had been admitting to turning sixty-nine for some fifteen years, was a direct descendant of a distant cousin of Paul Revere and had total recall for both the distant past and immediate present. She wasn't too bad at predicting the future, either. A maiden lady, she lived in a white clapboard house that was strategically located across from Aleford's green, with a perfect view down Main Street. Years ago, Faith had had the misfortune to break one of the town's taboos by ringing the great alarm bell, sounded only on Patriots' Day or to commemorate the deaths of presidents or someone from one of Aleford's original families. Faith rang it in true alarm upon discovering a still-warm corpse in the belfry, but Millicent and others continued to shake their heads over this rash act. To make matters worse, Millicent had saved Faith's life, and Faith was on the point of throwing the woman in the path of the commuter train, then snatching her back just in time to even the score. Still, Millicent was a veritable font of information when she chose to turn on the tap, and Faith thought she might pay a call on her to ask what she knew about Mansfield Academy.

'Have you seen them? Probably not,' Pix was saying. They were trudging back to the car, and Faith had been so lost in her thoughts about Millicent that she'd missed a vital reference.

'Seen what? Sorry. I was thinking about something else.'

'These computer games the kids play. We can control what Danny has at home, but not what he plays outside the house. Just take a look the next time you're in Toys 'R' Us or Staples. "Animated Blood and Gore" and "Animated Violence" – that's what it said on one he wanted to buy. It was labeled for seventeen and over, but I'm sure he could have bought it. He says it's just a game, that it doesn't mean anything, but it *does* mean something. I'm not about to get an ax and start smashing computer screens – although I've felt like it sometimes when he won't even look up at me – but I think it does say something about the times we live in.'

Ben had already moved on from total devotion to Mister Rogers to an obsession with Inspector Gadget, and Faith was pretty sure Captain Kirk would be next. 'I do agree with you. It's why we never let Ben have a toy gun. Yes, it's a toy, but it's a replica, and I don't even want one of those around. He can, and does, use his finger. A finger never hurt anybody – so long as it's not on a trigger. I wish all those people who are so crazed about banning Harry Potter because it's about witchcraft would focus on these dismemberment games instead. Not that any of it should be banned, but perspective, please. I'm beginning to feel like we're on NPR. How did we get on to the First Amendment? Oh, Danny and his games.'

'It's just another of the things that worry me about him. Why would he want to play them?' Pix sounded seriously concerned.

'Power, control – all the things a kid his age doesn't have.' As she answered Pix, Faith wondered about these as a motive behind the racial attacks on Daryl Martin. Power and control, strong adolescent urges. She, like Patsy and Daryl, were assuming it was a fellow student, someone with deep-seated racial hatred, and a sick need to bully.

'And these chat rooms,' Pix said. 'He says he doesn't go into them, and I have to believe him, want to believe him, but the idea of Danny going into one and thinking he's talking to another teenager about their favorite groups, when he's actually talking to an adult masquerading as someone Danny's age, is terrifying.'

They were at the car. 'Don't worry,' Faith said. 'This is Danny we're talking about. Your Danny. Everything's going to be all right. He's just going through a hard time.'

Pix sighed. 'Maybe I'm getting old. It takes so much energy to raise kids, although when he's out of the house, I'll probably cry every day.'

'No, you won't,' said Faith. 'You'll be able to wear sexy night-gowns and play *your* music loud.'

On the way back, Faith thought about Daryl's E-mail and the explanation he'd given Patsy about how the sender could conceal his identity. Danny was a computer-savvy person and close at hand. She should ask him more about how you could do this.

'I might want to ask Danny about some computer stuff. He may read manuals for fun, but I don't. Maybe he can stop by this weekend. He knows all about the Net and E-mail, right?'

'Oh yes, or he thinks he does anyway. The Internet. I sound like a Luddite, I know, yet I do wish it wasn't swallowing up our lives so completely.'

The Net. The information highway had some pretty strange off-ramps. For a moment, Faith felt a twinge of concern about

Danny Miller. What *was* it on the screen that was obsessing him so totally?

Pix pulled into Faith's driveway and Faith started to get out of the car. She would have to go pick up Amy soon.

'I may not know how to cook, but I do know what teenagers like to eat,' Pix said. 'I'll be glad to help you with your course. I'm assuming it really is going to be for idiots. You're not planning to teach them to make puff pastry or duck à l'orange.'

'Duck à l'orange is not that hard to make, but yes, I'm only going to teach them the basics. They all know how to use a microwave to heat a Hot Pocket. I'm going to take them a step further. Maybe two steps.'

'Why don't you throw in some simple etiquette? Napkin in lap, what to do with a salad fork, that type of stuff. Again, my children may not be well fed, but they are well bred. And yes, you may use that line.' Pix smiled for the first time since she'd knocked at Faith's door. Her kids were well bred, even aside from table manners. Everything was going to be all right. Sooner or later.

'That's a terrific idea. I read in the *Times* that teaching Miss Mannering to young Wall Street hotshots and others eager to climb ladders has become a booming business. I'll end the course with an elegant but easy dinner prepared by the students and take things over from work so they can set a nice table. They can invite faculty members and show off.'

'Invite some girls from Cabot instead. More fun showing off – and not so much pressure,' Pix advised.

'Much better idea. I haven't met any of the faculty yet. The headmaster invited Tom and me to their weekly sherry hour today. But you're right – if I were a sixteen-year-old boy, I'd rather cook dinner for a sixteen-year-old girl than for my math teacher. Call me. I'd love to have your help. And don't worry about Danny,' Faith repeated. 'He's a *teenager*.'

Faith got out of the car, acutely aware of the number of italics she'd thrown into the conversation, and went into the house to thaw out. She dearly loved Pix, but she wished her friend's idea of an expedition tended more toward a stroll through Barneys in Chestnut Hill, with lunch at Figs afterward, than brisk walks with an inevitably squashed sandwich in one's pocket.

Two

At precisely 3:30, the appointed hour, a tall, attractive woman in a houndstooth-check suit, only slightly bagged out in the seat, came striding over – hand already extended in greeting – to Faith, who'd been sitting in the hall outside Mansfield's main office, leafing through outdated issues of the *Atlantic Monthly*.

'You must be Mrs Fairchild!' The woman's enthusiastic tone would not have been out of place on the sideline of a lacrosse match going into sudden-death overtime.

'And you must be Ms Reed!' Faith replied in as close an approximation as she could muster.

'Do call me Connie. Everyone does. We are terribly grateful to you for pitching in like this.'

'Oh, it's nothing. My pleasure – and please call me Faith.' Everybody didn't, but she felt compelled to match point for point. So far her contact with Mansfield had resulted only in dredging up reminders of her own school days – memories she would rather have consigned to the oblivion they had happily occupied since graduation. Connie Reed was the embodiment of all her games mistresses – they had used the British term at Faith's school – as well as every Joyce Grenfell character in the British comedies Faith had seen. Connie even had a slight over-bite. Faith's main goal in phys ed had been to avoid as many classes as possible, which won her the title 'Queen of Cramps' from her more athletically inclined or envious friends. Hope, of course, had led the school to victory after victory on all sorts of playing fields, and her name was inscribed on a number of the shining silver cups on display outside the headmistress's office. Faith had heard that Aleford High School offered such things as yoga and even walking for phys ed nowadays. They didn't even call it phys ed anymore, but wellness. She had definitely been born at the wrong time. Connie Reed, on the other hand, was born for all seasons – emerging from her mother's womb with field hockey stick in hand. The image made Faith wince and smile.

'Everything all right?' Connie didn't miss much. 'Let's be off, then. We don't have that much time. Mustn't be late for our sherry!' She gave a jolly laugh that sounded very much like a whinny. 'We'll start at Carleton House, where the course will be meeting.'

Faith trotted obediently alongside Connie, sensing that if she did not, she might feel the flick of a crop.

As she'd driven up the drive leading to the cluster of main buildings, she had been struck by the beauty of the campus – and the quiet. The school had been marked only by a discreet wooden sign suspended from a post, the entrance flanked by two ivy-covered stone pillars. The late-afternoon sun promised a brilliant winter sunset and its slanting light bathed the buildings she'd passed in a warm glow at odds with the temperature. There was a variety of architectural styles, yet they were all very much in keeping. Dropped from the sky, Faith would still instantly have known that she was at a New England prep school or small college campus. Some of the buildings were clapboard, a few Victorian, and a stone chapel sat complacently on a rise overlooking the lot where Faith had parked in a visitor's space. The buildings were set on well-tended grassy open spaces, paths lined with ancient hardwoods, their branches denuded now. Yet pressing in on this microcosm was a dark forest of pines. In the fading light, they had looked impenetrable. There were few students out, but Faith had passed several lone figures and one small group, all of them walking quickly through the frigid air, figures casting long shadows, eager to get inside.

'Our new sports center is in this direction.' Connie waved briskly to the left, where Faith could see a large building looming far away on the horizon, perpendicular to the woods. Mansfield seemed to own quite a substantial piece of Aleford – and in Aleford, as in all the western suburbs, land was at a premium, with developers paying the equivalent of the debt of a small country for lots on which to build multimillion-dollar mansions complete with great rooms, central air, and Jacuzzis in all five baths.

Connie was still urging the sports center on Faith. 'Do make time to take a peek while you're here. We're very proud of it. Our headmaster ran a marvelous campaign and actually raised more money than we needed! Mansfield has always believed in a sound mind in a sound body.' She gave a little chuckle to let Faith know that it was a cliché – but Faith didn't believe Connie for a minute. It was no cliché; it was dogma.

'Here we are.' She led the way up the front stairs and across the large porch of a comfortable-looking white Colonial house. 'This is one of our older dorms and it's not fully occupied this year, just some of our overflow seniors. That's why the kitchen is free. Normally, we'd have resident houseparents, but Professor Boothe is acting as dorm master, and he preferred the suite on the top floor. He's a single gentleman and eats his meals with the boys or elsewhere. He should be taking your course!'

Faith remembered the name. This was the history teacher Daryl had mentioned to Patsy. The one with the 'cult following'.

'He must be teaching one himself.' Faith decided taking Connie's jocular remark at face value might yield some information. It did.

'Oh my, yes, his is always one of the most popular. I believe this year he's doing something called Alger Hiss's Pumpkin:

Animal or Vegetable? Do not ask me what that means, because I have no idea. The only animals I'm afraid I have much interest in are my corgis.'

Dogs. Faith knew it.

'Like the queen's?'

Connie beamed at what she assumed must be a kindred spirit.

'I don't have as many as Queen Elizabeth, but I dare say my Bonnie and Heather would fit in quite nicely with their cousins across the sea.'

She closed the front door behind them. They were standing in an elegant foyer with curving twin staircases on either side leading to the second floor. Looking through an arch to the left, Faith could see a living room with comfortable couches and armchairs. There was an upright piano and bookshelves filled with books. A fireplace was at one end. A school banner and framed Currier and Ives prints hung on the walls. It looked like a cozy place to sprawl out and read or do homework. On the other side of the hall was another opening. This led to what might originally have been a dining room, but which was now fitted out with large library tables and several computer stations. It, too, had bookshelves. Connie led the way into the room.

'In the old days, students ate in their dorms, but when Robert, Robert Harcourt' – there was no mistaking the reverent tone – 'came in, one of the first changes he made was to have everyone eat together. Community building. The kitchen, though, is still right through here.' She opened a door.

It wasn't as bad as Faith had expected. It must have been updated for the dorm parents. There was a good-sized gas range – she hated cooking on electric burners – a large fridge, a dishwasher, and plenty of counter space.

'Do you have any idea how many boys I'll have in the course?' she asked.

'Probably no more than ten. You can always limit it, if you want.'

Ordinarily, Faith would have, but in this case, the more Mansfield students she could attract, the better.

'Ten, or even a few more, will be fine.'

She opened some cupboards and drawers. There was an odd assortment of china, glassware, and cutlery. The same was true for pots, pans, and utensils.

'I should come back when I have more time and make a list of what I'll need to bring from work,' she told Connie. She hadn't found a whisk – or any cutting knives.

'The door's always open. Come whenever you like. Now, there's a bathroom at the end of the hall, and I think that's all you need to know, unless you have any questions.'

'No, not really. I'm assuming the rest of the house has student rooms, that sort of thing.' She wouldn't have minded a peek at Paul Boothe's suite to see what was hanging on his walls and filling his bookshelves, but she couldn't think of a legitimate reason for asking. She pulled open another drawer. It was filled with pot holders and plastic spoons. Nobody had done any serious cooking in this kitchen for a very long time.

But she did have a question after all. 'Will it be all right to eat in the other room? I'm not sure we could get everyone around this table.' A Formica-topped table from the fifties and four chairs had been pushed against the wall under one of the windows.

'The big tables in the other room will be fine. Just make sure they don't spill anything on the computers. Normally, we don't allow food in that room, but you'll be there to supervise.'

Suddenly, the impact of what she'd agreed to do hit Faith with the force of a blow to her solar plexus. She'd fallen down the stairs at her grandparents' once as a child and had the wind knocked out of her. Lying on the floor, terrified, she hadn't been able to make a sound. She opened her mouth now and was not surprised nothing came out. Supervision! Responsibility! She'd been so caught up in the real reason for being at Mansfield that she'd pushed the ostensible one way to the rear.

Teenaged boys! They might give her a hard time, not want to learn what she'd be teaching, say it was all boring, make farting noises under their armpits, put straws in their nostrils, laugh uproariously when she talked about breast of chicken – the list was endless. Was it too late to back out?

It was.

'I hate to ask you to do anything else for us after you're already doing so much.' Connie's eyes locked on Faith's and Faith could feel the force of Ms Reed's so very sincere gratitude bore a tunnel straight to the lobe housing Faith's own conscience. She had agreed. It was like swearing an oath. 'It won't take long, and you might be interested to see the big kitchen.' Connie invested the last words with all the promise of a very special treat – hot chocolate *and* s'mores. 'I'd like to introduce you to Mrs Mallory, the school cook.'

Compared to what she had already so heedlessly agreed to do, this was very small potatoes, and Faith found her voice. 'Of course, I'd be delighted.'

Outside, night had fallen fast and hard, as it does in January. Faith could see only Connie Reed's face when they passed under one of the lampposts. The woman was nattering on about the school and her dogs, which appeared to occupy equal places in her heart. Faith learned that Connie had come to Mansfield after a brief secretarial stint with a Boston law firm before she'd found this, her dream job, in rural Aleford the year Harcourt resurrected Mansfield from its ashes. As her panic ebbed, Faith hoped it would be as easy to get information from everyone at Mansfield as it had been from Ms Reed – but she doubted it.

Approaching a large brick building, Connie stopped abruptly under one of the lights and cleared her throat. A slight unease was dimming her previously genial expression.

'Mrs Mallory – a wonderful, wonderful lady. The boys adore her, and of course she's a superb cook. Mrs Mallory,' Connie started again, 'apparently is a tiny, tiny bit miffed at not teaching this course herself, but it would be impossible with all her other duties. Still, I thought if she met you and perhaps—'

Faith thought, Why put the woman through any more misery? and interrupted Ms Reed. 'I understand completely. The kitchens of Mansfield, be they big or small, are her bailiwick.' Why was she speaking this way again, the way she had when she'd talked to the headmaster on the phone? She took a firm hold of herself. She'd be dashing off five-paragraph standard-form history essays soon. 'I will be happy to make nice on your cook.' That was better, although Connie looked slightly startled.

'Well, good. Good, good, good. She'll be busy with dinner preparations, but I'm sure she can spare a few moments.'

Making nice on Mrs Mallory was not easy. Bearding the dragon would have been a more appropriate way to describe the endeavor. Mrs Mallory was almost the size of one and her lair – with an enormous cast-iron stove, blackened and encrusted from many years' worth of chicken à la king, meat loaf, and tomato sauce – was as hot as dragon's breath. Connie nervously introduced Faith, and Mrs Mallory swiped at the torrent of sweat on her brow with her stained apron, grunting something that might have been an acknowledgment of Faith's existence – or not.

'Something smells absolutely wonderful. What are these lucky boys getting tonight?' Faith gushed, since she hadn't thought to bring a sword.

Mrs Mallory seemed to consider this a deeply personal question and one Faith had no right to ask.

Connie began to babble on about the length of Mrs Mallory's tenure – she was one of the holdovers from the original Mansfield – and about how they didn't know how they could ever get along without her.

Mrs Mallory's presence had so dominated the room that Faith didn't realize anyone else was there until a slender African-American woman who looked to be in her mid-sixties – impossible to guess Mrs Mallory's age without counting the rings

– opened the oven door and slid a tray of biscuits in, then retreated for another one.

'And this is Mabel. Mabel, this is Mrs Fairchild, who is here just for Project Term to teach the boys to make some snacks.' Mabel nodded and Faith took note of the emphasis placed on the words *just* and *snacks*. She also noted that Mabel was introduced only by her first name, as opposed to both herself and Mrs Mallory. *Mrs* Mallory – surely, like all those British *Upstairs Downstairs* cooks, her title was honorary. She wore oven mitts like gauntlets, so it was impossible to see if the woman by some remarkable chance was wearing a wedding band.

Faith gave it one last try. An appeal to Mrs Mallory as cook to cook. Or, more appropriately, woman to behemoth.

'I understand that you would have been doing the course, except Mansfield would have had to starve.' Smile, smile. 'But perhaps you could do a guest lecture or two – teach them to make some of their school favorites?'

Hard to tell what Mrs Mallory thought, but Connie was looking at Faith in awe.

'I might.'

The two words turned out to be the sum total of the cook's verbal interaction with Faith. Even her 'good-bye' and 'thanks' met with a mere nod.

Back outside, Faith felt a strong kinship with Connie as they let out their breath in unison.

'You were marvelous. However did you think of offering to have her come teach?'

'I have no idea,' replied Faith, who didn't. 'What was for dinner, do you know? It really did smell good. I'm sure she's a fine cook.'

'She is – although the beef liver and onions don't usually go over well. I think tonight it's chicken croquettes – "mystery balls", the boys call them. They really are naughty.'

They laughed together as they walked toward the headmaster's house, and Faith realized it would be a big mistake to stereotype Connie Reed as a straitlaced old maid. She'd been at a boys' school for over twenty-five years and she knew her students – naughty and nice. The question was whether she knew anything about what was going on with Daryl – and if she did, how would she react?

Seeing Tom, sherry glass in hand, standing before the fire in Robert Harcourt's living room had all the appeal of an oasis in a desert, a Saint Bernard with a keg of rum, an island as the life raft's logs split apart. Faith was very glad to see her husband.

The man next to him stepped forward. He was tall and must have been very handsome in his salad days. He remained attractive, despite a hairline that had receded from what was surely a more rounded face than that of his youth. His eyes were very blue and the hair that was left – still a healthy crop – was blond. When he greeted Faith, his handshake suggested a firm tennis grip. His brightly polished blazer buttons displayed a crest. A quintessential WASP. Robert Harcourt, the headmaster.

'Ah, Mrs Fairchild. Welcome. I've been having a delightful chat with your husband, and we're all so pleased you could make it.' Every word rang true. Robert Harcourt was always, she suspected, in earnest, dead earnest. It was abundantly clear why Daryl Martin had opted for Patsy – and Faith.

'Lovely to be here,' she replied, taking a glass of sherry from the tray being handed around by Connie Reed and then moving closer to both Tom and the fire. She could be earnest, too.

The warmth of the hearth was short-lived, however, as Robert Harcourt diligently shepherded the Fairchilds around the room, introducing them to the faculty. Hors d'oeuvres of a type Faith was used to from her years in Aleford were set out on various pieces of furniture in the Harcourts' living room. Nice pieces of furniture, Faith noted. Real Sheraton and real Chippendale, not Ethan Allen. Robert must have inherited them. He could never have afforded them on a headmaster's salary. Although, she realized, since he'd been able to buy the school, he no doubt came from money.

It was quite a beautiful – and luxurious – room. Not at all what she had expected. The floor was covered by an enormous Sarouk, its colors picked up by the heavy rose damask draperies at the windows and subtle Brunschwig & Fils fabric on the couch. The artwork was an eclectic mix of Hudson River School and more modern landscapes. Faith was startled to see an entire wall covered with extraordinary Russian Orthodox icons. The wall itself had been painted a deep crimson, and fiber-optic lighting, partially concealed in the molding, illuminated the jewel-like hues and gold leaf below.

Unfortunately, this exquisite taste had not extended to the cuisine. No caviar. just the usual Wispride and Triscuits, carrots and celery strips, and, perhaps in Faith's honor, sautéed chopped mushrooms rolled in slices of flattened white bread, then cut into pinwheels. She knew them all. The faculty seemed intent on drinking the sherry as quickly as possible so as to guarantee a refill, while decimating what food there was, perhaps in the hope of skipping the mystery balls on tonight's dinner menu and making do with an egg on toast or something similar later on.

They looked much like teachers everywhere. All sizes and shapes – but not colors in this crowd. There was the intellectual group, the women still clinging to their long hair, despite a preponderance of gray; the men holding on to their beards – these badges of youthful rebellion and optimism in the sixties. Several green canvas book bags were piled in a corner of the room. If there was singing – and there was a baby grand next to the French doors, which presumably led to a patio – one of them would surely suggest 'Where Have All the Flowers Gone?'

Then there were quite a number of well-preserved specimens close to retirement age, the men in Harris tweed sports jackets, the women in Lanz wool dresses from Talbot's – attire that had stood the test of time. Some of this group had devoted their lives to teaching for the joy of it; some were putting in their time, due to lack of imagination or energy, until they could reasonably cash in their TIAA-CREFs. Faith wondered how many of the staff had been ousted when Robert Harcourt took over. As he introduced them, it soon became apparent that most of the women in this group were faculty wives, not faculty.

But which one was Mrs Harcourt? Connie Reed had been passing the drinks – and no doubt counting them. It seemed odd that the headmaster's wife was not doing the honors as hostess – at her husband's side to welcome guests. Perhaps she wasn't even in the room. Out of town – or so fed up with sherry hours that she was having a martini upstairs and watching the news.

'This is Paul Boothe. Paul is in our history department and lives at Carleton House.'

Boothe was one of the young faculty. They formed their own distinct group. No one was dressed in jeans. Mansfield had a strict dress code. The boys wore jackets and ties – with the option of a V-necked sweater or turtleneck underneath in the wintertime – every day except Saturday afternoons, when there were no classes, and Sundays, after a mandatory but, the catalog stressed, nondenominational religious service in the chapel. There was an oxymoron in there somewhere, Faith had noted when she read the brochure. Paul Boothe looked as if he would have liked to be wearing jeans, pressed jeans, well-cut jeans, but jeans. Jeans with his crisp snowy white oxford-cloth shirt. He'd taken his jacket off. He wore suspenders – red suspenders. His dark black hair curled Byronically at the nape of his neck. But the perhaps coveted image of romantic hero had been blighted by his acne-scarred face and the thinness of his lips. And he was not a muscular hero – slight and not very tall. His face was as white as his shirt. He looked like someone who had avoided natural light for most of his life. He wasn't actually repellent; in fact, there was a strange magnetism in his appearance – Mannerist

School. Most of his charismatic appeal – and it was easy to see how susceptible his students might be – came from his eyes, which were almost violet and put in, as the Irish say, with a muddy finger. They dominated his face.

'I'm not overly interested in food,' he said, shaking her hand with the tips of his fingers.

Faith was tempted to reply that she was not overly interested in history, especially kitsch history, as the title of his course suggested it to be, but she knew that it would make her look like a philistine in present company – and besides, it wasn't true.

Tom jumped in. 'My wife's food is the equivalent of the siren's song. You may find yourself looking for wax once the smells start drifting your way.'

Surprisingly, Paul laughed, heartily. 'I just might have to at that. Good to meet you both.' His head swung around at the sound of someone entering from the hall. He moved quickly in that direction.

'That was so sweet, darling,' Faith whispered in her husband's ear. It was nice to have someone who would leap to your defense this way. And there was no question about Tom's interest in food. At thirty-three, he was still a big hungry boy and seemed to burn up his calories before they even entered his metabolic system.

'Good. My wife's arrived,' Robert Harcourt commented, looking past the Fairchilds, 'She was, uh, unavoidably detained. Good, good, good.' Had Robert picked this up from Connie or vice versa? In any case, Faith was sure that if she spent much time in their company, she'd hear the repetition a lot. Robert had also rubbed his hands together. These weren't traits she wished to assume.

'Can you forgive me?' A sultry voice, with a slight Russian accent, filled at the moment with deep regret. And there she was – a bird of paradise scattering the drab mud hens, her plumage and song drawing every eye and ear. The headmaster's wife.

'I am Zoë, Zoë Harcourt, and you are, of course, the Fairchilds, since I know everyone else in the room for centuries. The traffic was a nightmare.' She smiled. The fire seemed to burn brighter. Faith was intrigued, not by her grammar, which seemed like an accessory, but by the woman's entire presence. How could Faith have lived in Aleford all this time and not heard about Mrs Harcourt? Mrs Harcourt – dressed at the moment in a shocking-pink silk sheath with an immense royal blue pashmina shawl draped around her shoulders, a shawl that she rather dramatically tossed as she walked toward them, revealing a hint of cleavage. She teetered ever so slightly on her Manolo Blahnik slingbacks, and the only jewelry she wore, apart from some impressive stones on her fingers, were heavy gold Tiffany Schlumberger earrings. Sherry hour? Sherry-Netherland hour was more like it, and Faith wondered what on earth this exotic creature was doing sequestered in a staid New England prep school with Mr Chips. It was unlikely that Zoë Harcourt had anything to do with the Daryl Martin matter, but Faith resolved to find out all she could about the woman.

It wouldn't be hard. Zoë loved to talk – and, as was soon apparent, loved to talk about herself.

'Normally, I would not be in this cruel climate now, but my plans changed, so here I am.' She tucked one arm through Faith's, the other through Tom's. At least we'll both smell strongly of Shalimar, Faith reflected.

'I am sure Robert has introduced you to everyone.' Zoë lowered her voice and whispered in Faith's ear, 'Each and every last boring one. But I am being too mean. They are not all so bad.' She laughed and pulled them toward the wall with the icons. She took her arm away from Faith but kept a firm grasp on Tom, gesturing toward one icon in particular – a Madonna with huge soulful almond-shaped eyes, looking out from a gem-studded frame. 'From my mother's family. They fled from the Bolsheviks, carrying only a few of their treasures. My grandmother used to tell me stories of the old days. Visits to Tsarskoye Selo, poor Nicholas. He gave her the Order of Saint Catherine.' Zoë sighed theatrically. 'Such a sad end to such a beautiful time.'

It hadn't been very beautiful for most Russians, especially the peasants starving in those so very picturesque villages and the soldiers starving in the nightmare at the front, but Faith kept her mouth shut. It was a performance, after all. She stepped back and almost collided with one of the elderly faculty members – a tall man with a shock of white hair. He was grinning in a conspiratorial manner.

'Our lovely Zoë. Definitely makes life more interesting here. Always has. But do not be deceived, my dear.'

Noting Faith's surprised expression, he hastened to add, 'Oh, the icons are real enough. Some of them superb. Mrs Harcourt has excellent taste and a good eye, but the only things Zoë's ancestors ever brought to this country were empty pockets. Granted, they filled them quickly enough. My name is Winston Freer, by the way. I teach English. Most particularly Shakespeare, as in "It's junior year, so it must be Shakespeare and Freer".'

He was really very sweet, Faith decided, and his courtly manner was quite appropriate to his subject matter.

Zoë had moved on, Tom in tow, to examine one of the landscapes.

'My name is Faith Fairchild. I'll be teaching a cooking course during your Project Term.'

'Oh, we know all about you. This is a very, very small community. Word gets around. No secrets here.'

But there was a secret. A very big secret, and as Faith listened to Professor Freer's advice about how to be firm with the boys, she gazed about the room. A number of the faculty had left. It was getting close to dinnertime. Those remaining were standing about in small groups, talking. They did this every week. Surely they must get tired of the command performance, the enforced collegiality. It had made sense to assume that whoever was attacking Daryl was a fellow student, yet there was no reason to make that assumption. It could just as easily be one of the faculty. One of the faculty, a twisted bigot. One of the faculty in this very room.

Faith and Tom were almost the last to leave, much to Faith's embarrassment. Never arrive first or leave last was a credo of hers. But Zoë had spirited Tom away for a 'real drink', some vodka, and a look at more of her treasures in another part of the house.

'Here we are, darlings,' announced Zoë, addressing the remaining stragglers. 'Where does the time go?' She flashed a dazzling smile at them. 'Call me, Faith, and I'll come teach the boys how to make a fabulous Stroganoff,' she said, then she was gone. No polite excuse or explanation. She simply left the room. But of course, Zoë was the type of woman who never apologized or explained.

As Faith was musing over Mrs Harcourt's behavior, Connie came bustling up – the flip side of the coin.

'Would you mind quickly filling this form out? I meant to give it to you before we left the office, but I was eager to squeeze in a visit with our Mrs Mallory and thought I could give it to you here.'

'Certainly.' Faith reached for the paper and pen Connie proffered. Much more important to placate the cook. She glanced at the form. It was a boilerplate disclaimer: If Faith managed to scald herself with hot water or one of the boys tripped her when she was carrying said pot or anything else untoward happened on the school grounds, it would be no never mind to Mansfield. They also needed her Social Security number.

Finally outside in the freezing night air, the front door closing firmly behind them, Faith took Tom's arm and drew him close. 'I don't think we have to go to any more of those, not being real faculty.'

'Good God, I hope not. Once was enough.'

'What about the charming Mrs Harcourt?' Faith asked teasingly.

'The charming Mrs Harcourt has an overabundance of hormones. But,' he added, laughing, 'if I were to go back, she'd definitely be the reason.'

Faith agreed. 'What were her etchings like?'

'Etchings? Oh, the things in the other room. Not etchings at all, but some rather nice Russian bibelots – Fabergé type, and each with a poignant story. Maybe we should go next week, so you can hear about Cousin Dimitri and poor, poor Sasha.'

They were walking toward the spot where Tom had parked.

'How old would you say she is?' Faith asked, knowing full well she could go to sherry hour for the next twenty years and never be invited to see Zoë's treasures. 'Robert Harcourt has been the headmaster here for twenty-six years and he'd been a teacher and administrator for some years before that in Connecticut. So say mid-fifties. But Zoë doesn't look that old.' Faith wasn't jealous of Zoë – it wasn't just a matter of age, although the words *older woman* took on a new meaning when applied to Mrs Harcourt. But not Tom's type at all. Faith was Tom's type.

'I'd say late forties, but I'm sure she'd change forties to thirties. I'm also sure a lot of her vacations have been to the plastic surgeon. I hope you never go that route. I like a woman with wrinkles, especially if I have them, too. Look at my parents. They match.'

This was true. The elder Fairchilds could almost be brother and sister. Yet, they had started out looking completely different – a redhead and a brunette, one with a high complexion, one with cheeks of ivory. Now both were always slightly tanned from working in the garden and both had hair that had gone completely white. Faith had no intention of either accepting crow's or any other feet on her face or looking like her husband. But they'd cross that bridge when they came to it. Or rather, she would, then double back.

'They could never have furnished that house on a headmaster's salary. One, or both of them, must have money.'

Tom nodded. 'Money to buy the school in the first place, and although I'm not an expert on these matters, I'd say Zoë's frock wasn't from Marshall's.'

Faith was amused – amused by the whole conversation. Fortunately, Tom, despite his collar, was a good gossip and not above discussions of extremely secular matters. And he was right – the dress wasn't from Marshall's. Not unless Chanel had misdirected a shipment to Saks lately.

They were at the car.

'Jump in, honey, and I'll take you to your car,' Tom offered.

'It's just beyond the next building, and I'd really rather you got home. I promised Danny we'd be back before seven, and it's getting late. I left dinner for him and the kids, but I don't want him to have to cope with bedtime. You know how hard it is to find baby-sitters, especially ones who live next door.'

'You're sure? It's cold,' Tom said.

'Good for me,' Faith called over her shoulder as she strode off.

'We'll make a New Englander out of you yet.' Tom's voice was barely audible over the noise of the engine, but Faith heard him.

'What an idea,' she murmured. It would be like a sex change.

She reached the parking lot and noticed that the car in the space behind hers was running. She could see two dark silhouettes, heads close together, in the front seat, and as she passed the driver's door, she smelled cigarette smoke drifting out of the slightly cracked window. Smelled cigarette smoke and something else.

Shalimar.

Three

Carleton House was completely empty. Faith hadn't expected a red carpet, but she had thought there would be someone to greet her at the first class. Connie with an attendance sheet or Daryl. She'd arrived twenty minutes early to set up for the class and had been glad of the lack of company then. But now, thirty minutes later, at ten minutes past nine, when Cooking for Idiots was supposed to start, she was puzzled, and slightly annoyed. If there had been a change, why hadn't someone called her? Maybe no one had signed up? But as of Monday, there had been ten kids enrolled. What had happened over the next day? Had she gotten the time wrong? No, she was sure Connie Reed had said nine o'clock.

The front door opened and banged against the wall. A breathless voice shouted, 'Mrs Fairchild? Are you here?' Faith went through the dining area into the foyer, almost colliding with a young black teenager.

'You must be Daryl,' she said.

'I am and get your coat. I'll explain while we're walking. I didn't think you'd want to miss this.'

Faith grabbed her coat from the coatrack and hurried after him.

'Miss what? Where is everybody? What's going on?'

Daryl Martin smiled. It *was* a beautiful sight. Patsy had described him accurately. His deep brown eyes seemed to melt into his smooth skin. He was tall and moved with the grace of an athlete. His well-shaped head was defined by a thick tangle of dark hair, cut short.

'At the end of breakfast, just when everybody was getting ready to split for their projects, the headmaster comes running in and announces that there's an all-school emergency meeting in the chapel at nine-thirty.'

'Do you think it has anything to do with what's going on with you?'

'That was my first thought, too, but I didn't see how he could know anything about it unless you or Mrs Avery said something, and I was sure you hadn't.' There was no mistaking the emphasis he put on those last words, that implicit warning for the future.

'Then I thought it was probably the usual,' Daryl continued. 'He'd found a joint someplace or an empty beer can. Project Term is a little – very little – looser than school usually is, so I figured he wanted to read us the riot act and set the tone. He's a big one for setting the tone. But I was wrong.'

They were almost at the chapel and boys were continuing to stream in.

'So what is it?' Faith stopped. Once they were inside, Daryl would have to sit with his class, while she made herself as inconspicuous as possible in the rear.

'Somebody's ripped off something from Mrs Harcourt and she's bullshit. Wants to address the school. Have everybody turn their pockets inside out.'

'How did you find out?'

'Went into the kitchen and asked Mabel. In the kitchen, they know everything that goes on in the school. Well, maybe not everything, but a lot. And Mabel's always been very good to me. One of my people.'

Faith nodded. 'I met her – and Mrs Mallory.'

'Now, she is definitely not one of mine, and I'm not sure she's one of yours, either. Some kind of whole separate race thing going on there.'

Faith laughed. It had been less than five minutes, but she knew why Patsy was so taken with Daryl and why she had agreed to help him on his own terms. If the situation weren't so deadly serious, she might even describe herself as having fun. Someone had stolen something from Zoë and Zoë meant to get it back. It should be quite a show.

'Meet you at the class. We don't know each other, remember. I'll stay after and we can talk then.'

Faith nodded and thanked him loudly for informing her about the schedule change. Connie Reed rushed past her, uncomprehending, flushed and obviously upset. Efficient as she was, it obviously hadn't occurred to her that Faith would be cooling her heels at Carleton House. Whatever was missing must be significant, Faith thought. Daryl disappeared into a sea of bobbing heads and chatter. The whole school was excited. She slipped into a seat at the rear of the chapel and kept her coat on. It was cold in the chapel – cold as only an old New England stone edifice in January can be. There were no pew cushions – too unmanly – and the chill seemed to travel straight from the depths of the frozen ground through the slate floor, up the sides of the mahogany pew, and directly into every bone in Faith's body, starting with her coccyx.

Robert Harcourt stepped forward to address his flock. There was instant silence.

'I have called you all here together due to a most grave matter, and it saddens me that we are to start our annual Project Term with a dark cloud hanging over us. Someone in our community is a thief.' He paused and directed his gaze like a searchlight over a prison yard upon each and every face. 'Mrs Harcourt is missing several items of great value – and I need hardly say that the sentimental value is the one that most concerns us here today. They belonged to her family and—'

'My grandmother! My grandmother's pillbox.' Zoë leapt from the high-backed chair near the altar. A moment before, she'd been immobile, sitting slumped over, the picture of woe, wrapped in an enormous shearling, as if she'd just stepped in from the steppes. Now she was the picture of rage.

'I want them back. You're all to look for them. Some boy' – these last words were spoken in a death knell, her accent more pronounced, her voice almost a baritone – 'some boy has taken them from *my* house to sell for a fraction of what they're worth to buy who knows what. Invaded *my* house!' She raised her arm and shook her velvet-gloved fist. 'But you are to find them. I had photographs, fortunately, and you will study the copies.' She was really, really scary. The expressions on the faces Faith could see were easy to read. This wasn't like Mom and Dad pulling a nutty over a broken curfew or a *D* in French. This was Mount Saint Helens, Mount Vesuvius, Mount Zoë.

Robert stepped up and put his arm around her, guiding her firmly back to her seat. He proceeded as if the interruption hadn't occurred.

'The objects belonged to family members of Mrs Harcourt's and, although worth some considerable monetary amount, would be very difficult to dispose of. The police have copies of the photographs and are circulating them throughout the area. We have also posted copies on all dormitory and classroom bulletin boards. There is one in each of your mailboxes.' Faith had a sudden image of Connie racing around the campus with a staple gun and an armload of posters. The whole episode was somewhere between high drama and comic opera, music by Mussorgsky, film by Eisenstein.

Robert Harcourt's sonorous, slightly ecclesiastical voice continued on. His calm tone was in marked contrast to his wife's, but the effect was much the same. An implied threat – retribution, hellfire. Faith forced herself to listen to his words and ignore her thoughts.

'But I have complete confidence in the kind of community we have here at Mansfield. It may have been an impulsive act. In fact, it must have been an impulsive one, and I'm sure whoever gave in to this weak lapse will feel all the better for returning the objects. And if you happen upon them and are not the culprit, you do not have to tell me where you found them – unless you wish to, of course. Simply restore them to me and we will assume that the act will never be repeated. But I want to make one thing absolutely clear. We cannot survive in an atmosphere of distrust and suspicion. I will not tolerate this kind of behavior. Therefore, I want this matter settled immediately. The items are to be returned by dinnertime. A note slipped into my mailbox or under my door, telling me where they are, however you wish to handle it. Now, please rise and we will sing the school anthem.'

Zoë didn't move from the Niobe pose she'd resumed, and Faith almost toppled over as she stood up. She'd lost all the feeling in her right foot and most of what was in the left.

Beneath the chords of the rousing hymn to Mansfield, Faith picked up a comment or two from behind. She couldn't be sure who was speaking, though.

'Don't remember this much of a fuss when someone swiped McCord's Palm Pilot.'

'Amen.'

'What makes Harcourt so sure it was someone from the school? Couldn't it have been an itinerant tramp?'

Faith peeked over her shoulder at this notion and saw the remark had come from one of the older faculty wives. In all Faith's years in Aleford, she had never laid eyes on an itinerant tramp, or a tramp of any kind, unless you could count Cindy Shepherd, but it wasn't nice to speak ill of the dead. Yet the notion was sound. Why was the headmaster so sure Zoë's treasures had been pilfered by one of the boys?

She had her answer sooner than she could have imagined. As she joined the orderly and subdued throng leaving the chapel, someone tapped her on the shoulder.

'Not showing our best side, I'm afraid.'

It was Winston Freer, the Shakespeare professor.

'I suppose theft is always a problem in any school,' Faith said. 'But I'm puzzled why the Harcourts are so sure the culprit was one of the students. Surely there are people coming and going all the time on campus who may even have seen the things through a window – meter readers, delivery people. Wouldn't one of the boys have been more apt to steal money than pillboxes and icons, or whatever it is Mrs Harcourt is missing?'

'You are embraced by the gift of logic, Mrs Fairchild. I myself would have assumed the same had I not been apprised of the situation during the department heads' meeting in Robert's office early this morning.'

He smiled, and for a moment Faith wondered if that was that. Perhaps the headmaster had enjoined them all to secrecy. Fortunately, he hadn't – or Winston didn't care. He was clearly enjoying the situation.

'They found a button. Too, too Conan Doyle. One expected Robert to announce from the pulpit just now that the criminal was five foot ten, with a mole behind his left ear, and had recently suffered a cold.'

'A button?'

'A very distinctive button, to be sure. From a Mansfield blazer. It must have been hanging by a thread, a navy blue thread, and *plop*, there it was on the floor, complete with the manufacturer's initials on the back. A thoughtful clue, don't you think? It would have been foolhardy for our Zoë to be so accusatory otherwise. Parents don't care for that sort of thing.'

'Probably not,' Faith replied somewhat vaguely, since her mind was racing in quite another direction. How very convenient. A button at the scene of the crime.

'Well, I must leave you here. My path diverges. You must come for tea soon. An old man such as myself longs for new faces.' He smiled and so did Faith.

'Thank you. I'd like that.'

'I have a small cottage, not far from the lake. Anyone can tell you where. Now, about this other matter. The boy will be caught soon and/or Zoë's precious trinkets returned. Perhaps not by dinnertime. Robert is a bit optimistic, I'd say. But there are always boys who will squeal on other boys, and the thief himself may break down. As Will put it so aptly in *Henry the Sixth*, "Suspicion always haunts the guilty mind; The thief doth fear each bush an officer". Now, I must away.'

He left, his dark green Tyrolean coat fluttering slightly behind like a cape. Faith quickened her steps toward Carleton House. She'd had a sudden thought. If you really hated someone, hated him enough to send a steady stream of vicious bigotry his way, wouldn't framing him for a crime like this be the next step? She had to get to Daryl before the class started and send him back to his room to check his school blazers.

Button, button – who's got the button?

'Are any of you Daryl Martin?' Faith asked, addressing the small group of boys who had already arrived and were assembled in the kitchen. Thank goodness Daryl *was* there.

'I am.' He stepped forward.

'Good, I understand that you are my student liaison. Since I don't know Mansfield, I'll be relying on you to tell me how to find my car again and what to do when the oven sets off the smoke alarm, as it's bound to do. Perhaps Ms Reed told you?'

Daryl picked right up on it.

'Yes, I'm your guardian angel. Anything you want to know.'

The other boys had stopped talking when Faith asked her question but now had resumed. A couple of them were studiously examining a color Xerox of what Faith assumed were the missing goods. It was easy to draw Daryl away and quickly tell him what she had learned from Professor Freer. He was out the door immediately, ostensibly in search of a campus map for

Faith. He was gone for about fifteen minutes, but Faith had still not started when he returned. Several of the boys were late, arriving with apologies – and almost all of them clutching the wanted posters.

One of the latecomers rushed in, started to speak, and then stood shock-still.

'Mrs Fairchild! I didn't know you would be teaching this course! Um, I mean, hey, that's great.' It was Brian Perkins, Danny Miller's friend, and from the glum look on his face, Faith's presence was anything but great.

'It's good to see you, too, Brian. I think you'll have a lot of fun and you'll be able to impress your friends and relatives with your advanced culinary skills.' Over the years, Faith had gotten to know Brian through Danny and the two had jointly baby-sat a few times, taking the kids to the playground or the green. Brian had been a roly-poly kid with a ready grin. He'd shot up and slimmed down. The grin was in hiding. If he was unhappy at Mansfield, Faith would have thought the sight of a familiar face would have brought a remnant of his cheerful expression to the fore. Why had he been so dismayed to see her? What else was in hiding? It wasn't as if she knew him well enough to embarrass him in some way. She wasn't carrying any pictures of baby Brian lying bare-bottomed on a bearskin rug. The boy had seemed genuinely upset, though. One more complication in a place that was fast becoming as puzzling as Rubik's Cube.

Daryl walked into the room and gave her a surreptitious thumbs up, accompanied by a sewing motion.

She'd been right. Her enthusiasm for teaching Cooking for Idiots fell as fast as a soufflé after a slammed oven door.

Faith looked around the kitchen of Carleton House at the boys standing in various typically adolescent postures – heads down, heads up, a leg twitching, a finger tapping, a hand immobile. Two, whom she pegged as ninth graders, based on a paucity of facial hair, were noticeably flushed and excited, an indication of the brouhaha just raised in the chapel. The rest of the faces were clothed in studied nonchalance. Daryl's face, too, was a mask, a mask she imagined must be a familiar one for him – self-effacing attentiveness. Protective coloration. Only one boy seemed totally at ease and relaxed. He wasn't moving, yet there was a suggestion of movement about him, a great and vital energy. He was extremely handsome, Apollo Belvedere by way of J. Press. During Project Term, the school's dress code was somewhat relaxed. The boys didn't have to wear jackets and ties, although they could if they wished. Most had elected to wear turtlenecks under a V-necked sweater with the Mansfield crest. But there were subtle differences, and Faith was reminded of the way she and her friends had sought to assert their personalities, individualizing the school uniform by pushing the accessories envelope – barrettes, knapsacks. The same was true at Mansfield, and Faith was quick to note that the paragon wore a gold signet ring and a Rolex. His nails were manicured and he wasn't getting his shining blond hair cut at the Aleford barbershop.

Another boy stood out. The chip on his shoulder was almost visible, and if the school had permitted body piercing and tattoos, he would have sported them. His dark green school turtleneck was much too large and was untucked. His nails were bitten to the quick and he wore a curious silver ring with a highly impressionistic skull etched on the surface. Any barber could tend to his coif, which was as short and close to his head as he could get away with here. Each of the two boys had carefully crafted an image, and the messages were clear: winner and loser. And the loser, Faith was sure, would say not caring about winning was what it was all about. She sensed she was going to be learning a lot more than she wanted to know about the murky teen waters of the twenty-first century.

'Let's get started, shall we? I certainly won't make you wear name tags, but please go around the room and give me your names so I can check them off this very official list.' One had been left, of course, by the efficient Ms Reed. 'And I may even remember them by the end of the course.'

On the assumption that all boys this age were hungry all the time, she'd brought oversized chocolate chip and oatmeal cookies, with milk, plain and chocolate, to go along with them. The food was disappearing rapidly as she called roll and briefly outlined what they were going to do.

'There's no magic to cooking; only magic in eating.' She paused. It was a nice line. She'd have to try to remember it to tell Niki, who appreciated this sort of thing. She missed her assistant. The latest postcard from Australia was of a beach and had only two words on the back: 'Boogie boarding!'

'We aren't going to have as much time today as I'd hoped.' She paused again, and only the two ninth graders showed any reaction. They both turned bright red and looked guilty as hell. Highly suggestible. The others nodded politely in acknowledgment of the time constraint.

'Therefore, I'm going to get right to it. We'll start at the beginning – breakfast, which can also be brunch, and even dinner, if you're so inclined.'

'Like those diners that serve breakfast all day and night,' one boy offered.

'Exactly. One of the main reasons to do your own cooking is that then you can make what you want to eat when you want to eat it. I've prepared a rough outline of what we'll be covering, with all the recipes, plus a table of measurements and a glossary of a few essential cooking terms. We'll also spend some time on "gracious living" ' – she hoped they could hear the quotation marks – 'such as which fork to use at a dinner party and what to do if you spill spaghetti sauce on your date. We'll conclude with a dinner party of our own, and I'd like you to think about whom to invite. I understand some of the Cabot girls might not mind sitting down to a meal prepared by the opposite sex. It could give them hope for the future.'

'Hear, hear,' a tall, skinny boy with wire-rimmed glasses and too much chin called out.

'Okay, now please count off and we'll divide into two groups for today.'

The boys obligingly started to count. Before they got to the end, Faith noticed the boy with the Rolex, Sloane – a name she knew she wouldn't forget – slipped behind another to make sure he was in the second group. Why? She quickly looked at all the boys in the first group. Whom had he wanted to avoid? Some long-standing quarrel – or was it Daryl? Daryl, who had counted off 'One' when it was his turn?

There were ten boys, creating two manageable groups.

'I'm starting you off with pancakes. You get the egg lecture tomorrow, when we have more time. Today, it's good old-fashioned pancakes – with some additions, if you wish. Of course you can buy pancake mix, but by the time you add an egg, liquid, and shortening, you might as well make them from scratch.'

'My Dad calls pancakes "flapjacks",' commented a boy whose voice was in the process of descending from the attic to the basement.

'Flapjacks, griddle cakes, batter cakes, pancakes – they're all the same, and each part of the country has some special variation. In Rhode Island, they eat johnnycakes, which are pancakes made with cornmeal. The Native Americans made them first, of course, and the settlers must have been happy to have something to add to their dreary diet, especially after they also learned from the local tribes how to tap the maple trees. We have maple or blueberry syrup today. The important thing to remember about syrup, besides getting the real thing, is to warm it. There's nothing worse than a stack of steaming-hot pancakes dripping with cold syrup.'

The boys were smiling – some with genuine anticipation, one or two, Faith was sure, in self-congratulation – literally a gut course, with only a log to keep. And Faith had made even that easy by providing her little booklet.

'Both groups' – Faith pointed to both sides of the room – 'are going to make the basic batter; then we'll use one to make apple pancakes and one for plain ones.'

Soon the room was filled with activity as the two groups measured and sifted, broke eggs, poured milk, melted butter, and stirred.

'You can add chopped nuts, blueberries, or replace the whole milk with buttermilk.' She showed them how to test the griddles on the top of the stove by pouring a few drops of water on them. The water sizzled and she demonstrated the way to make a well-rounded pancake by pouring the batter from a spoon held close to the griddle's surface. Soon they were all giving it a try and watching eagerly for the bubbles on the uncooked side to appear before flipping them over.

'How's this?' The boy with the skull ring, whose name was Zach, expertly flipped a pancake into the air. It landed perfectly back in place.

'Show-off.' Faith couldn't tell who'd said it, but there was no mistaking the tone. She quickly said, 'I think we have a ringer here. Where did you learn to do that?'

'I washed dishes in a restaurant kitchen last summer and the cook showed me a few things.' He was scowling.

'That's great. Restaurant kitchens are like no place on earth. The pace is frantic – a whole world apart from the calm dining room only a few feet away. Even a different language.'

'Like Adam and Eve on a raft?' Daryl said. 'Two fried eggs, sunny-side up, on toast, right?'

'Right,' said Faith. 'And don't forget, Adam and Eve on a raft – wreck 'em'

'Scrambled!' Zach exclaimed, smiling, before he remembered he was supposed to be presenting a different image and the scowl returned.

'Zach, show me how to flip these. I want to impress my

mother next time I'm home,' Daryl said, moving over to the stove. He passed in front of Sloane, who took a step back.

'Excuse me,' Sloane said with exaggerated politeness.

'Well, excuse me, too,' Daryl said with guarded amiability.

He was just past Sloane when the boy remarked, 'I'm surprised you haven't already attained this pancake skill.'

Daryl turned around, eyes narrowing. 'What are you talking about, Buxton?'

The room grew quiet and the boys who had been setting the table in the other room returned, their radar infallible.

Faith had opened her mouth to speak – a word about silver-dollar pancakes, crepes, anything – but Sloane Buxton smoothly answered Daryl. 'Nothing much. Just had the impression you liked to cook. That's all.'

Of course it wasn't, and the shadow of Aunt Jemima was as clear as if Sloane had traced her kerchief-headed silhouette in black paint on the kitchen wall. The table-setters drifted back. Faith handed the warm platters, filled with pancakes, to several boys and they all prepared to break bread together.

By the time they'd cleaned up and talked about what they wanted to get out of the course – one of the ninth graders wanted to learn how to make baked Alaska; most of the rest had riffed on the themes of quick, edible, and impressive – class time had run out. Sloane was the first to leave, giving Faith a polite compliment on the class and thanking her for giving up her time to teach 'a motley and ignorant bunch such as we are'. He seemed so sincere and was truly so lovely to look at that she wondered whether she'd been wrong about the interaction she'd witnessed. Maybe he did merely think that Daryl liked to cook. Daryl, in fact, did, and he had promised to give Faith his grandmother's recipe for smothered pork chops.

Zach Cohen departed quickly also, tucking his shirt in before he left. Aside from these two, none of the boys had stood out particularly.

Faith had arranged for Tom to pick Amy up. It had been a busy couple of days and there had been no time to get back to Mansfield to check out what was in the Carleton House kitchen. She'd brought everything they needed for today's class, as well as some staples, which she started to stow in the canisters she'd noted when she'd been here with Connie Reed. Daryl had gone off with the others, but she wasn't surprised when he returned through the back door of the kitchen.

'Well?' he said.

'Well?' she replied.

He sat down, pulling a stool from the corner. Unlike those of some of his classmates struggling with various dermatological vicissitudes – there had been a distinct smell of Stridex in the air – Daryl's face was unblemished and smooth. His appearance reminded Faith of the other handsome boy in the group.

'If I had to pick someone,' she said, 'I'd go for Sloane Buxton. But Zach Cohen has neo-Nazi written all over him. Perhaps written a bit too boldly to be taken seriously.'

Daryl nodded. 'Can't figure Zach out. His freshman year, he looked like all the rest of us – not me, of course, but the standard-issue Mansfield young gentleman. Came back in September looking like this. Something very heavy must have happened over last summer. I've never had any problem with him. He's a total techie, and I like that stuff, too, but he mostly keeps to himself. He is one of my suspects, though, and I steered him toward the course, which wasn't hard after I heard he'd worked in a restaurant kitchen.'

'He seems like a very angry boy, and you're right – it could explode in your direction. What do you know about his family?'

'Nada. As I said, we were never that close. And anyway, it's not the kind of thing guys talk about usually. I don't know much about anybody's background here, except that it's definitely different from mine. And' – he smiled ruefully – 'so far I haven't been invited to meet Mommy and Daddy at the condo in Aspen or the family's summer place in Newport.'

'Sloane projects that image for sure,' Faith commented, wondering if she was also going to start sprinkling her conversation with 'likes'.

'He lives on the North Shore. I do know that much – and he always looks the way he did today. Perfect. Something weird about him, though – aside from his obvious belief in the superiority of the white race. But in that department, he's always very careful. If I called him out, say on the pancake business, he'd express polite surprise and suggest that whatever the problem was, it was my problem, not his.'

'Anyone else I should keep an eye on?'

'The tall kid with the wire-rimmed glasses, John MacKenzie – a senior – is the leader of what we call the Boothe Brigade. Again, it's just a feeling I get. Mr Boothe talks like a liberal, but some of the kids who hang on to his coattails are a little strange. John was going on about Herrnstein, *The Bell Curve* guy, in psychology class before exams and the whole notion of intelligence being genetic – code for race-related. There are certain words, certain names that always make me sit up and take notice. And they were all coming out of this kid's mouth. Now he may just be in love with the sound of his own voice – a lot of Boothe's kids are like that – and not paying much attention to what the words actually meant—'

'Or it could be something more,' Faith finished for him.

'Exactly. I've really been looking at the kids here hard, even before the noose thing – back when the E-mails and articles started coming. It may be someone I haven't thought of, but at least these three give us a place to start. Or I should say, you. Sloane and John both live here in Carleton House, which makes it convenient. John, obviously to be as near as possible to the master; Sloane because he snagged a great room. Zach is in my dorm, but it's not far. It won't be hard for you to slip into their rooms during lunch, or, if you don't mind getting up early, when we're at chapel.'

'You have chapel every morning?' Faith was surprised.

'It's not usually as interesting as it was today. Mrs Harcourt was something else, but yes, we meet every morning for announcements and Dr Harcourt's words of wisdom. Sometimes a student is in charge or one of the faculty, but usually it's just the headmaster with an inspirational thought or three.'

It struck Faith that Daryl was very articulate himself – and a good judge of human nature. If he felt these boys were the ones they should start with, she was sure he was right.

She had a question. 'Why is John taking my course and not Boothe's? I would have thought he'd naturally want to sit at the master's feet and absorb his wisdom.'

'Good point. But you know these teachers like Boothe. It's supply and demand. Now Boothe creates demand by keeping the supply very select. His courses are both the hardest academically and hardest to get into on campus. It's like your parents have to sign you up at birth, and when you take one, you have to do nothing but Boothe work. To get into the Project Term course, you had to write a ten- to twelve-page essay on what you could contribute and what you could get out of it.'

Faith was amazed. 'He must be putting something in the water. I can't imagine all these kids doing this. So John had had enough and didn't do the essay?'

'Wrong' Daryl grinned. 'John did the essay. Sweated bullets over it, I hear, especially as it was during exams. Boothe didn't announce the course topic until then. No, John wasn't tapped as one of the elect.'

'He must have been furious. And what a sadistic way to run a course. Talk about separating the sheep from the goats, or is it lambs from the sheep? I never can remember.'

'More like men from the boys here. But John wasn't mad. Professor Boothe makes the losers feel like it's an honor even to be considered. That's what I mean by this cult stuff. It's like that old movie with Svengali. He showed it in class once.'

'So you've taken his class.'

'Two of them. Guess I must think or look right.'

'What about Sloane Buxton? Is he one of Boothe's followers?'

'That guy only follows himself. Besides, he could never get in. Not the brightest bulb on the tree where academics are concerned. Too smart by a mile otherwise. Kind of lazy, besides, when it comes to work. Always happy to buy a paper.'

Faith had known people like this during her school years.

'Yet he is in Carleton House, and so is Boothe. It could mean something.'

Daryl nodded gravely, then said, 'Or nothing.' He jumped up from the stool. 'I thought of one thing you could look for in their rooms. Check to see if they have last year's yearbook and turn to the pictures of sophomores. One of the clippings I got had my picture, my yearbook picture, pasted over the dude being arrested. Whoever did it is going to have an empty spot in his yearbook. I've already checked the library's and the copies in the yearbook office. Now, we just have time for a quick tour of the campus before lunch ends and everyone will be around.'

'Connie Reed already gave me the Mansfield tour.'

'Ah yes, but not the tour of the Mansfield students' campus.'

Worlds within worlds. And at Mansfield, there were many. Daryl provided a running commentary and Faith began to feel as if she were in someone's 'excellent adventure'.

'Starting right here at Carleton House,' he said, leading her to the back stairs and up three flights to the attic, 'we have one of the favorite fair-weather smoking lounges.' He reached behind an old wooden file cabinet and produced a key, with which he unlocked a door leading to a flat roof surrounded by decorative brickwork. The snow that had drifted against the door made it hard to open all the way, but Faith got the picture. 'There's one of these on either side of the main peaked roof, and as you might imagine, it's the perfect spot for all sorts of activities. Most of the regulars have their own keys, thoughtfully handed down to someone in the younger generation after graduation.'

It was the perfect spot, high enough to escape detection from the ground and secluded from the rest of the house.

'What about Mr Boothe? Doesn't he live just below on the third floor?' It would be relatively easy to avoid the houseparents' quarters on the first floor, but surely Paul would hear kids going up and down the stairs.

'An opera buff – headphones on whenever he's not teaching or promulgating. Plus, I don't think he'd really care so long as no one pitched over the side, although there have been some near misses, I've heard.'

'Drugs, alcohol?'

'Both and sex and rock 'n' roll.'

Faith wished she didn't know so much about being a teenager. She and Tom had vowed the instant she knew she was pregnant with Ben that they would lie their heads off when their wee babe grew old enough to ask about his parents' activities at various points in their lives. It would be 'Do as I say' all the way. She planned to adopt the same attitude with Daryl and let him assume she'd spent her adolescence in a convent.

'Where do the kids get the stuff?'

'Second half of senior year is when the campus really buzzes – literally. Seniors can have cars then, and most do. Other times, people are always going home for weekends when it's not vacation. Plus, there are the day students.'

The day students! Faith remembered the look of dismay on Brian's face when he saw her – and everything Pix had said about Danny came rushing back. What had these two boys gotten themselves into?

Daryl continued the catalog. 'Then there are the Cabot girls. A dealer or two over there. You know, when you've just got to have that Abercrombie sweater and mean old Pops won't buy it for you.' He laughed. 'Am I disillusioning you? It's not all the kids – or even most.'

'No, you're not – and maybe that's what's making me feel bad. I wish you were. But lead on, Macduff. What next?'

'You didn't have Mr Freer, obviously. It's "Lay on, Macduff", but no matter.' He chuckled. 'You should have seen the guy when we did *Othello*. He didn't know where to look, and I swear few classes have ever whipped through that play so fast – or so superficially.'

'Does this happen a lot? Teachers uncomfortable when a race-related topic comes up?'

'Yes and no. The ones I like are the ones who neither go out of their way to avoid it nor emphasize it. Those are the worst – the emphasizers. To them, I am the house Negro, the spokesman for my entire race. "Now, Daryl, what are your thoughts on affirmative action?" Or the ones who make sure I know they've read everything Richard Wright ever wrote but who then explain he just doesn't fit into the curriculum as well as John Steinbeck, Ernest Hemingway, or some other white guy. I don't care! Just let them be honest about it all.'

They were walking rapidly toward another dorm – Daryl's. It was newer than Carleton House and larger: a square stone building with Doric pilasters on the front, vaguely reminiscent of a bank. On each floor, the rooms lined the corridors on either side, Daryl told her. His was on the second floor, Zach's on the third.

'Can't get to the roof here,' he pointed out as they passed by. It was shingled with copper and sloped sharply.

The campus was deserted, but glancing at her watch, Faith realized it wouldn't be for long.

Daryl saw her movement. 'You're right, but I want you to know the layout. We'll be quick. This path leads to the lake.' They walked briskly; ancient rhododendrons towered above them, their leaves palsied with frost.

'Give me your map and I'll mark the other places kids go when they don't want to be found. The new sports center went up right over one of the old favorites, I've heard – almost like Harcourt knew what he was doing. But with a campus this large, it's impossible for the faculty to keep an eye on us all the time. Especially late in the day, between the end of classes and dinner. Off-campus faculty are leaving; on-campus faculty have had enough of us. And the security staff is a joke. One of them was caught smoking dope with a kid last year and he got booted out, but the kid managed to stay. He was a senior and only a week from graduation. Lame. Very lame.' Daryl appeared to be considering the frailties of his fellow students. He looked at Faith in mock seriousness and pointed straight ahead. They had reached their destination. 'You have to hope they never drain the lake. There's probably a few stories of empty beer cans at the bottom.'

If there were, the ice gave no sign, smooth except for a few holes cut for ice fishing. It was a beautiful spot. The trees had been cleared on the side where they were standing, but the rest of the shore had been left unmanicured. Cattails and tall grasses gave way to towering pines.

'What's all this?' Faith asked, pointing to piles of wooden crates and assorted tree limbs not far from where they were standing. It seemed an unlikely location for Mansfield debris.

'The makings of a bonfire. A humongous bonfire. One of the Project Term traditions. We all sit by the bonfire drinking hot cocoa, warm in front, our asses freezing. It's pretty cool, though. You should come.'

'When is it?'

'Sunday night.'

It might be fun for the kids, Faith thought. It would also give her another opportunity to be at Mansfield.

Daryl gestured toward the fuel for the bonfire. 'Maintenance totally gets into it. They're the ones who build it with the senior class each year, although I can't say that everybody participates. Mostly, it's the jocks and preppies like Sloane and his buddies who seem to feel the need to erect something really big.'

The allusion was not lost on Faith, and she laughed. They were walking back toward the main part of the campus.

'For the maintenance guys, it makes a change from the routine; plus, they get a chance to get rid of all sorts of crap. They save the really good stuff all year, like those crates. The new pianos for the music department came in them.'

Suddenly, there were boys on the paths everywhere, running, pushing, shouting. Pix's unerring nose had been right and there had been a snowfall over the weekend. Not a major No'theaster, but enough for snowballs, and they were whizzing through the air now. Faith and Daryl parted ways, and ducking a snowball, Faith returned to Carleton House, finished stocking the larder and taking inventory, then put on her coat to leave. The temptation to begin her search was overwhelming, and she was just about to creep up the back stairs, ostensibly in search of a bathroom – she'd removed the toilet tissue from the one downstairs – when Sloane Buxton entered the hallway.

'I was looking for a bathroom. The one down here seems to be out of supplies,' she said quickly, uncomfortably aware of the two rolls of Charmin in one of the zippered tote bags she'd used to transport what she'd needed for the morning's class.

'I've been taking an inventory and stocking the larder. It seems no one has used the kitchen in a while.'

Sloane Buxton had not expressed any surprise at seeing Faith still there, nor had he questioned her, but she found herself rattling off explanations in a disjointed and highly unprofessional way. It was Sloane who appeared to be the calm and canny sleuth, not Faith. He reminded her of her friend and sometime partner, Detective Lt John Dunne of the Massachusetts State Police, who could get more information by not asking questions than anyone Faith knew. He simply kept his mouth shut, and after a while you would say anything to fill the empty air, and that anything was usually what Dunne wanted to know.

'Why don't you come and use the facility on my floor? I can assure you it is well stocked.'

Was he being ironic? She felt herself blushing. Damn it! The kid was seventeen or eighteen years old. He had no business being so poised, so Charles Boyer.

The facility *was* well stocked – to the point of slight effeminism. A terry-cloth bathrobe with the school crest on the pocket hung neatly from a hook on the back of the door. The towels were clean and fluffy, stacked precisely on a shelf that also held various toiletries – no Right Guard in sight; rather, Calvin Klein and several varieties of Penhaligon's cologne, which Faith herself bought for Tom at Louis, carefully removing any price tags. When she met him, Tom had been strictly a soap and water man – and the soap was Ivory. The soap in Sloane Buxton's bath – and Faith wondered whether he shared it with anyone else – was French, Roger & Gallet, sandalwood. She dried her hands on a tissue from her purse. She didn't want to touch anything.

He was waiting outside the door.

'Sorry you were inconvenienced. I'll make sure it doesn't happen again. The maintenance people don't get here all that often. It's a bit out of the way from the rest of the dorms.'

Faith was unpleasantly aware of that – and aware that they were apparently the only people in Carleton House at the moment. He followed her down the stairs just a little bit too closely, and when they got to the front door, he leaned against it, blocking her exit.

'I'm really looking forward to your course – and getting to know you better.'

'I'm glad you're interested in cooking,' she said, reaching for the knob. He reached, too, covering her hand with his and smiled confidently as she pulled back.

'Until tomorrow then, *Mrs Fairchild*.' There was no mistaking the emphasis – or the look in those devilishly piercing blue eyes. Sloane Buxton thought he was God's gift to women – and maybe he was.

Faith walked into her house feeling as if she had been away somewhere for days. And judging from her emotional and physical exhaustion, that somewhere had been trekking in the Himalayas.

She could hear Tom talking on the phone. He sounded more excited than usual. She quickly took off her coat and threw it over the back of the chair. Ben wasn't home from school yet and presumably Amy was napping. What was going on?

'Yes, yes, of course I will. Don't worry. *Please.* I know what you must be going through, but we'll talk tomorrow. Faith just walked in; I'll let her know immediately. Just stay calm. I'm sure everything will be fine. Tomorrow, then. Okay. Good-bye.'

Tom hung up the phone, then turned to Faith, anything but calm himself. His face was agitated, and instead of reaching out to greet her, he ran both hands through his hair, tugging at the roots.

'That was my father. Mother's leaving him!'

Four

'I don't believe it!' Faith echoed the shocked amazement in Tom's voice. Dick and Marian Fairchild heading for Splitsville? Sooner Ozzie and Harriet or the Cleavers or the Waltons or even her own parents – and that would never happen.

'You must have misunderstood what he was saying.' Dick Fairchild, semi-retired from Fairchild Realty in Norwell, down on the South Shore, was a man of few words, and those words usually had to do with interest rates and radon detection.

Tom shook his head slowly. ' "Hello, son. Your mother's leaving me. Can you meet me for lunch at the Oyster House tomorrow?" That was about it.' Tom sat down heavily in a spindly Windsor chair left by prior occupants. Faith kept it in the hall corner, next to the table with the phone, lest anyone be tempted to find comfort in it. Now it was as if Tom couldn't trust his legs to take him as far as the living room, with its soft couch.

Faith pulled him to his feet.

'Come on. Let's sit in the other room.'

'Mom and Dad. I never thought that they'd ever break up.' Tom's shaky voice was a poignant reminder that whether you're four or thirty-four, you want Mommy and Daddy together, for better or worse, and preferably in the house you grew up in. 'Do you think I should call Bill and Judy?' These were Tom's brother and sister.

'Not yet.' Faith was firm on this one. 'I'd be surprised if Judy didn't know.' Still very much Daddy's little girl, and his favorite. 'And Bill, too. But if they don't, then your father has some reason for not telling them. And maybe the reason is that this isn't really happening. If you want to call anyone, call your father back – or your mother.'

It was Tom's turn to protest. 'Mom may not know he's told me, and I don't want to add any more fuel to this fire, whatever in blazes it is.' Tom was waxing metaphorical. 'And clearly Dad didn't want to talk on the phone. It will have to wait until tomorrow.' He sighed deeply. Tomorrow was a long way away.

The old Union Oyster House was Dick Fairchild's favorite restaurant and had been since college and courting days. It was where Faith had been introduced to Tom's parents, and she reflected that clearly Dick thought of it as a haven, his turf. And he might also be in the mood for baked scrod.

'No, if anyone calls Mother, you should,' Tom said. 'In fact, why don't you go down and have lunch with her while I'm seeing Dad? Take Amy.' He looked so pitiful. Faith envisioned the scene in his mind. Faith and sweet little Amy dressed in one of her granny's smocked creations, standing on the doorstep – maybe carrying a basket of baked goodies. Think of the children, Marian. If not your sons and daughter, then your grandchildren! 'Oh, sweetheart, I'm sorry. I can't. I'm teaching at Mansfield, remember, and I really can't miss the second class.' Besides, she added to herself, I have a lot of work to do. She hadn't been able to search a single room yet. 'But why don't you suggest to your father that they come here for the weekend, or at least for Sunday. You know how much they love to hear you preach; then after lunch, we might be able to talk things out. They could stay Sunday night and go to the bonfire at Mansfield. It sounds like fun. The boys sing, drink hot cocoa, and there's skating on the pond.' Faith had stopped by Connie Reed's for particulars after hearing about it from Daryl. The bonfire was just the sort of thing Fairchilds loved – outdoor activity offering minimal comfort.

Tom nodded approvingly. 'Better plan – although Dad won't want to miss the Super Bowl. I don't, either. But the rest of you can go to this bonfire thing. We don't want to make too much of this. Or put Mother on the spot.' He ruminated, then said, 'Poor Dad. He sounded totally bewildered. My God, Faith, they've been married almost forty years!'

Faith instantly quelled the little voice inside her head that nagged, Maybe that's the problem. She decided to dwell instead on the English clergyman Sydney Smith's words: 'Marriage resembles a pair of shears, so joined that they cannot be separated; often moving in opposite directions, yet always punishing anyone who comes between them.'

The room was completely devoid of what Faith had come to call *Eau d'Adolescent Homme* from her brief forays into the Miller boys' rooms and memories of those of male friends during high school and college. Those rooms had smelled like unwashed garments, especially socks, forgotten food of various sorts, and, underlying it all, a powerful whiff of boy funk. There was no boy funk present in Sloane Buxton's room. No man funk, either. The air was clear, with only the faintest suggestion of leather – from an easy chair next to the desk – and the citrus of his aftershave. It was as unnerving as the boy himself.

She got to work quickly. The boys would be finished with chapel soon and arriving for her class downstairs in the kitchen.

He *had* snagged a great room. There was a window seat beneath two large windows that offered a beautiful view of the campus facing the lake, the ice sparkling in the distance. The sun streaked the snow-covered ground with blinding light, but not enough warmth to melt the drifts or the deadly-looking icicles that hung down like medieval daggers from the roof. But she wasn't here for the scenery. She turned resolutely and surveyed Buxton's room.

It wasn't large, but it had a fireplace surrounded by what

appeared to be Minton tiles. The school-issued furniture had been augmented by the leather chair, an attractive paisley bedspread and matching curtains, several framed prints of English hunting scenes and a Daumier caricature. A small worn but authentic Oriental lay on the floor by his bed. It was really too much. Too Max Beerbohm or Osbert Sitwell. She wasn't sure what she was looking for – rope, scissors and newspapers? A copy of *The Life of John Birch*? An application to Bob Jones University? She scanned the small bookcase. His courses marched along the rows – thick copies of Janson and Brinton for Western Civilization; *Beowulf, Sir Gawain, Macbeth* – for British Lit; a physics text, several math books, *Les Fleurs du Mal* in French – maybe something there. A copy of *Mein Kampf*. She took it out and leafed through it, as she had the others. Portions of the text had been underlined. She would have to ask Daryl if Mansfield used it for any course. There was a well-read copy of *Gatsby*. She was not surprised. What was surprising was that there weren't any yearbooks. She'd have thought Sloane would have them so that someday he could show junior what a hotshot his old man had been in prep school. Maybe he kept them at home.

In the closet, besides the school blazers – buttons intact – and gray trousers, there were several Brooks Brothers suits and a Ralph Lauren overcoat. His shoes were arranged in neat rows, each with its own wooden shoe tree. She pulled the desk chair over and checked the top shelf. Sweatpants, sweatshirts, running shoes and not much else. No copies of *Hustler* pushed to the rear.

Sloane's chest of drawers yielded nothing, either, besides the fact that he preferred boxers and his sweaters were cashmere. A silver-backed clothes brush, hairbrush, and comb set were arranged on top. A gift from the 'rents, no doubt, but no Moroccan leather framed photo of Mummy and Daddy. No pictures of anyone. She opened the desk drawers. Paper for his printer, ink cartridges, pens, pencils. A couple of computer manuals the size of Gutenberg Bibles. No scissors, no rope. No letters. The room had a characterless feel to it, or rather, it seemed as if it *did* belong to a character, a character in some play. It was like a stage set.

She lifted the top of the large window seat. Ski boots, gloves, goggles. A hockey stick, tennis racket, skates – and an elaborate traveling bar in a leather case from Mark Cross. Scotch. She shut the lid and sat down. The computer on his desk was silent, but a tiny orange light glowed. It was on sleep. She got up and hit the return key and the screen came to life. It was as organized as the rest of Sloane's existence. There was a folder for each subject he was taking, and she noted he'd already started keeping the log for her class. Two sentences: 'The first class was devoted to the art and manufacture of pancakes, a more versatile food than I had previously imagined. My group added apple slices as the pancakes cooked, and the result was extremely satisfactory.'

What a prig.

There was a folder labeled 'Games'. Maybe Sloane was into the slash-and-burn stuff – Duke Nukem, Quake. But no, only a couple of sports games, plus chess. Nothing to indicate an addiction – hours in front of the screen.

She connected to Netscape and opened his E-mail. No new messages. And not too many old ones. There were a number from Winston Freer. Apparently, Sloane had been getting some SAT prep from him. Most of the messages were to arrange meetings and assignments: 'Same place, same time,' 'Repeat the exercise', that sort of thing. She was struck with the respectful, almost worshipful tone of Sloane's messages to his professor, and it was clear that Freer also thought well of his student. Winston Freer had struck Faith as a keen – rapier-sharp – judge of his fellow human beings. He'd certainly been on the mark about Zoë Harcourt. Maybe there was something she was missing about Sloane. She continued to search his E-mail. Well, well, well. Maybe the boy wasn't such a prig after all. The majority of his correspondence was with someone named Heather at Miss Porter's. Very hot and heavy, with extremely satisfactory results apparently. It turned out he *did* have some photographs. Faith put the computer back on sleep and made a thorough search of what was left, looking under and in the bed, lifting the chair cushion, feeling in the cracks – zilch. There was a wastebasket next to his desk. Carefully, she smoothed out the pieces of paper that had been balled up and tossed into it. There were sheets with columns of numbers and some graphs. Apparently math class efforts, exam review. She scrunched them up and put them back. The last piece of paper was more interesting: a copy of the notice posted about the theft that every boy was to have received. Obviously, Sloane wasn't putting his in his scrapbook. And if he had one, Faith had failed to turn it up so far. She studied the sheet intently. She hadn't seen one yet. Zoë had indeed had some treasures, and Faith was willing to bet that it was their value on the open market and not sentimental, real or no, that was behind the woman's emotional outburst in the chapel. What was pictured was worth a king's – or rather, a czar's – ransom.

There were four items on the glossy colored Xerox. One was an enameled snuffbox with an oval portrait of a Russian gentleman – Nicholas? – in the middle of the lid. The next was the famous pillbox of grandmother fame – small, but its ivory enamel was decorated with gold filigree and what appeared to be an emerald in the center. And there was a Fabergé, or school of Fabergé, egg. It wasn't one of the imperial eggs, yet it was very, very nice. Canary yellow, with thin gold bands studded with diamonds. The photo of its interior revealed a deep blue star-filled sky.

The descriptions were simple – color, size, not materials. Faith was sure the Harcourts didn't want the boys, particularly the guilty one or ones, to know just how valuable the objects were. The piece that caught Faith's eye was a lady's compact, a powder case, so-called. It was enameled in deep emerald green and the top was covered with a lacy web of diamonds, dripping with tiny drops of bejeweled dew. There was no sign of the spider, the arachnid that had created this artifice of nature. She skimmed the rest of the text on the sheet. It was basically what Harcourt had said in the chapel. She wondered if the deadline had been met. She'd know soon. All she had to do was look at the ninth graders. Today's chapel gathering would be a reprise of yesterday's, notched up, if the articles hadn't been returned by dinner last night. And Faith agreed with Winston Freer: It wasn't going to be that simple.

Noting again the absence of things she'd expected to find in the room of a kid this age – a stereo system (there wasn't even a radio), stuff, as in souvenirs from trips, a mug or two, silly presents from girlfriends, a lava lamp, whatever – she left, the air as empty as before.

She reached the kitchen, eager for the clamor the boys would bring. Sloane Buxton's room had definitely creeped her out.

They arrived as noisily as she had predicted.

And once again, the two ninth graders looked like they'd been caught with their hands in the till. So, Zoë's heirlooms were still missing. To make sure, Faith asked jauntily, 'How was chapel?'

Sloane Buxton answered politely. 'We sang, "Turn back, O Man, Forswear Thy Foolish Ways", Professor Freer read "The Darkling Thrush" by Thomas Hardy, our headmaster informed us that his wife's possessions had not been returned, and we closed with "Wonders Still the World Shall Witness".'

Someone had a sense of humor, Faith thought as she suppressed her own laughter. The organist? Surely not Robert Harcourt.

'Well, that's too bad, but I'm sure it will all be straightened out. Now to the lovely, *edible* egg.' She realized she was thinking of the missing golden one in contrast. I should be taking the theft more seriously, she chided herself. But that was hard, given Zoë's histrionics and the much, much more serious matter at hand.

Still, she'd have to watch herself. Even kids as young as Amy had built-in X-ray vision, able to spot adult subterfuge at ten paces – and the students in front of her had had many more years of practice. She continued brightly: 'The egg – your best friend in the kitchen. If you have eggs, you always have a meal.'

She went through the basics, showing them how to crack an egg – reminding them to discard any eggs that were cracked to start with – and how to use the shell to fish out any pieces that might have dropped into the bowl. She showed them how to separate eggs, told them the importance of keeping eggs at room temperature before cooking, and how to make a perfect fried egg, sliding it gently into the pan from a saucer.

Some boys took notes, including Sloane and Brian Perkins – Sloane for his erudite log, Brian because he wanted to avoid her eyes. What was the matter with the boy? He hadn't been able to look at her since his startled entry the day before. He sat apart from the others and was not involved in any of the banter. It was apparent he was as miserable as his friend Danny. Faith felt annoyed. She didn't know his parents, but she had a sudden vision of them: Oh, yes, Brian's at Mansfield this year. We thought it would be better for him. Better for them, more likely, and some notion of status. Aleford High School was one of the best in the state and outranked Mansfield academically. But it wasn't a private school – or rather, an independent school. Patsy had told her this was their preferred appellation. It sounded so much more PC. Faith cracked the egg she was breaking for an omelette so viciously, it exploded. She was doing them one-handed now and promised by the end of the course everyone would be equally proficient.

'It's all in the wrist, Mrs Fairchild,' said Zach Cohen as he grabbed an egg and neatly cracked it into the bowl with one hand. Another thing he'd picked up in the restaurant kitchen last summer.

'Cohen, you are such a brownnoser,' someone called above the general cries of derision that greeted his performance.

Faith just laughed. Patsy was right – she was having fun, and the kids – make that most of the kids – were great.

'Now, I've given you the recipe for spaghetti carbonara in your packet, and it's very easy to follow. When we get to pasta, I'll go over it with you, but it's one to remember when you think about eggs. All you need for it is a half a pound of bacon, a clove of garlic, three beaten eggs, and half a cup of Romano or Parmesan cheese. I like to mix the cheeses and use pancetta, an Italian bacon, but anything you have at hand is fine. Right now, half the group is going to practice making omelettes. I've brought all sorts of fillings: cheese, ham, a mixture of herbs. I'll show the other half how to make a kind of spaghetti pie, a pasta frittata, with eggs and leftover pasta. We'll eat, and if there's time, we'll switch and make them again.'

'I assume we'll keep the same groups as yesterday?' Sloane asked.

Faith hadn't thought about it. 'Yes, I suppose so, if that's all right with everybody.' No one objected.

'Okay, now wash your hands. You can't do that too much when you're cooking. Also clean all your work surfaces. You omelette guys should be all right on your own, but yell if you need help.' She pretended not to hear the muffled 'helps' as she turned to walk the frittata group through this easy, satisfying recipe. She'd brought pesto, which she'd made and frozen last summer, to add to the pasta, in this case capellini. She'd chosen it as the 'leftover' because of the speed with which it cooked.

'The eggs bind the pasta, and you can also bake this in the oven, instead of doing it on top of the stove the way we are today.'

Daryl was the one who turned the crusty mixture out of the pan on to a large plate, then slid it back in to cook on the other side. The kitchen was filled with the mouthwatering smells of olive oil, garlic, basil, and cheese. Soon they were in the other room, sitting down to sample the fruits of their labors.

'Never, never toss out your pasta dish from the night before. And if your date eats like a bird, be sure to get a doggie bag for that fettuccine,' Faith advised.

The guys laughed, and ate so fast, Faith realized they would just have time to repeat the exercise.

'Sorry, I forgot to pour the milk,' Sloane said, and a few glasses were quickly filled with plain or chocolate. John MacKenzie took a deep swallow – and choked, spewing milk across the table.

'That's not funny, MacKenzie!' one of the boys who'd been splattered said in outrage. But his words were immediately eclipsed by a duplication of MacKenzie's act by the other boys drinking the chocolate milk.

'What on earth ...' Faith stood up, alarmed. It had all been going so well. No farting noises, but now milk was coming out of their noses!

'Taste it,' John said weakly, pushing the pitcher toward Faith. She poured some into her glass, took a sip, and gagged. It wasn't just sour; it was horribly salty. It was possibly the worst thing she'd ever tasted.

'Are we going to die?' asked Brian Perkins, clutching anxiously at her sleeve.

'No, no, of course not,' she said with a confidence she hoped she felt. She'd bought the milk yesterday at the Shop and Save with the rest of the provisions. They'd had some of it with their cookies. 'Sour milk can't kill you. It just tastes vile.' The boys who had swallowed the disgusting drink were in the kitchen gulping water and trying to rinse the taste from their mouths. Faith followed them, looked in the refrigerator, and immediately noticed that the caps were off all the gallon containers. She didn't have to pour more samples to confirm her suspicions. The bottles had been closed when she left. She looked on the counters and in all the cupboards, particularly the ones where she'd put things. Behind the flour she found a large, almost empty bottle of soy sauce with mushroom flavoring. She sighed in relief. She'd been about to call Poison Control to be sure. The bottle had been full – and unopened – yesterday. She held it up in front of the boys, some of whom were looking quite dreadful.

'Here's our culprit.' She tried her mother's old trick and stared into each boy's eyes intently. They were either awfully good or awfully innocent. Each met her unspoken challenge: Can you look me straight in the eye and say that you didn't do it?

But if it wasn't somebody in her class, who was it?

As she slipped across campus to Daryl's and Zach Cohen's dorm, Faith tried to feel reassured by Daryl's parting words: 'Just some asshole. Don't worry about it'. Sloane had been the one who reminded them he hadn't poured the milk. Was this his idea of a joke? Neither he nor his groupies, which was how Faith thought of the two boys in the class who not only hung around with him but mimicked his dress and speech, had drunk any milk. But then they were more of a scotch and soda crowd. It was probably someone who wasn't even in the class. Maybe some merry trickster who lived in Carleton House. Faith vowed to check every ingredient from now on.

Before she'd gone into Sloane's room, she'd checked Paul Boothe's, which was on the same floor. It was locked, as she'd assumed it would be. Mansfield's open-door policy would not apply to its on-campus staff, who needed whatever privacy they could get. She thought again about the way he manipulated his students by setting such high hurdles for entry to his classes, thereby increasing his hold over them. It was all one big ego trip for this type of teacher, and kids this age were so impressionable. It was the odd paradox of adolescence that rebellion was accompanied by total subservience to the Paul Boothes who strode across their stage.

She went into the dorm through the back door and up the stairs, taking a quick look at Daryl's room. No nooses. Just a neatly made bed. A bureau crowded with photographs, some stuck in the mirror – Mom and Dad, a bunch of kids standing in front of canoes, Daryl at the beach with a lovely young thing, and a lot of his dog – a caramel-colored mop of a mixture leaning toward spaniel. Music system, stacks of CDs, and a bookcase crammed full of all sorts of reading matter besides his texts. A carelessly tossed pair of pajamas on the desk chair completed the picture. No designer bedspread, just the school-issued blankets and plain muslin curtains. She closed the door, but not before she saw the one thing that was unusual in Daryl Martin's room. You could clearly see lines on the floor – like skid marks at a fatal crash – made from pushing the bureau into position against the door each night.

It would take me a week to search Zach's room thoroughly, Faith thought in dismay as she opened the next door. It was like a teen Costco, a Costco that was getting its merchandise not by trucks but by what had fallen off them. Like Daryl and Sloane, Zach had a single. Unusual for a sophomore, she'd have thought. Daryl had told her that only seniors had singles, and, he added, 'exceptional underclassmen such as myself'. Was Zach another 'exceptional underclassman', and how so? Certainly he looked different from the majority of the Mansfield student population, but there were a few others pushing it, too. Were they also segregated into singles for fear of contamination? Meanwhile, what was he doing with all this stuff, and where had he gotten it? This wasn't simply a case of overindulgent parents. Computers, printers, scanners, laptops, sound systems, electronic things that could have been nuclear warheads, so foreign were they to her, were piled all over the place. Stacks of CDs – Orbital, Prodigy, Juno Reactor – Zach was heavily into techno groups. She turned one of the cases over and read Prodigy's song titles – 'Voodoo People', 'Firestarter', 'Breathe', and 'One Love'. She could identify with the last at least. There was lots of software: StarCraft, Unreal, Diablo,

Grand Theft Auto. No question about what Zach was doing with *his* free time.

She made her way across the room. The shades were down and she'd switched on the light when she came in. Clothes were strewn on the floor. She took a breath. Ah, that old familiar smell. The funk. It was there. What about room inspection? She laughed at herself. Would Zach care? This was a boy who had made a very abrupt turn, according to Daryl. Was it a turn to the left or right? The bookcase was crammed with computer manuals and magazines, a lot of sci-fi and, surprisingly, all the Harry Potters. No neo-Nazi stuff, or if he had it, it was hidden. And no yearbook.

A new Special Edition iMac sat on his desk. It was not on sleep, and Faith turned it on. The screen saver was a still from *The Matrix*. All his files were locked. She shut down. His unmade bed revealed nothing until she slid her hand under the pillow. There was something in the case, and that something was a very sharp switchblade. She left it; she had to, yet the thought of why he might need it was unsettling – defense or offense? His dresser drawers were filled with clean clothes – the boys did not have to do their own laundry – and what wasn't for school was black. The only picture in the room was a large poster of Albert Einstein thumbtacked to the wall – another Mansfield no-no. Nothing affixed to the walls, except with proper picture hangers. There was a dartboard on his closet door. The Harcourt wanted poster was pinned to it, one dart squarely between the eyes of the Russian on the snuffbox. Snuffed.

Gingerly, she opened the closet door. A tangle of shoes cluttered the floor and Zach's blazers were slipping off the hangers. No buttons missing. Nothing in the pockets. She sighed. She had to get back. Tom was with his father in town and she had to pick up Amy. She dragged the desk chair over to look on the top shelf – nothing noteworthy except for a piece of petrified pizza that might interest the Smithsonian. She was returning the chair when she bumped against one of the sound systems, nearly sending it toppling to the floor. She reached to put it back in place and stopped. The owner had written his name on the back in indelible marker. The proud owner: Danny Miller.

What to do? What to do? *What to do?* She had several choices, and as she drove toward the center of town, they played leapfrog in her mind. Talk to Pix? Talk to Danny? Talk to Tom? Talk to Pix and Danny together? Talk to Pix, Danny, and Tom together? Talk to no one? She was favoring the last option as she pulled into the nursery school parking lot and prepared for the wall of guilt that would fall upon her since her child was the last one to be picked up. Yes, for the moment, keep her mouth shut. Or better, talk to Daryl. He had to have some idea of why Zach Cohen's room was crammed with consumer goods. What had Danny said to Pix about his prize possession? He'd loaned it to a kid he knew? But Zach obviously didn't need to borrow it – and how had Danny gotten to be such buddies with Zach in any case? Brian Perkins was a freshman, and upperclassmen didn't talk to freshmen, at least not in a way that would warm a mother's heart.

Amy was drowsily nibbling on the sandwich Faith had prepared for her lunch, and she greeted her mother with her usual slightly perplexed look. If Amy was at her friend Jeremy's house, this look would soon be accompanied by heartrending cries of 'No, I don't want to go home!' Pix, the teachers, and Jeremy's mother, whose son exhibited the same behavior, had all told Faith this simply meant Amy wasn't 'good at transitions'. Faith could identify with this and hoped her daughter would outgrow the crying part – or would at least sob in secret.

They waved good-bye to the teachers, who had told Faith it didn't matter they were staying late anyway so many times that she felt worse than ever, and got into the car. Amy promptly fell asleep and Faith faced another transition – lugging Amy up the back stairs, through the kitchen, and into bed. When this was accomplished, she felt like a nap herself. Between teaching, snooping, and all the other tasks of everyday life, she was exhausted. Instead, she made herself a cup of coffee and waited for something else to happen.

The something else she was expecting was a call from Tom, or maybe he'd stop by after his lunch with his father. But the phone never rang. Finally, she called next door, and Rhoda Dawson, the church administrator, told Faith that the Reverend wasn't there and she hadn't heard from him. He'd cleared his afternoon, so she presumed he was still in town with his father. Faith presumed the same thing and hung up to wait. She wasn't sure whether it was a good sign or a bad sign that Tom was spending so much time with her father-in-law.

She went through her Mansfield plans for the next day. She wouldn't be able to do any more room searches – she wanted to case out John MacKenzie's – because she planned to speak to Mrs Mallory about teaching a class or two. Mansfield classes met on Saturday mornings, and her hope was that the cook would take one or both of these. Project Term ended February 9, which was a little more than two weeks away. She had a great deal to cover in that time. And she had to schedule Zoë's Stroganoff class. Somehow, she had the feeling it was not uppermost in that lady's mind at the moment.

Ben burst through the kitchen door filled with news from the first grade front.

'We are studying whales, and I need to bring my tape in tomorrow. Some of the kids didn't even know that whales sing, MoM!' Faith didn't care for the slight note of scorn she was picking up.

'All right, sweetheart. I'll leave a note on the door to remind us, but you just happened to get that tape for Christmas. You wouldn't have known about the whale songs, either.'

'Still.' Ben didn't give up easily.

'Still nothing. Bring the tape and enlighten others. Now, when Amy wakes up, we need to return our library books and go to the market. Until then, why don't you have a snack and look at the whale book that came with the tape?'

'Great! And maybe the library has more. We're going to draw whales in chalk on the playground, *life-size!*'

Education was certainly much more creative than Faith remembered. First grade was a very distant memory of workbooks and a teacher who smelled like lilies of the valley.

The phone still had not rung by the time Faith left for her errands. When they got inside the library, both kids made a beeline for the children's room. She followed them in and helped Ben find whale books, which he immediately took to one of the comfortable nooks that had been part of the plan for this new addition. Besides the nooks, there were computer stations, but the puppet theater in a nook of its own had been preserved from the old children's room and reassembled. Generations of Aleford kids had put on shows for real and make-believe audiences with an assortment of hand puppets. It was Amy's favorite place, and now she had Oscar on one hand and some sort of mythological beast on the other. They were hugging and Amy was crooning softly to herself. One of the librarians was at her desk nearby, and Faith told her she was just going to go into the main library for some books for herself and would be back in a minute.

'No problem, Mrs Fairchild. I'm engaged in the pleasurable task of ordering new books. The kids are fine where they are.'

Faith scanned the shelves marked NEW BOOKS to try to find something to fit her current mood. No mysteries. Too confusing – and irritating. The way everything was so neatly, and quickly, solved. Contemporary novels about relationships. Elizabeth Berg had a new book out. She thought about Marian and Dick. Almost forty years, as Tom had pointed out. Was there a novel about them? Finally, she turned away and went off to the stacks for some cookbooks, comfort food for the mind, and a copy of Anthony Bourdain's *Kitchen Confidential*, which she hadn't gotten around to reading yet. The account of his 'adventures in the culinary underbelly' – restaurant kitchens – might be just what she needed to distract herself from the academic underbelly she was experiencing.

Millicent Revere McKinley was shelving books, and she looked disapprovingly at Faith for taking one down. Faith knew what she was thinking. Not only was there an unsightly gap now but in the near future, someone, probably Millicent, would have to put the volume back again. Better simply to leave the books alone.

'Hello, Millicent,' Faith said. 'Are you working here now?'

'Friends of the Library has always pitched in as shelf detectives – making sure all the books are in order and reshelving those that are not.'

If ever there was a calling for Millicent, this was it. She would pounce on a misplaced book with the fervor of a very hungry lioness on a hapless wildebeest.

'I hear you have a job yourself. Teaching at Mansfield.' Millicent smiled complacently. She liked knowing things and, even more, liked people to know that she knew them.

'Project Term. A cooking class. It's been fun.'

'Such dear boys. I usually participate, but this year I was too busy.'

Dear boys was not the term Faith would have chosen, even for the ones she cared for, but she nodded. Maybe she could steer Millicent away from the boys and to the staff, particularly the headmaster's wife. She wondered if Millicent knew about the theft.

Of course she did. Faith's tentative remark about a bit of trouble was met with an immediate 'Oh, you mean the break-in at the Harcourts'?' Her eyes were sparkling under her Mamie Eisenhower fringe.

'I'd never met Mrs Harcourt until recently. I hadn't realized that we had such a collection of Russian artworks in Aleford.'

Millicent narrowed her eyes, 'What you hadn't realized was that we had someone like Zoë Harcourt in Aleford.'

'That, too,' Faith confessed. Damn Millicent.

It was one of Miss McKinley's more expansive days. She must have found a great many books out of order.

'Of course when they first arrived – it must be more than twenty years ago – she made a stir. She's a good bit younger than Robert, although not so much as she'd like you to think. We used to see her around quite a bit. She had a little sports car – and then there were the clothes. Bright colors and sables in the winter, until she must have gotten nervous about having paint thrown at her, because those disappeared. And, gradually, Zoë disappeared, too. Began to travel a great deal. Robert would go with her in the summer. I hear she has an apartment in New York City.' Millicent emphasized the last three words as if she were intoning 'Sodom and Gomorrah'.

'Apparently, the items taken had come down through her family.'

'Oh, she's Russian all right. At least her grandparents were.' Millicent's specialty was ancestry and she was equally adept at deciphering a Cyrillic family tree as her own heavily laden New England boughs. 'But her parents grew up in New York – Brighton Beach; then her father invented some kind of part that every airplane has to have, and by the time Zoë came along, the family was in Westchester and Palm Beach.'

So Winston Freer had been right about the provenance of Zoë's treasures.

'It's all her money. The school, that is. Robert Harcourt never had two nickels to rub together.'

But wouldn't Zoë have wanted her husband in some other sort of profession? International currency trading, politics? The governor's wife, the senator's wife? Even – Faith could see the inaugural gown – First Lady? But perhaps Robert was not so inclined – or gifted.

'She didn't strike me as a typical headmaster's wife.'

'She's not. But I suppose the life suits her. No responsibilities, aside from pouring tea or sherry occasionally and handing out a prize or two, and over the years, she's done less and less of that.'

'Have you ever heard any rumors about—'

Maddeningly, Millicent did not let Faith finish her sentence.

'I'm sorry, Faith dear, but I do have a great deal of work to do, and aren't those your children at the circulation desk?'

Yes, those were her children. Millicent's tone of voice had raised the suggestion of dubious parentage, just as she had intimated that she knew exactly what Faith was going to ask – whether there had been rumors about Zoë and other men. She raised her arm to put a book on the top shelf, darting a tantalizing smile in Faith's direction, making it clear by her gesture that she was putting a tidbit of knowledge up and out of Faith's immediate grasp.

Ben was tugging Amy along behind him.

'Where have you been, Mom? I'm bored, and Amy's bored, too. We told the librarian we were coming to find you and she said okay.'

Amy didn't look bored. She still had her puppets on like mittens and she looked as if she was going to let out a wail of protest at the prospect of being parted from them. Not in the library, Faith prayed fervently. Not in front of Millicent, she added in a PS to God.

'Come on, chickadee, and give me a puppet show. Ben can watch, too, since he's so bored.' She gave him a withering look. 'Six-year-old children do not get bored, especially in libraries.'

Ben scowled. 'I wanted to go home and look at this tape I found.'

'Okay. That's what you tell me. Not that you're bored. We'll watch Amy – *for a little while*.' She emphasized her last words to take the sting away of her earlier scolding. Ben picked up on it and brightened.

'Got you, Mom. Hey, they have a whale puppet. I'll be in the show, too.'

When they finally got home, the only message on the machine was a brief one from Pix, wanting to know where Faith was and what she was up to, and an even briefer one from Patsy that simply said, 'Anything to report?'

Nothing from Tom.

The days were getting longer and every increment of light was a blessing. She had never gotten used to how dark it was in New England during the winter. Seasons changed in New York, but man had made up for nature's deficiency and it was light year-round. She put the whale tape on and was rewarded by the sight of Amy and Ben snuggled together watching it. Faith had decided not to believe in sibling rivalry when Amy was born. It took too much energy away from more interesting and rewarding things in life. Tom agreed, so like little brush fires, they assiduously stamped out any possible occurrences. Brush fires. That reminded her of the Mansfield bonfire. She thought they only did things like this at large southern universities before football championships. Maybe Robert was from the South. She knew very little about his background. His voice was generic Yankee, but he wouldn't have been the first one to assume it to complete the picture he was trying to present.

She called Patsy back, but there was no answer at home and Faith didn't want to bother her at work. She left a message that there wasn't anything yet but she was working on it. Strictly speaking, that wasn't true. Yes, she was working on it, but she'd found out a great deal. The problem was, she couldn't see any way that what she'd discovered related to the racist attacks on Daryl.

Faith hadn't liked the tone in Pix's voice, but she didn't call her back. Now that the leaves were off the trees, she could see the

Millers' driveway clearly and Pix's Land Rover, which only went into the garage during storms, wasn't there. She also wasn't sure how she was going to handle the discovery of Danny's sound system in Zach Cohen's room.

She had just put the water on to boil for the egg noodles, which would accompany the Swedish meatballs she'd made yesterday, when she heard a car pull into the drive. It was Tom at last. She'd thought she would have to feed the kids first.

'Honey, what's going on? I've been on tenterhooks all day. Why didn't you call?'

Tom folded her in his arms. His coat felt cold and rough and wonderful beneath her cheek.

'I've been with my father all this time. Lunch took a while; then he decided as long as he was up here, he wanted to walk around to some of his old haunts. Old haunts that are gone now, of course. Scollay Square, Cornhill, the West End. He was in that kind of a mood. My feet are killing me and it was freezing.'

Rare to hear a Fairchild mention a thermometer reading except in delight. Tom had had a hard day. He took off his coat and gloves, rubbing his hands together. Faith poured him a glass of the Coudoulet de Beaucastel Côtes du Rhône she'd been planning to give him with dinner and said, 'So, tell me! I can't stand the suspense. Are they splitting up?'

Tom sat down at the kitchen table.

'Mom redecorated the living room,' he said in a hollow voice.

Faith's first reaction was that this didn't sound like a woman who was planning on moving out.

'Yes, and that means ...' She realized this was going to take some time.

'It's obvious. She's like a different person. She's ordered new dining room furniture, too!'

The Fairchild dining room, like the living room, was – or, in the case of the living room, had been – furnished with a few good family heirlooms and a whole lot of well-worn, well-sat-in pieces they'd accumulated since they'd moved to the house, when Tom, the eldest, was born. The dining room set had come from Paine's – your basic highly polished mahogany table with extra leaves in the closet, a sideboard, and rather uncomfortable matching chairs.

'She put the old living room stuff in the attic.'

So the woman had not gone totally berserk. Marian's leaving the odd ottoman on the sidewalk for the trash collector would have been of real concern to Faith. If there was even the slightest possibility that someone might have a use for an item, it went into the attic, which, needless to say, was overflowing with everything from boxes of worn linens – potential rags and drop cloths – to wrapping paper, creases ironed out for reuse.

'But what about this business of leaving your father?' Faith asked, trying to steer Tom gently back on track.

'Modern. She wants a more "contemporary" look. Now, does that sound like my mother?'

Actually not. Marian still wore shirtwaists, and in the winter, her tweed skirts matched her Shetland cardigans.

'Maybe she felt she needed a change.'

'Change! Why on earth would she need a change? Hasn't she always been perfectly happy with the way things have been?' Faith was sure this outburst was a direct quote from Dick Fairchild.

'People can be perfectly happy and still want a change after a while.' Say forty years, Faith added to herself. She got up to put the noodles in the boiling water. They might as well eat, and maybe by the time she went to sleep she'd know what was going on.

The entry of the kids, hungry and eager for Tom's attention, put a stop to all grown-up conversation. They hadn't been able to talk about anything serious in front of the kids since Ben was two and a half. Faith remembered it all too well. Precocious Ben, blond hair gleaming, blue eyes big and round, had toddled up to

Ruth Simmons and asked her how her 'sunuvabith' was. Faith had whisked him away after stuffing a cracker in his mouth, fearful that he would add the word *husband* to what she hoped were otherwise-indecipherable words.

Tom wasn't hungry. He ate only one large helping of what was one of his favorites.

At 7:45, children disposed of appropriately, Faith sat him down on the couch and said, 'Now, I've been patient enough. What exactly is going on between the two of them?'

'I wish I knew. Dad wishes he knew,' Tom said mournfully. 'You have got to talk to Mother. What she's doing is going on a cruise. A cruise!'

Faith sighed. All was clear. A cruise. To the Fairchilds, at least the Fairchild men, this meant the *Love Boat*. Marian, an attractive woman, would fall into the clutches of some Lothario, a babe magnet. Marian herself perhaps was trolling for just such a contemporary adventure to go with her new furniture.

'Well, why doesn't your father go with her?' The obvious solution.

'It's complicated. You know he doesn't like to travel, and Mom has always seemed content with the place at the Cape and a few ski trips to Vermont in the winter.'

Death, thought Faith. Death. It would be like death. Keep house, then go to the Cape and keep house. Rent a condo and ski, and keep house some more. Granted, Tom and Faith had a small cottage on Sanpere Island, off the coast of Maine, yet she had made it very clear to her husband that this was not to replace foreign travel. Travel often, without children and with someone else making the beds.

'She just presented it as a done deal. She's got her tickets, everything. Told him she's tired of asking him and said if she's going to see anything of the world, she'll have to go without him.'

It was straight from the pages of *Ladies' Home Journal* –'Can

This Marriage Be Saved?' She has an itchy foot; he just wants to stay home.

'But let me get this straight. She's not talking about a divorce, right? She only wants to go on a trip.'

'So far.' Tom's tone was portentous.

'Your dad thinks it's the thin end of the wedge. Today Nassau or wherever she's going, tomorrow Reno.'

'This is really nothing to joke about,' Tom protested.

Faith was immediately contrite. These were Tom's parents, after all, and men didn't have much of a sense of humor when it came to this sort of thing, even when not related to the persons involved.

'I'm sorry, darling. And of course I'll talk to your mother.' In fact, Faith could hardly wait. 'But I think you and your dad – and the rest of the family, if they're upset, too – should let Marian enjoy her trip and welcome her back. Lots of couples take separate vacations. Not that I'm advocating it,' she added hastily. There was no way Tom was going anywhere without her. 'But think of the Millers. Sam goes on fishing trips without Pix.'

'That's different,' Tom said. 'Pix has to take care of the kids.' He stopped. 'Omigod, what a stupid thing to say.'

Faith gave him a big kiss. He was coming round. Perspective was everything.

'Anyway, Mom's not going to Nassau. She's going to the Galapagos. They have lectures and everything. Dad would hate it. She's right.'

'Did you invite them for the weekend?'

'Yes, and Dad said he'd call. It was so sad, Faith, the way he was pointing out all these places they used to go. They had their first date right at the Union Oyster House, you know.'

'I know,' said Faith. 'Don't worry. Everything will be fine. Your mother just needs a little space.'

'That's what *she* said,' Tom remarked, the small cheerful spark Faith had ignited totally extinguished by the sigh that accompanied his words.

The phone rang exactly at nine o'clock, the cutoff time for calls in Aleford and the like. Tom picked it up, expecting his father, but it was Pix, wanting to talk to Faith.

'Sorry to bother you this late, but I had to go to a Planning Board meeting.' The Millers were extremely involved in town politics. Faith used Tom's position as an excuse to remain bipartisan and thus unable to attend meetings, et cetera, unless she really cared deeply about an issue. Then she made an exception – just this one time. So far, the strategy had served her well.

'It's not late. Don't worry. What's up?'

'It's Danny.'

Faith's heart sank.

'I got a call from school today,' Pix continued. 'He's failing math and barely passing everything else. Sam is still away, and Danny refuses to talk to me about it. I'm going crazy.'

'I'll be right over,' Faith said.

'You're wonderful, but I don't want to sit talking about him when he's right upstairs. Tomorrow?'

'As soon as I get back from Mansfield, I'll call you. And I know this isn't a big help, but try not to worry. Kids go through times like this.'

'I'm trying to remember that,' Pix said. 'At least I know what's going on.'

Faith said good-bye and hung up. Now was definitely not the time to tell Pix about Danny's sound system.

Five

How are things going?' A bright and cheery voice greeted Faith as she walked toward Carleton House the next morning. It was Connie Reed.

Tempted as she was to answer, My in-laws' marriage may or may not be on the rocks, I haven't made much headway in finding out who's attacking Daryl Martin, someone is sabotaging my ingredients, my best friend's son has gone haywire, and I'm catering a luncheon next week and have no idea what to serve, she settled instead for 'Fine. The kids really seem to be enjoying themselves, and,' she added hastily, since the aim of education at places like Mansfield was not enjoyment but achievement, 'they're learning a great deal. You may want to think of opening up a café on the school grounds.'

Connie frowned, and Faith belatedly recalled her impression that the woman had virtually no sense of humor. 'I don't think the headmaster, or the trustees, would be in favor of a commercial enterprise, but I'm glad the boys are taking the course seriously. Why don't you come have a cup of coffee with me? You're a bit early. Chapel is just starting.'

Faith had planned to taste-test any ingredients left on campus, then take a quick look at John MacKenzie's room, yet she didn't want to hurt Ms Reed's feelings. Maybe she had friends among the faculty, maybe not. She lived in a small house on campus, one of the buildings left from the estate that had preceded the school.

'That sounds great. Where to?'

'Mrs Mallory keeps a pot going all day for the faculty and generally leaves a plate of cookies or muffins to go with it in one of the rooms off the kitchen. Faculty members eat with the students, and this is the nearest thing we have to a lounge, although each department has created its own.'

Well, back to plan A. Faith had planned to see Mrs Mallory before class and had only changed her mind in the wee hours of the morning, when she realized she hadn't searched MacKenzie's room yet.

When they were seated with their mugs and cinnamon scones, still warm from the oven, Faith mentioned that she wanted to schedule Mrs Mallory for tomorrow's class, Saturday. 'And I thought I'd ask Mrs Harcourt for the next. At the sherry hour, she offered to teach the students how to make beef Stroganoff, a traditional family recipe, I gather. I know she must be terribly upset about the theft, but I hope it will all be cleared up by then.'

'Mrs Harcourt teach the boys?' Connie sounded dubious. 'I'm not sure that's totally appropriate, or rather,' she said hastily, 'that she meant to seriously offer her services. She's never actually taught, you see, and it might be a bit much for her. Perhaps she could just give you the recipe.' Connie beamed at her solution.

Zoë, armed with sour cream, a good knife, and her own commanding persona, not able to control a roomful of teenage boys? Hard to imagine. Why didn't Connie want her to take the class?

The woman was talking rapidly now, burying the previous subject. 'Of course, we are all appalled at the theft. This kind of thing just doesn't happen at Mansfield. Robert, Dr Harcourt, sets such a high moral tone. We searched the boys' rooms immediately but didn't find any of the articles, and they still haven't been returned.' She sounded oddly triumphant. Faith had a wild thought. Was it Ms Reed herself? Pocketing Zoë's bibelots to teach her a lesson? And what lesson? To behave more like a headmaster's wife and less like an escapee from the Bolshoi?

'Did you check the blazers, too?' Faith asked. 'I mean for a missing button.'

'I suppose that's common knowledge, though I'm surprised it got as far as you,' Connie replied somewhat absently. 'Yes, we checked, and all buttons were in place. Of course, the first thing the boy would have done when he realized it was missing would have been to sew another one on. Boys are always losing buttons, and there are plenty of various sizes in the sewing kit we issue them in ninth grade, along with other necessities.'

Faith wished someone had issued Tom a sewing kit at some point, since he'd gone straight from a mother who'd mastered the Singer around age four to a wife who was severely challenged in this department. When he handed her a sock to mend, Faith replaced it with a new one she'd washed a couple of times and then buried the old one in the trash. It wasn't that he'd care about the substitution, but he'd protest the disposal. Old socks were handy for polishing – or she could make hand puppets for the kids from them. Thrift. Yankee thrift. She sighed and tuned back in to Connie's paean to her boss. She'd moved on to Project Term in general and what a visionary concept it was. Faith had had enough of Robert worship, so she explained she just had time for a word with Mrs Mallory, thanked Connie for the coffee, and headed into the kitchen.

Only a few breakfast dishes remained – bowls encrusted with oatmeal, plates streaked with egg. The room was warm and moist from the steam of the dishwasher. Mrs Mallory was nowhere in sight – and had she been around, there would have been no mistaking her presence. Mabel was sitting on a stool, reading the paper. She looked up and smiled at Faith.

'The boss will be back in a minute. Have a seat. Want some coffee?'

Faith hadn't seen Mabel face-to-face at their earlier meeting, and she now realized the woman was much older than she had thought.

'Thanks, I just had a cup, and a delicious scone.'

Mabel nodded. 'We're known for our baked goods. Freshmen go home at Thanksgiving looking like the butterballs on the table.' She laughed. Faith did, too.

'You must get to know the students pretty well over the years.' The boys rotated table-waiting and other jobs.

'That we do – and some of them come back to see us after they graduate. Bring their families sometimes.'

'I've gotten to know a few of them myself since I've been teaching them this cooking course. Daryl Martin is in the class, and I like him very much.'

Mabel looked at Faith appraisingly. 'Daryl's a good boy. Smart boy. He knows how to get along here.'

'What do you mean? I'm sorry, I don't mean to sound like I'm quizzing you.'

'But that is what you're doing, isn't it, child?' Mabel laughed again at Faith's discomfort.

Impulsively, Faith reached for the woman's hand. 'Yes, it is. No one else knows, but Daryl's been getting ... well, some nasty messages on his computer and in his backpack. I'm trying to find out who's doing it.'

Mabel gave Faith's hand a little squeeze. 'I knew something was troubling him. Don't worry, I won't say a word to anyone. But you've got a big job on your hands.' All traces of amusement had vanished. 'Could be almost anybody.'

She's right, Faith thought dismally as Mrs Mallory loomed in the doorway.

'But I'll do what I can,' Mabel whispered, then returned to her perusal of the obituaries. It was Faith's grandmother's favorite section of the paper, too; she always turned to it before the headlines. Faith was never sure whether this was for information or reassurance. Probably both.

She stood up, walked over to the cook, and got straight to the point, asking her if she would take tomorrow's class. It was time to get over to Carleton House. In addition, she couldn't think of any other way to approach the woman. Flattery was out.

'I don't know ...' Mrs Mallory began.

'Soup and sandwich lunch on Saturdays. Do the soup today and nothing much else to do tomorrow morning that the rest of us can't handle,' Mabel said.

'Well ...'

'Teach those boys to make the cookies they like – chocolate chip, hermits, and those peanut ones. They'll bless you for the rest of their lives.'

Whether it was due to the prospect of a perpetual state of grace or the assumption of her rightful position as purveyor of culinary expertise at Mansfield, Mrs Mallory agreed.

'Tell the boys I will not tolerate lateness and I will bring everything that I will need.'

Faith thanked her profusely, and as soon as she was out the door, she ran as fast as she could, since she was loaded down with the assorted equipment and ingredients for today's class. She was late herself.

Angry voices greeted her as she pushed open the front door. Good Lord, she wasn't all that late. She heard what sounded like a chair falling over, then abrupt quiet, followed by Daryl Martin's voice, choked with anger: 'I'm going to kill you, Buxton. You'd better watch your back.'

'What's going on here?' Faith's own voice was raised as she stepped into the room.

Sloane Buxton very deliberately righted the overturned chair. 'I'm afraid we got a little rowdy, Mrs Fairchild. I'm sorry. It won't happen again.'

His loyal lieutenants, who had been standing on either side of him, echoed the sentiments. All three were the pictures of innocence, appropriately chastened. Daryl's face was impassive – the mask in place – impossible to tell what he was feeling or thinking. The ninth graders, all three, including Brian Perkins, looked terrified. John MacKenzie was pointedly staring out the window and Zach Cohen – Zach Cohen was laughing.

Faith went right to tuna fish.

'Easy, tasty, good for you, but you have to remember to drain the oil or water it's packed in before using it.'

As she expected, Daryl returned after the class was dismissed, slipping in the back door. Faith was busy tasting what was in the canisters. Someone had mixed salt with the sugar and the flour was flecked with black – coarsely ground pepper, obviously meant to suggest mouse turds. She'd have to come back later and replace the contents. Mrs Mallory said she was bringing every-thing herself, but Faith didn't want to take any chances. She could just see her running out of sugar or flour and thinking Faith herself had contaminated the ingredients.

'Hey.' Daryl's soft voice startled Faith.

She shook her head. 'Soy sauce in the milk, salt in the sugar, and God knows what in the flour. And a brawl. What is going on here?'

'I can't stay long. I have to go to lunch today.' He smiled ruefully. 'Pride, you know. When you've been dissed, you don't crawl into bed and pull the covers over your head.'

'As much as you'd like to,' Faith said.

'Yeah.'

'So what happened?'

'It was dumb. I was dumb. I lost it – and I hate that. We were all here waiting for class to start. I opened my knapsack and took out the folder with the packet you gave us. I found this inside.' He handed her a folded piece of paper, which he had taken from his pocket. It was a Xerox of one of the original Aunt Jemima pancake mix ads. Someone had added to that offense by further thickening her lips with a marker and drawing obscenely large breasts.

'Sloane was next to me. He was smiling. "Wouldn't have thought you'd go for older women, Martin", he said, and his buddies laughed their heads off. I was going to smash his ugly face in, then stopped and kicked the chair instead. You heard the rest.'

'It's sick.' Faith stared at the picture. Where had Sloane gotten it? Because it had to be Sloane, after the business in class about the pancakes.

'I am so sorry, Daryl.' Seldom had words seemed so inadequate. 'I don't know what to say.' She felt sick – and angry. She'd like to smash Sloane's face in, too. 'Let me keep this and I'll call Patsy as soon as I get home. The only good thing is that this makes it clear who's been doing all this. I searched his room and found nothing, but he'd be too smart to leave anything incriminating lying around. Maybe I should check his two friends' rooms. It could be a group of them.' Strength in numbers. Mobs. Lynch mobs.

'Not a bad idea. And in the meantime, I'm going to be keeping my eye on Mr Buxton.'

She remembered she hadn't told Daryl about the knife or other stuff she'd found in Zach's room. When she did, Daryl's reaction was typically calm.

'I'll take the knife. He's either going to hurt himself or someone else with it. Best put it out of his reach.'

'But won't he miss it?'

'Sure, but things disappear from people's rooms all the time. The good old open-door policy. The school covers itself by telling us not to keep valuables on campus.'

'What about all his computers and the other things, sound systems?'

Daryl laughed quietly. 'Zach has been known to buy, sell, and trade. And he told me he has all the serial numbers. None of it is going anywhere unless Zach gets his money or something in trade – barter is mostly what he does. He's a computer hack himself – the kid is so far out of anyone's league here, including the computer science teacher – and he knows what everyone has and thinks he knows what everyone needs.'

Faith shook her head in amazement. 'Now, what we *need* is to put everything together, tell the headmaster, then confront Sloane. He might confess when faced with the evidence.'

'That kid wouldn't confess to anything if his own mother was on the rack. No, we have to catch him – and we will. Now, I'm out of here.'

Faith wanted to give the boy a hug and did. 'See you at the bonfire. Maybe by then this will all be over.'

Daryl hugged her back. 'Don't get your hopes up.'

Faith had made sure to be one of the first mothers at nursery school that afternoon, and the only problem with that was it meant peeling a reluctant Amy from a riding toy before the eyes of all those who followed. They made it home; Faith put Amy down for her nap, then checked the answering machine. There was one message. It was Tom.

'Hi, honey. Hope your class went well. I shouldn't be late today, and my sermon's pretty much done, so we can do something tomorrow.' His tone was determinedly jaunty. Faith was immediately suspicious. 'I don't know about Mom and Dad, because ... Well, the thing is, Dad called, and he hasn't told Mom he had lunch with me and that we know about everything. So he can't ask her about the weekend.' There was a longish pause. Faith was surprised at her father-in-law. What was this, junior high? 'Anyway, could you call Mom and invite them? Tell her about the bonfire thing and that I'm pretty free tomorrow? I'll talk to you later. Love you.'

As if she didn't have enough on her plate. Faith was annoyed, but she reminded herself that this was not the Fairchild men's area of expertise – relationships, communication, especially close to home. Tom was great with other people. She punched in her in-laws' number and Marian answered. After the hello, how are yous, Faith asked her mother-in-law to come for the weekend.

'We haven't seen you in a while, and there's a big bonfire at Mansfield Academy on Sunday night. They sit around, drink cocoa, and sing songs. I know the kids will love it, and it would be even more special if you were there.' Faith meant it. She was very fond of both Tom's parents, and the kids adored them.

'That's very sweet of you to think of us. Of course we'll come, but I'm afraid I can't get away for the whole weekend. I'm in the middle of replacing the living and dining room drapes. I never really cared for the old ones, which I cut down from some my mother was getting rid of when we moved here. As I'm sure Tom told his father when they had lunch yesterday, I'm leaving soon for a little trip and I want them up before then, so Dick will have a place to sit down. Right now, fabric is spread out all over the place.'

No flies on Marian.

'How—'

'Left the credit-card receipt on his night table, and who else would he be meeting there?' Marian said before Faith could finish her question. 'Now, I must be going. I have a million things to do to get ready. We'll see you at church.'

'Are you sure you won't come earlier – Saturday afternoon? We could go shopping.' Marian loved to shop.

'No, but thank you. I've ordered everything I need from TravelSmith. See you soon, darling. Bye.' Marian Fairchild, explorer, world traveler. She reminded Faith of all those wonderful female Victorians who scaled mountain peaks, penetrated jungles, and shot rapids with aplomb – and always took time for tea.

She had no sooner hung up than the phone rang again. It was Pix.

'I was just about to call you,' Faith said truthfully. 'Amy's napping. Why don't you come over?'

'I can't. I have to pick up Sam at Logan. I don't know when I've been more glad to have him home. Danny wouldn't talk to me last night or this morning, except to say I was getting bent out of shape about nothing and that he wouldn't be answering to "Danny" anymore.'

'Not answering to Danny?' Faith was confused. Had the boy adopted one of his computer passwords as his name to drive his mother even more crazy?

'Dan. We have to call him Dan now. Of course, when we named him, I assumed he'd be Dan at some point, but not until he was older. We'll just have to get used to it. My mother said it was about time when I told her, that he wasn't a little boy anymore – which I know – and it's easy for her to say, since she's always called him Daniel anyway, and I assume he'll respond to that.'

Ursula Rowe, Pix's octogenarian mother, was invariably correct, although not in a Millicent McKinley sort of way. Ursula was more circumspect, and this quality of gentle omniscience was one Faith treasured – at the same time, she was glad her own mother lacked it entirely.

Having ranted, Pix spoke more calmly. 'He's going to be getting extra help in math at school, and I've hired a tutor to work with him on Saturdays on math and whatever else he needs.'

The Pix machine had gone into action.

'But won't that interfere with hockey?' Danny – or rather, Dan – was on the JV team.

'No,' Pix said wearily, 'apparently he left the team before Christmas. Why one of the coaches didn't get in touch with us, I am at a loss to understand. But I do understand why Danny, Dan, hasn't been eager to have us come to his games lately. I feel bad, because I've never been a big hockey fan and was just as glad to stay home. I should have suspected something.'

'Oh, Pix, how could you know? And you've always gone to everything.' Too late, Faith realized that that was the point.

'Exactly. All three of us have to look at how we've been

behaving. I should have been in closer touch with his life, particularly regarding school. One thing is clear, though. The computer goes. I told him at breakfast. If he needs to do research or write a paper, we can plug it in and either I or Sam will monitor what he does. He's addicted and it has to stop.'

Faith did not feel in a position to give child-rearing advice to the woman on whom she depended for her own, but this did sound a little like Big Brother, or Big Mother – and Dan would view taking away his computer like cutting off a limb. She immediately decided not to say anything about the sound system, but she'd tell Tom about the whole mess. Pix was scared. And when people are scared, they'll do anything. Especially when it comes to their kids.

'The traffic is going to be terrible coming home. I have to go. Sam offered to take a cab, but I want time alone with him to tell him what's been happening.'

'Let's talk more tomorrow.' Faith said good-bye and hung up the phone. She picked it up immediately to call Patsy. Dire as the Miller situation was, it was nothing compared to Daryl's.

'The whole point is that we *are* different. There was this girl on my hall in college who used to say, "Patsy, I wouldn't care if you were purple with polka dots. Color is only skin-deep". After a while, I gave up trying to make her understand that it wasn't. She'd worked the whole thing out for herself and felt just fine about the race thing.'

Patsy was at Faith's, Ben was at a friend's, and Amy was sitting in her old high chair, finger painting on the tray. After she'd shown Patsy the Aunt Jemima ad, Faith had tried to describe how she'd felt – sick, angry, and guilty. Ashamed for her race, and that had led to Patsy's statement.

'All I could say was, "I'm sorry". I couldn't say I knew how he felt, because I don't know how he feels. I can suppose, but not presume. Does that make any sense?' Faith asked.

'Lots,' Patsy said, and reached for a piece of shortbread. Faith always had good things to eat. 'I've done some workshops with teachers who tell me proudly that they don't see color. They treat all their students alike. Well, bullshit, excuse me, madam. If you don't see what color your students are, you are missing the whole picture. And nobody treats everybody alike.'

'So, what I do is ...' Faith frowned.

'What you do is what you've been doing. You didn't choose being white, but you can choose the kind of white you are. Now, should we take this pile of sorry stuff to Harcourt and have him haul the little bastard in, or do we give Daryl some more time?'

'We give Daryl some more time – and me, too. But a deadline. Monday. I'd like to have a look at the other kids' rooms, including this boy John MacKenzie, who makes me a little uneasy. I can slip away during the bonfire on Sunday night.'

'Sounds reasonable. Now, we'd better clean that child up. She's got more paint on her face and in her hair than anywhere else. She's the whole Rainbow Coalition in one.' Patsy laughed and Amy joined her. After a moment, Faith did, too.

When Patsy left, Faith realized she hadn't checked her E-mail and should have while her friend was there. Daryl had said he'd keep in touch that way when he couldn't see her. Normally, Faith checked it every morning, but more frequently now. There were three new messages. One was from Sandra Katz, a member of the very informal Uppity Women's luncheon club. The group was meeting at her house next week and she said the only thing she wanted on the menu was fresh raspberries; otherwise, Faith could surprise them. 'We need fruit – and color – at this time of year!' she'd written. Faith quickly replied that Sandra could consider it done. Maybe she'd build the whole luncheon around the fruit – salad with a framboise vinaigrette, game hens with a raspberry glaze, and for dessert, raspberries – au naturel, with slightly sweetened crème fraîche for those who wanted it and plates of *friandises* – chocolate truffles, oatmeal lace cookies, bite-sized macaroons, and shortbread hearts.

The subject of the next message was 'Not Your Average Sheila' and Faith didn't recognize the name of the sender, Patrick McClaine. It was from Niki.

G'day Faith!
Patrick's putting some steaks on the barbie, and when I saw a computer sitting on his desk, of course I asked if I could use it to let you know that I am alive, but kicking is not necessary in this incredibly laid-back country. Patrick informs me that with the start of school vacation today, I have selected perhaps the worst time to be here. The roads and beaches will be jammed. But I don't care. The more Australians I meet, the better.

I took the Indian Pacific from Sydney to Perth, totally amazing trip. Went on part of the longest straight stretch of track in the world and through what has to be the most isolated town. I'll never tease you about Aleford again. Cook, the 'Queen City of the Nullarbor' – which means 'zero trees' – has a total population of three. Tough for play dates, or much else. Picked up a car in Perth. Thank God for air conditioning and have maybe gotten the hang of driving on the wrong side of the road. Aussies are very kind about this. Ended up here in Cervantes. Australians are into unusual names. Like the aboriginal ones best – Yallingup, Manjimup, Kalamunda, etc. No windmills at Cervantes, but did find a Don Quixote at the Pinnacles – incredible limestone spires, hundreds of acres of them. Patrick was photographing them for some magazine (he's a photographer, duh). After a while, though, we decided seen one ... Anyway, here I am at his house overlooking a gorgeous beach (may start working for the Australian Tourist Board, with all these adjectives).

Despite the gallons of sunblock I'm going through, don't miss New England winter at all, but do miss you guys. Am pretty sure we won't be checking E-mail after we eat, but try a reply.

xoxo,

Niki

P.S. A sheila is a girl, by the way. Got to love the lingo.

Faith sent a chatty message back, omitting virtually everything that was currently going on in her life. For a moment, she'd let herself relax and join Niki gazing out at the ocean and feeling the sun on her face – she didn't care how hot it was.

She almost overlooked the last message. No subject, and the name of the sender was 'Cyberite'. She assumed it was some sort of spam and hesitated for a moment. The last thing she wanted was to unleash a virus, yet, like Pandora, she couldn't resist. She clicked, but it wasn't plagues, sorrows, and misery for mankind that appeared on her screen; it was one very specific, very terrifying message just for Faith herself:

MIND YOUR OWN BUSINESS AT MANSFIELD,
BITCH, OR YOU'LL BE VERY, VERY SORRY.

Tom did come home early, and Faith took the opportunity to run back to Mansfield to replace the ingredients with unadulterated ones. Her initial frightened reaction to the anonymous E-mail she'd received had abated as she realized that it had to have come from Sloane, warning her not to get involved in what she'd observed between Daryl and him in class. And perhaps he knew she'd searched his room. He was the type to slip a hair in the door or some other James Bondian trick to tell if anyone had been there. It could have been on his computer – the files would have shown when they were last opened. Normally, people didn't notice this, but then, Sloane was definitely not normal.

'Cyberite' – a play on words for *Sybarite*? She wouldn't put it past him.

'I won't be long, honey,' she said as she left. Friday night was pizza and salad night at the Fairchilds', and Faith had prepared the dough already, stretching it into shape. They always made two: one Amy and Ben's creation, one Tom and Faith's. She had some chorizo sausage, mushrooms, caramelized onions, and ricotta cheese for theirs; tomato sauce, sliced peppers, pepperoni, and Parmesan for the kids. Ben had recently demanded pineapple and ham after tasting Hawaiian pizza at a birthday party. Faith explained that this was not a native Hawaiian dish and he'd have to eat it elsewhere or wait until he was a grown-up with his own kitchen. 'Yes,' she'd told Tom, who looked as if he were about to protest, 'I am a food snob and I intend to raise my children without American Chop Suey or Hawaiian pizza.'

There were a couple of kids at the computer terminals in Carleton House's former dining room when Faith walked into the room on her way through to the kitchen. She smiled and said hi to the first group, causing obvious consternation to the one farthest from the door.

'Mrs Fairchild!' Zach Cohen jumped out of his chair and stood in front of the screen, turning off the power button on the surge protector with his foot. The computer obligingly crashed instantly. The boys on either side of him were no less dismayed.

'I left a message for my mother telling her where I was,' Dan Miller said defensively, blushing. He always blushed when he was upset – or angry.

Of course he knew his mother wouldn't receive it until she got back from the airport with his father.

Faith didn't want the boy to think she was spying on him – and she wasn't. 'I had to bring some things over. Mrs Mallory is taking the class tomorrow and I thought she might need them.' Zach and Brian – it was Brian Perkins who rounded out the group – nodded.

'That should be interesting,' Zach said, and everybody looked at each other for a few seconds more before Faith said, 'Well, I have to be going. Do you want a ride home, Dan?'

'You've been talking to my mother,' he said, not defensive now, but accusatory. Didn't mothers in Aleford have better things to do than talk to one another about their children? It was written all over his face. He was blushing again.

'She did mention something about your wanting to be called Dan, yes. I happen to think it's a fundamental human right to be called anything you want to be called, so long as you don't scare the horses.'

They didn't get the allusion, but that was all right. They got the drift.

'I have a cousin Robert who was always called Rabbit, until a couple of years ago he did the same thing and just said it wasn't his name anymore,' Brian said. It was the most Faith had heard him say since she'd seen him the first day in class. Friendship is a wonderful thing.

'See you guys in class and perhaps over the weekend. Dan, Mansfield is having their bonfire on Sunday night and we're going. Why don't you come with us?'

'I think I'm grounded until my fortieth birthday, but I'll ask my mom.' The other two laughed. Dan didn't.

She walked away, her thoughts focused on what had been on the screen that they didn't want her to see. The most obvious possibility was porn of some kind. She knew it was ludicrously easy to access just about anything sexual two – or more – human beings might engage in. Make that animals, too. Given the state of their hormones, porn was the most likely. But could it have been something else? Something violent? Something forbidden? She tried to erase the notion of the three boys hacking into some sort of missile-control system or even the system at Aleford High to boost Dan's GPA from her mind. 'Cyberite' – that was the nom de plume used to disguise her correspondent's identity. It sounded like something these guys would pick, but why? No, it had to be Sloane.

It didn't take long to empty the canisters, clean them out, and replace the contents. She was almost finished when Paul Boothe entered with a package of frozen enchiladas from Trader Joe's. He was quite surprised to see her.

'Mrs Fairchild! This is devotion. And on a Friday. I've just decided to forgo dinner and have my own little TGIF celebration in my rooms with this and a goodly amount of scotch.'

It seemed that he had already imbibed a goodly amount of said liquor.

'Mrs Mallory is taking the class tomorrow and I had to get some things ready for her. No gathering at the headmaster's?' Faith realized she hadn't received an invitation. Perhaps it had been a onetime courtesy.

'Canceled. Our beautiful, magnificent, outrageous Zoë is not permitting anyone to enter her abode until she has her trinkets back. But I speak too lightly. It was a major theft and I can well understand why she's furious.'

'But she couldn't possibly suspect one of the faculty!' Faith exclaimed.

He grinned slightly lopsidedly from the liquor. His pock-marked face assumed an altogether different look – rakish, roguish, and definitely leering. She was glad to hear the *click, click* sound of the keyboards coming from the room next door.

'The faculty,' he answered her, 'are no better than the boys, and in some cases, quite a bit worse. Plus, we don't make very much money and the Harcourts' missing items would go a long way toward raising one's quality of life – if not now, then in the not-too-distant future.' He stared pointedly at his frozen entree.

'Do you have anyone in mind?' Faith intended to take full advantage of the man's loose lips.

'That would be telling, but I will say it is not I. Too déclassé, and it's up to us superior beings to keep standards high. I reveal myself as a social Darwinist, but then, you are probably not familiar with the concept, its having no culinary implications except in relation to food-gathering techniques.'

He popped his dinner in the microwave and pushed some buttons. Faith thought little of his food-gathering skills, but, ignoring the put-down, she said mildly, 'Yes, I know what a social Darwinist is and am glad not to be so self-described.' His reference to scotch and now social Darwinism, that intellectual exercise to justify the superiority of one's own gene pool just what Mansfield kids needed – reminded her of Sloane Buxton. Sloane's room wasn't far from the teacher's. Was he, even now, sitting in front of the fire in Boothe's room with his Mark Cross travel bar open, waiting to resume their mutual-admiration society? Sloane, the perfect specimen, seemed tailor-made to be one of Boothe's followers.

'Have you ever had Sloane Buxton in class?'

'Our own Adonis. No, I'm afraid little Sloane has never made the cut. Smart boy, just not intelligent. He's in a kind of discussion club I run, though. An informal grouping. We meet in my rooms to talk about various things. Our last topic was the roots of Aquinas's *Summa theologica* in Abelard's and Anselm's thought.'

That must have had them on the edge of their seats, Faith said to herself as she left the room. There must be more to this select little club than medieval philosophy. What else was Boothe passing on – or out? She left the teacher to his dinner preparations, and stepping into the next room to get to the front door, she noted Brian, Dan, and Zach were just in front of her. She debated offering Dan a ride again, but let it go. Clearly, the boy wanted no part of the adult world – or at least the one he associated with his parents.

It was quite dark and she was hurrying along the path, her head down as the biting wind blew straight into her face.

'Whoops! Sorry, Mrs Fairchild. I wasn't looking where I was going.'

'Neither was I.' It was Sloane and they had collided. His laptop case had fallen to the ground, as had Faith's pocketbook. For a moment, they were occupied gathering up their belongings and repeating apologies. In his Nautica jacket, school scarf wound around his neck, and earmuffs, he could have stepped from the pages of Mansfield's glossy brochure – the picture of healthy young manliness. A sound mind in a sound body indeed. The school's motto was *Veritas et Bonitas* – Truth (and a nod to Harvard) and Goodness. At the moment, Sloane seemed to embody it. But it was all on the surface. She was sure of that. The temptation to bundle the boy into her car and drive straight to the Averys' house for questioning was almost overwhelming. Monday. They were going to wait until Monday.

'I've been enjoying your class. What's on for tomorrow?' he asked politely, both of them with teeth almost visibly chattering, wishing to be on their way.

'Mrs Mallory will be imparting some of her baking secrets to all of you – old favorites, I gather. But don't let me keep you out in the cold. See you Monday, or Sunday at the bonfire.'

'Ah yes, the bonfire. My last one. Would you like me to walk you to your car? It's so dark now, and what with Mrs Harcourt's recent experience, there's no telling who might be lurking about.' He seemed to relish the thought.

'That's quite all right,' Faith said crisply. 'Thank you, but I'm just over there.' She pointed to the lot by the main building. She couldn't leave without trying to get some information from him, though.

'The argument – the one you were having with Daryl Martin before class today – what was it about?'

If he was startled by the abruptness of her question, he didn't show it.

'I wasn't arguing with Daryl. You must have received a mistaken impression. My friends and I were fooling around, kidding each other. Possibly he misinterpreted something. But I have nothing against Martin. Diversity is the cornerstone of our democracy.'

Faith felt herself gag and vowed to make regular meetings with Patsy or someone very much like Patsy part of whatever was going to happen to Sloane Buxton.

There was a second or two of silence. 'Well then,' he said, 'I'll take my leave.' And he did.

What was it about this place? Sloane, Paul Boothe, Winston Freer, Zoë – they all talked and acted like caricatures of themselves. Puzzling about the school, Dan Miller, and whether Tom would remember to preheat the oven for their pizza took her all the way home.

Tom's parents had beamed all through the service, and while Faith thought the sermon topic, 'Commitment, Not Confinement', was a bit pointed, even that went over well. As usual, Dick Fairchild repeated that he was darned if he knew how he had ended up with a preacher for a son to any number of parishioners at coffee hour and Marian sought out the women she knew, sitting as far away as possible. Faith rushed home with the kids, fed them, and put the finishing touches to the traditional Sunday dinner she'd prepared: roast beef, Yorkshire pudding, green beans almondine, and Parker House rolls, along with cups of potato-leek soup to start and a mile-high apple pie to finish. Her hope was for profound postprandial drowsiness to settle over the men as they watched some sort of sporting event on TV, while she pumped Marian, who ate like a bird, for information during the washing up. Her mother-in-law would insist, and this time Faith wouldn't refuse her offer of help. Ben would enjoy sitting with his father and grandfather. Amy, who would probably awaken from her nap just as the pie was served, could make Play-Doh food at the kitchen table. Unlike Ben at this age, she would drift into her own world and the adults around her could speak freely.

Dick Fairchild scraped the last morsel of his second piece of pie from his plate. 'You'd be the death of me if we lived any closer, Faith. I am well and truly satisfied.' He stood up and pushed in his chair. 'Son, why don't we menfolk watch the pregame show and leave the ladies to enjoy each other's company?'

It was well and truly embarrassing.

'Sure, Dad, you go on in. I'll just help get these dishes off the table.'

'Now, now, I'm sure Faith doesn't need any help about the kitchen.' He frowned. Didn't Tom get it?

'Your dad's right, honey. You watch the game. There isn't that much to do here,' she lied.

Marian stood to one side, smiling slightly during the exchange. She helped Faith clear, then when her daughter-in-law voiced her token protest – 'Oh really, you don't need to help' – Marian replied, 'That's sweet of you, dear. It's nice not to have to clean up every once in a while. What I'd love to do is sit with my granddaughter and read to her. How about that, Amy? Do you want to go to your room with Granny and pick out some books?'

Amy, of course, squealed with delight, and after they left the room hand in hand, Faith wanted to squeal in dismay. It wasn't that she felt driven to have this little heart-to-heart with Marian. It was facing Tom and his father with the news that she was as clueless as they were. No, that was wrong. She wasn't clueless. She knew exactly what Marian was doing and why, but she hadn't actually heard her say anything.

Maybe there would be time later.

But there wasn't. Faith walked into the den, to find only Ben awake, watching clips from Ravens and Giants games so intently, he didn't hear her. Dick Fairchild had nixed the bonfire because he had previous plans to watch the Super Bowl with his brother, Ed (Fairchild Ford in nearby Duxbury). Marian and Dick would be leaving at five. It was getting to be 'now or never' time for Faith's talk with her mother-in-law. Faith went upstairs. Amy and Granny had moved from books to dolls and were having a grand old time.

'Such a treat for me,' Marian said. 'I can never get enough of this special little girl.' The special little girl threw herself into her grandmother's arms. Faith didn't have the heart to intrude on this lovefest, and besides, there could well be a special circle in hell for mothers who would.

She went back to the kitchen and made chicken soup with chickpeas, onion, tomato, ditalini, and rosemary for supper. She'd send some home with her in-laws, along with some baguettes and some cheeses from Formaggio Kitchen – Cheddar for Dick, Camembert for Marian. They'd have the same themselves. No matter how much they'd eaten at dinner, they'd still need something before they went to the bonfire.

The bonfire. Ben was tremendously excited to be staying up this late on a school night. There had been a break in the recent cold spell and the sun had shone all day. The moon had been the merest hint of a smile last night; it would be a grin tonight in the clear, star-speckled sky. Faith was excited, too. She planned to slip away and give John MacKenzie's room, as well as those of Sloane's friends, who were also in Carleton House, a quick once-over. They were pretty sure it was Sloane, yet they didn't know if anyone else was involved or not. She thought about Paul Boothe's little club. She'd like to get into his room and look around. Check his linens, for example. Make sure the only white sheets were on his bed.

Things were strangely silent next door at the Millers'. Pix's car hadn't left the driveway. They'd been in church – Dan, too – but hadn't stayed for coffee hour. Pix had given a little wave and smiled. One of those only-with-your-mouth smiles. Faith had told Tom all about the situation yesterday morning before they went off to the New England Aquarium with the kids. He was understandably concerned, but he agreed with Faith that she should try not to get between Dan and his parents. Dan was in the church youth group and Tom thought the best place to start would be for him to have a talk with the boy. They'd always gotten along well together. Then, with Dan's permission, Tom could speak with Sam and Pix or all three of them.

'It's about time he told them not to call him Danny. All his friends call him Dan, and Danny is a little kid's name,' Tom had said.

And he's not a little kid anymore, Faith had thought, flashing back to the hidden computer monitor at Mansfield.

Marian and Amy came into the kitchen.

'Do you think we should wake our boys up?' Marian asked. 'They look so peaceful, but it's getting late.'

'I think this is a job for Amy. Be gentle, sweetheart. Don't jump on Daddy and Grandpa. Just give them a kiss or a little tap on the shoulder.'

The three-year-old raced off gleefully.

Marian, not a demonstrative woman, give Faith a slight squeeze.

'I know you probably wanted to talk to me today – or rather, that your husband and my husband wanted you to talk to me today – but there really isn't anything to say. I'm not a young woman, nor would I want to be. I've enjoyed my life so far. I simply want to do a few things I've never been able to fit in. I'm sorry Dick is upset, but he'll get used to it.'

'Both of them seem to be overreacting a little,' Faith said.

'I'd say a lot,' Marian corrected her. 'And there will be more to come. One of the blessings of age is that you begin not to be so concerned with what other people think of you.'

Faith was a bit taken aback at this. What was Marian talking about? She couldn't keep herself from asking, 'Even your husband?'

'Even your husband,' Marian replied firmly. 'Now, you can

tell them everything's fine and you're going to come down and have lunch with me soon. That should hold them, and I want you to see my new furniture.'

What was it that was so seductive, so mesmerizing about fire? The sight of the gigantic crackling bonfire, jagged tongues of flame shooting straight toward the heavens, was so overpowering that Faith stopped dead at the end of the path. The scene before her was mythic. Boys were darting to the side for more fuel for the fire, dark figures suddenly illuminated as they threw branches and other pieces of wood on to the blaze. Boys were sitting on logs, drinking not mead but cocoa from mugs. Boys were singing campfire songs – 'Red River Valley' and 'Freight Train' – a harmony of voices that had changed and voices that hadn't.

'Holy smoke,' a man behind her blurted out. The people around him all laughed. He was talking to a boy next to him, presumably his son, a Mansfield student. 'When you said a bonfire, I figured the kind we make at the beach to roast hot dogs and toast marshmallows. Not the Towering Inferno. They must have had to use a cherry picker to build it. Any marshmallow you put near this would incinerate a few feet away!'

It was true. And the staff was keeping everyone at a safe distance.

Faith walked on, feeling the warmth of the blaze. Showers of sparks fell like shooting stars on to the icy surface of the lake. She was alone. Tom had not even pretended to want to come with her and miss the game. Ben was torn. Why did there have to be two things he wanted to do? In the end, his parents decided for him. Faith had promised to take him next year. She was relieved at the outcome. Having Ben along would have cramped her style. She couldn't very well drag him behind her while she searched the students' rooms.

Connie Reed was coming toward her. 'Welcome, welcome,

Faith! Get something to eat, drink, and pull up a log. Are you on your own?'

'I'm afraid the Super Bowl won out. A tough choice.'

'I quite understand – just look at all the transistor radios. But this is the night we've always had the bonfire, so neither Ravens nor Giants can stand in our way.' She'd made a joke, seemed a little surprised, and chuckled.

Faith got a steaming mug of cocoa and sat down on one of the logs, next to the family that had been behind her on the path. The father was reminiscing, speaking almost reverently as he gazed into the flames.

'I remember watching the Vendome fire,' he said. 'It must have been around '72 or '73. I was at B.U. A bunch of us heard about it and went down Comm. Ave. to watch. The Vendome was empty. It wasn't a hotel anymore. They were converting it into condos. We all thought it was terrific. Watching something burn like crazy when you knew nobody could get hurt.' He paused. 'We didn't find out about the nine firemen who died until the next day.' Seeing an anxious look on the face of the little girl beside him, he added, 'But I love bonfires. Nice, safe bonfires like this one, where we can look all we want. Now, that flame right in front of us reminds me exactly of one of Harry Potter's dragons. See the shape? What do you think, Katie?' The dad swung his child on to his lap.

'It does! And at the bottom of the fire, it looks kind of like a face. And the whole thing looks like little cities. Skyscrapers. And there's another face.' The Vendome tragedy was totally forgotten.

For the moment, Faith allowed herself to feel content. It was a beautiful night. She was with people who seemed happy simply to be together. The singing stopped and for a while there was nothing but the sound of the boys' voices, with an occasional touchdown reported or a shout as a piece of fuel ignited, intensifying the flames. Orange, many reds, yellow, a flash of white, a flash of blue – Faith tried to sort out the colors. The air smelled wonderfully of smoke, pine-scented smoke from the fir boughs the boys had gathered. As the branches burned, the fire raced into each needle, creating a blackened skeleton before it disintegrated. The corrugated cardboard from the cartons they were throwing on turned into fans of fine ash like the pleats of a Fortuny gown.

Then suddenly there was a voice – a full-throated alto. A woman's voice, mournful and tender. Everyone stopped talking to listen to the song. Zoë's sad Russian song. It was followed by another and another. One of the music teachers accompanied her on the guitar. It was magical. She was magical, standing in front of the fire, swaying slightly from side to side, her hair long and loose.

Then it was over; she moved away.

' "Love is a spirit all compact of fire, / Not gross to sink, but light, and will aspire". Will must have been staring into the hearth.' It was Winston Freer. He'd added a jaunty tartan tam-o'-shanter to his Tyrolean greatcoat, and the effect was more that of a lawn figurine than an international man of fashion. The fire had deepened the pink of his rosy cheeks and static from his cap had caused wisps of his white hair to cling to the wool.

'Which play is the line from?' Faith asked. 'It's beautiful.'

'Not one of the plays. *Venus and Adonis*. Like many modern mystery scribblers and the like, who long to be remembered for the literary novel they've managed to get published, Shakespeare apparently valued the poems above the plays, his bread and butter. Of course, *Venus and Adonis* was well regarded by the Elizabethans. The age-old tale of an older woman seducing a handsome younger man.'

Faith was sure it was not her imagination that a decidedly lascivious note had crept into Freer's discourse on the Bard.

'Speaking of which, I must go and congratulate Zoë on her performance. The songs, I mean.'

He really was very, very wicked. Faith couldn't help smiling as he made his way closer to the headmaster's wife.

Faith knew she should go to Carleton House – she didn't know how long the students would stay here by the fire, by the lake – yet the scene held her. She didn't want to leave. She saw some of the kids in her class, Daryl included. Robert Harcourt was throwing a crate into the fire. He seemed as enthusiastic as the students. Spying her, he raised a hand in greeting. She walked over toward him to thank him, although it had been Ms Reed who had issued the invitation. He was busy with another crate and she didn't want to bother him – or get quite that close to the bonfire. The heat baked her face, her eyes smarted, and she stepped back into the shadows, joining the group gathered there. The darkness, intensified in contrast to the blaze, blanketed them. She could hear the boys behind her talking, and all at once she became very, very interested.

'What an asshole. I mean, he's a senior. He's only got a semester to go. Why would he want to screw everything up? And you *know* Harcourt will tell the colleges he's applied to.'

'Yeah. But don't be so sure. He's one of those guys who can get out of anything. I'm sure that's what he's thinking right now. Right now, wherever he is, getting laid and stoned is my bet – probably in front of a TV. I wish.'

They laughed.

'I mean, it was a total accident that his parents showed up to take him out for lunch. No one would ever have known he wasn't here, since it's Project Term.'

'He's going to kill them. 'Rents. They do the stupidest things. I'm glad my old man and old lady are divorced. They never come to see me. We have a "You go your way, I'll go mine" thing going, which is fine.'

He spoke with bravado, but Faith wasn't convinced.

'Anyway, Sloane's going to be in a shitload of trouble, but it's only January, and he'll have landed on his feet by graduation. Bet?'

'You're on. Say fifty?'

'Fifty sounds good.'

They moved off out of earshot, but Faith had heard enough.

Sloane Buxton: AWOL.

Six

'What's all this about Sloane being missing from campus?' Faith asked, sidling up to Daryl.

'Yeah. His parents came to see him today and the boy could not be located. Harcourt started checking, and no one has laid eyes on him since Friday. He wasn't in class Saturday morning, but I figured he was sleeping in and his friends didn't say anything. Mrs Mallory didn't take attendance. By the way, we all like you better, but the cookies were fly.'

'I saw Sloane late Friday afternoon. He knew I wouldn't be teaching the class and that Mrs Mallory would.'

'There you go. Unless you passed your class list on to her, she wouldn't even know he was supposed to be there. You didn't give her your list, right?'

'You know I didn't. I forgot, plus I think the less she sees of me, the better for both of us.'

'You and the rest of the world. But the woman can cook. Anyway, Sloane's bed hasn't been slept in, so he must have split Friday night or early Saturday before anybody else was up. Harcourt is bullshit.'

'Does this happen a lot? Kids taking off?'

'Not really. It isn't that easy to get anywhere from here unless you have a car. Someone, probably one of his girlfriends, must have picked Sloane up. He is very popular with the ladies. He also probably planned to slip back tonight at the bonfire. One of his buddies has been by the path since we got here to head him off. They must have put a note in his room, too.'

'Will he get expelled?'

'No such luck. Think of the stink his parents would make, especially this close to graduation. The last thing the school ever wants is angry parents shooting their mouths off, even if their sainted son is in the wrong. I told you about the senior caught smoking dope, and look at that school in western Mass. where that kid – actually he was no kid; he was twenty – carved some antigay thing into another kid's back and got off with a suspended sentence and probation. He'd slashed somebody a week earlier, but that kid didn't tell his parents. It's a question of which parents apply the most pressure on the school.'

Faith shuddered. Then she brightened. 'Maybe this incident, paired with what Sloane's been doing to you, will convince the headmaster to take a tough stand.'

'But we don't have any real evidence yet. He'll deny it and his parents will back him up. Harcourt will do what we thought he'd do in the beginning – have a couple of chapels on diversity – and we're nowhere.'

Diversity. The word reminded Faith of Sloane's use of it. Daryl didn't need any more fuel for his fire, though.

'We're not nowhere; we're sure it's Sloane,' Faith protested.

'Yeah – and who else?'

The boy was right. Hate feeds on hate, and it seemed likely that more than one Aryan Nation type was involved in this persecution. 'I'm going to say good-bye to Dr Harcourt and case out a few rooms at Carleton House before I leave.' Paired with the first part of her sentence, it made for a weird 'To Do' list.

Daryl frowned. 'I can't leave yet; otherwise, I'd go with you. I'm in the chorus, and we sing a few songs at the end. Be careful – or wait until tomorrow morning. Right now, there's no one on campus to speak of. The security guys are all here to keep us from ending up as toast.'

'Then this is the perfect time.'

'For a lot of things – think about it.'

Faith did as she walked over to Robert Harcourt, who was now sitting down next to his wife, savoring his cocoa as if it were a rare elixir. Zoë had just poured something from a silver flask into her mug, but then, Zoë wasn't the cocoa type. An empty campus. An empty house. But the Harcourts' alarm system would be on – as it hadn't been before. What else was vulnerable? Or who?

'This was wonderful,' she said enthusiastically, sweeping her arm back toward the conflagration. 'I hope I can come back next year and bring my family.'

'By all means,' Robert said expansively, leaping to his feet like the gentleman he was. 'I'm glad you enjoyed it. It's always a special night at Mansfield, one of the old traditions we've continued.'

'We love traditions here. The older the better,' Zoë said. Whatever she was drinking had blurred her words slightly. She didn't get up.

'And the music, particularly your songs, was perfect. This is the kind of night I'm sure we'll all remember for the rest of our lives.'

Zoë nodded in acknowledgment. 'A few ballads from my homeland.'

'And I hear the class is going well. I should be taking it myself.' Robert gave one of those hearty ha-has that Faith associated with retired British officers who'd served in 'Inja, don't you know'.

It was a shame to take some of the bloom off, yet she felt she had to tell him what she knew about Sloane. And yes, she wanted to know just how deep the shit was that Master Buxton was in – ankle-, knee-, or shoulder-high?

'I overheard some of the students mention that Sloane Buxton, who's in my class, is off campus without permission. I thought I should let you know that I saw him late Friday afternoon. Or rather, early evening. It must have been around five-thirty.'

And what was she doing back at Mansfield at that time? The question was unspoken but clear. Harcourt's attention was diverted from the fire and Zoë stood up.

Quickly, Faith added, 'Mrs Mallory took the class for me yesterday. I like to be with my family on weekends and understood from Ms Reed that it would be all right to have your cook substitute. I didn't have time after the Friday class to leave some things for her; then I had to wait for my husband to come home to watch the children.'

'The children, of course,' Zoë purred. Millicent or someone else had said the Harcourts were childless. Out of choice? Maybe the Mansfield boys were enough, or maybe Zoë didn't relish morning sickness – or stretch marks.

'This is very interesting.' Robert was all business. 'Where did you see him? Was he behaving in an odd manner?'

He always behaved in an odd manner, but Faith couldn't very well describe her antipathy toward the boy without revealing his attacks on Daryl. But why the question? Was Harcourt already framing a defense for letting the boy stay on after breaking a major school rule? Poor Sloane was upset, depressed, acting irrationally?

'I was walking toward the main parking lot, where I'd left my car. It was cold and windy. We both had our heads down and bumped into each other. There was nothing unusual in his behavior. We picked our things up, spoke briefly about the class. I mentioned Mrs Mallory would be doing some baking with them the next day and we went our separate ways. He seemed to be heading back to his dorm.'

Harcourt nodded. 'Thank you for passing the information along. It doesn't look good, I'm afraid. He may have thought his absence would go unnoticed with a substitute, and things are a little more relaxed during this term. Frankly, I'm surprised he hasn't turned up here, mixing with the crowd.'

Obviously, the headmaster hadn't noticed the lookouts and realized Sloane would be warned by his friends. Maybe the plan was to appear at Harcourt's door, hat in hand, abjectly apologetic after the bonfire, when the headmaster was still basking in the afterglow. That's what Faith would have done.

With the chorus of 'Men of Harlech' ringing in her ears and the crackling flames growing dimmer, she walked back toward the main campus. It was dark and the total absence of any human beings was scary. For a moment, she was tempted to take Daryl's advice and wait until morning, but she shook off the thought and hurried to Carleton House. It rose out of the darkness, only the porch light on, looking not so much a ghostly galleon as a ghostly tea cozy. She went up the front stairs and walked in. A dark figure rushed toward her. She opened her mouth to scream and a gloved hand forced the sound back into her throat. She tried to break free and kicking wildly, sent them both tumbling to the ground.

'Shut up! Shut up!' her attacker whispered fiercely. It was a boy, and as her eyes adjusted to the dark, she saw who the boy was: Zach Cohen. The boy whose room she'd searched. The boy who kept a knife under his pillow.

'You scared the shit out of me – pardon my language.' He took his hand away and sat up. 'I'm sorry. I didn't know it was you. I mean, of course I didn't know it was you. I didn't know who it was. Everybody's down at the lake. I wasn't thinking. I just didn't want you to yell. I'm really sorry.' He seemed dazed.

Faith was feeling pretty dazed herself. She stood up to turn on the light, then thought better of it and sat down again. In truth, her legs were a little wobbly.

'What are you doing here?' she asked before he could.

He was dressed completely in black, a watch cap pulled down

over his ears, gloves, and a long black trench coat – the Peterman Company kind. Every parent's nightmare come to life since the tragedy at Columbine.

'The bonfire isn't really my thing. All that rah-rah stuff. I decided to stay in the dorm.'

'But this isn't your dorm.'

He looked at Faith sharply. 'You're right – it isn't. But a kid who lives here had something for me and I thought this would be a good time to get it, since I didn't have anything better to do.'

She realized he was carrying a laptop case.

'It's mine. I'm not into ripping things off from people,' he said quickly.

This made sense. He didn't need to steal, given what he had in his room from buying, selling, and trading.

Then he asked, 'Are you going to report me?' He sounded like a very little boy for a moment.

'Is the bonfire required? Are you breaking a rule by not being there?'

'I never heard that we had to go. It's not in the rule book anyway.'

It was no doubt beyond the headmaster's ken that any Mansfield boy would not want to be there, so a rule wasn't necessary.

'Then I'm not sure what I'd be reporting you for,' Faith reasoned. 'I'd like to see you in brighter colors, but the fashion police aren't around tonight. I'm also taking you at your word – that the computer is yours.'

It looked exactly like the laptop case Sloane had been carrying Friday, but to the untutored eye – and Faith's definitely was – one carrying case looked very much like another.

Zach visibly relaxed.

'Jeez. You are not like any adults I've ever known. Thanks a lot, and believe me, I won't forget this.'

While he was in the mood, Faith thought she might try to get a little information – about the boy himself and what he might have picked up about what had been happening with Daryl.

'Where do you live? Are you from Massachusetts?'

He appeared to find it a reasonable question – or maybe it was that anything would appear so after the events of the last five minutes.

'I've lived in a bunch of places. My parents like to travel. I've been in boarding schools pretty much since I was nine. Right now, my mother lives in France and my dad is in New York. They got divorced last summer and the joint-custody thing is mostly who can stick me with the other one. I don't care really. It's pretty much always been like this. They can't help the way they are. They never should have had a kid – and I guess I've heard that often enough.' He gave a little laugh, which sounded a whole lot like a sob, and Faith found herself close to tears – the sad and mad kind.

So this was what had caused the metamorphosis. One mystery was cleared up. If Zach was unwanted, he was going to behave and look as unwanted as possible.

'What do you think of Sloane Buxton and his friends? You were there on Friday in class. What was really going on?'

'I try not to have a lot to do with them. They're users – and bullies. Last fall, it was pretty bad, but they've moved on to other people. That's what usually happens. This type of guy has a short attention span.' He appeared happy to discuss his tormentors. 'Friday, they were yanking Daryl's chain. They are such morons. He's cool, and I've never seen him react before, but there was something in his notebook – I didn't see it – and he just exploded.'

Faith nodded.

'And what was going on later when I came back? When you were with those ninth graders at the computer?' But Zach had had enough of show-and-tell. He stood up and his face shut down. 'We were just playing some dumb games. Nothing special.

I have to go now. I don't want to run into anyone else. See you in class,' and he was out the door.

Faith figured Sloane's buddies would have rooms on the floor below his, and she figured correctly. But James Elliot's and Sinclair Smith's rooms were totally different from their friend's. A quick search revealed both were of the 'shove dirty clothes on the closet floor and leave as much athletic equipment, including jockstraps, strewn around as possible' school. Neither boy had anything except textbooks in his bookcase, although both had yearbooks for each year – Daryl's pictures all intact. Sinclair had a stack of *Playboys* in his desk drawer. James went in for *Hustler*. Sound systems, stacks of CDs, and computers loaded with games – very nasty games, James's taste leaning slightly more toward dismemberment than Sinclair's – completed the picture. The only thing of any possible importance was that James had a Hotmail account. She didn't know enough to figure out what name he was using. The icon had his own name, but he could make another one up, open an account, and close it in rapid order. Make it up with the name 'Cyberite', for example.

She was beginning to feel as if she could write one of those little books stacked next to bookstore registers like candy in the supermarket, *What I Learned About Life in the Teen Lane from Searching Their Rooms*. Or she could start her own Web site with a virtual tour of dorm rooms: 'And here we have what was probably an apple core but now resembles a desiccated body part, speaking of which, don't forget to peek at the vast array of condoms under Sinclair's underwear.' These rooms lacked Sloane's domestic touches, the boys having settled for school-issued interior decorating, save for an easy chair, apparently necessary for serious studying, or at least for serious magazine reading. Sinclair had a picture of a large sailboat, himself at the helm, and judging from the strong resemblance, it was his family that was beaming encouragement his way.

There weren't any other rooms occupied on this floor. She

went up to the next floor and tried Boothe's door. It was still locked. Not that she blamed him, but she wondered if she at least might be able to look in the windows from the fire escape that climbed the side of the house his suite occupied. Lack of a flashlight, remembrance of how cold it was away from the bonfire, and the possibility of getting caught dissuaded her.

John MacKenzie's room turned out to be on the first floor, not far from the landing where the two graceful front staircases ended. The house must have formerly been the headmaster's or built by one of the original faculty members, someone with independent means and good taste. It was a shame that it had been carved up into dormitory rooms.

There was no porn, no frivolity of any kind in John's room. Like Sloane's, there was a minimalist quality to it. No sound system, no stuff. But unlike Sloane's with its country house look, this room resembled a monk's cell. Nothing in excess. Except books. The bookcase was crammed full and there were stacks of books on the floor next to it and next to the bed. Philosophy, psychology, history – no fiction. She turned his computer on and, unlike the others, it was protected with a password. She typed in his name, trying a few variations, but nothing happened. What was it that John didn't want anyone to see? She shut down and looked through his drawers. Nothing of interest except a pile of papers labeled 'Papers from Professor Boothe's Courses and Rewrites'. She picked one up. He'd gotten a C. Boothe had written almost as much as John had. Attached to it was the rewrite. Apparently, John had shown the paper to Boothe, yet this time there was only one comment written at the end: 'Better, but not best'. What a pedant the man was! And dangerous. This was the kind of thing that drove kids into the vortex of depression. She felt a stab of pity for John, excluded from his mentor's current course. The message was loud and clear: You're not making the grade. She wished she could sit the boy down and tell him about the Paul Boothes of the world. What little, little men they really were. At the same time, she thought, What would John do to make himself feel better, feel superior? Go after Daryl?

She left Carleton House feeling depressed herself. What was this school really about? James and Sinclair, upper-class bullies, would graduate and go on to one of the Ivies, as had Dad and Granddad and Great-granddad, continuing to sail on through life. Angry Zach would eventually explode, harming himself or someone else. John would get rejected by Harvard, because Boothe would refuse to write him a strong recommendation letter, since to do so would mean lowering Boothe's standards, and John would kill himself or maybe the teacher. Too simplistic? At the moment, she didn't think so.

'Have a good time, honey? Kids are asleep and the Ravens won.'

Faith must have looked blank. Tom put his arms around her. 'Football team. The Super Bowl. Remember?'

'Sure. I'm very happy for you.'

'No, you're not. You're sad, because I'm a Giants fan. Plus, I lost five bucks to Sam. Noting the extreme interest you have in the subject, I'd suggest we head for bed and you can tell me all about the bonfire. Or we can skip it, baby, and you can let me light *your* fire.'

'Gambling, sex, thank God I married a minister.' Faith laughed, moving up the stairs with all due speed.

Sloane Buxton had still not returned to Mansfield by Monday morning. Faith thought he might have been pulled from her class as punishment and was sitting in the headmaster's office writing 'I will never leave campus again' forty thousand times, but it was clear both from the worried looks on his friends' faces and Daryl's slight shake of his head that Sloane wasn't back.

Today she was teaching them how to make a few soups that could serve as either lunches or dinners, especially supplemented by some of the sandwiches she'd taught them how to make on Friday, a salad, or any number of breads or rolls – focaccia, sourdough, buckwheat, olive, or a simple baguette. She also planned to teach them how to eat soup and launch the Miss Manners part of the course.

The time went quickly and soon they were ladling out bowls of pasta e fagioli – that hearty Italian soup with beans, to which they'd added some chunks of sausage – and heading for the dining room.

'All right.' Faith looked at the smiling faces of the boys gathered around the table. But then, looks can be so deceiving. She'd been in most of their rooms and she hadn't slept well last night, despite her husband's excellent ministering. Zach, dressed in black, kept leaping into her dreams.

'There are few things in life more pleasurable than sitting down to a good meal with friends and/or family. I make that distinction, because family dinners may not be your favorite get-together at the moment.'

'Or any moment,' piped up one of the ninth graders. 'Like every Thanksgiving is the same. My uncle Len drinks too much and starts listing all the mean things my mom did to him when he was a kid, and his wife gets mad, too, like she's never heard it before, and my cousins and I are out of there.'

Faith nodded. She catered a lot of family reunions and could count on one hand the ones that went off without a hitch. 'Blood is thinner than gravy,' she told the boys, and wondered what she meant. They seemed to understand.

'However, friends are the family you choose, so think about eating with them.' She picked up her soup spoon. She'd had the boys set the table with a full array of cutlery.

'It's very easy to know which piece of silverware to use. You go from the outside in. After you've put your napkin in your lap, of course.'

'Of course,' Zach said in a slight mocking tone. 'We attend

Mansfield Academy, remember? Where no napkin in the lap means nothing on your plate.'

'You always eat soup this way.' Faith demonstrated, spooning the soup away from herself and back toward her mouth in one sweeping motion.

'Why?' asked John.

'I have no idea,' Faith answered. 'Probably so you won't splash it on to yourself or the table. Many conventions have no explanations, but they have become accepted customs. When you don't follow them, you look—'

'Like a jerk.' Daryl finished for her and copied the way she'd eaten her soup.

While they were eating, Faith asked them to list the manners no-nos they already knew.

Brian Perkins, noticeably silent in class, as usual, recited in what had to be a dead-on imitation of his mother. 'Take your elbow off the table. Don't slouch. Don't talk with your mouth full. I told you not to slouch. Bring the food to your mouth, not your mouth to the food. If you keep slouching, you won't get any dessert.'

Everybody laughed and he looked pleased.

'Okay,' James said. 'I've got a few. Don't eat until everybody's served. Don't reach for stuff across the table. And my favorite, which my dad does all the time and it drives me crazy, don't make loud chewing noises.'

'And no reading or wearing your headphones, no matter how much you don't want to hear your sister whine,' Sinclair added.

'Don't eat with your knife,' John MacKenzie said solemnly, and seemed surprised when they laughed.

'We'll continue this discussion tomorrow, but you guys are very knowledgeable. Now, just the way you wait until everyone is served before eating, wait until everyone is finished before clearing. That said, we can get on with it and I'll see you tomorrow.'

She was sure it wasn't her imagination, but the class seemed more relaxed without Sloane. Even his friends seemed to forget about his absence. She wondered if they knew where he was. She was almost sure they did. They lived in the same dorm and traveled in a pack. The worried looks on their faces at the beginning of class might have been due more to concern about the trouble they could get into for not telling than any concern about good old Sloane.

'Faith?'

'Yes, Charley, what's up?'

Charley MacIsaac, Aleford's veteran police chief, never called without a reason.

'I understand you've been teaching a cooking class at Mansfield. Something tragic has occurred, and I'd like to come by and talk to you. The state police are in on it, too.'

Faith was alarmed. Had something happened to Daryl? Everything had been fine in class, and that had been only a few hours ago.

'Is it one of the students? You've got to tell me.'

'We're not a hundred percent sure yet, but we think so. They had a big bonfire last night.'

'Yes, I know. I was there,' Faith said impatiently. Why wasn't Charley getting to the point?

'This morning, some maintenance workers were clearing away the debris and ... well, they found human remains.'

'What!' Faith yelled into the phone. 'You mean all the time we were watching, there was a body in the bonfire?'

'That's what it looks like,' Charley replied. He made arrangements to come by and hung up.

Faith stood still, seeing the flames, and the voice she couldn't get out of her mind was that of the little girl talking to her father – 'The bottom of the fire, it looks kind of like a face'. There had been a face – or rather, a faceless face. And it had to have been

Sloane's face. She started to gag when she thought of them singing, sipping cocoa, sitting in the flickering shadows from that ghastly light, the shooting sparks, the fiery embers, the horrific fuel – a corpse – beneath the crackling blaze.

Sloane. He'd never left campus at all.

It *had* been his last bonfire, just as he'd said.

But who would want to kill him? He was just a kid. Not a particularly nice kid, but a kid, and it was hard to conceive of anyone harboring the kind of sustained psychotic anger required for this kind of murder. It had been well planned out. The timing was too perfect. Those large piano crates conveniently standing by the side of the lake, fodder for the bonfire. He had to have been killed on Friday night or very early Saturday, before the bonfire was assembled. And if it happened Friday, she might have been the last person to see Sloane Buxton alive. And that was why the police would be ringing her doorbell any minute.

Ben would be home from school soon. She called Pix and enlisted her aid. Pix, who didn't ask any questions, just came over and scooped Amy up to come play with the dogs, promising also to meet Ben's bus. So the house was empty when Charley walked in, followed not as Faith had expected, by Detective Lt John Dunne of the state police – the man Faith liked to think of as her assistant – but by a trim, impassive young woman in uniform. She had shoulder-length wavy red hair pulled back in a low ponytail and the wrong color lipstick.

'Lorraine Kennedy.' She extended her hand. 'I've heard about you from Detective Lieutenant Dunne. He's out of state, taking a course.' She managed to convey that everything John had said about Faith was negative and that whatever course he was taking was none of Faith's business. It was not a good start. Her accent placed her squarely in South Boston or maybe Charlestown. Dunne was from the Bronx, and his voice always made Faith nostalgic for egg creams and the zoo. Lorraine Kennedy's made Faith feel that she was one of those people 'from away'.

Faith shook the woman's hand. Ignoring the reference to Dunne, she said, 'I can't believe something like this has happened. It must be the missing boy, Sloane Buxton.' Then she motioned toward the living room and they all sat down. She didn't offer coffee. It wasn't a social occasion. She repeated her assertion as a question. 'You do think it's Sloane, don't you?'

Charley answered. 'We're waiting for his dental records, but he's the most likely possibility. Been gone for a few days. Didn't tell his friends he was leaving, and they swear if he'd been planning to take off, he'd have told them.'

'I think that's true. If only so they could cover for him.'

'You didn't like him, did you, Mrs Fairchild?' Lorraine Kennedy asked abruptly. It was the kind of question that wasn't a question.

Faith could play the same game. 'Why on earth would you assume that?'

'You don't seem to be too broken up about one of your students being cremated right before your eyes.'

Charley looked uncomfortable, but didn't say anything.

'Believe me, I am "broken up", as you put it. He had his whole life before him, and this was a gruesome act. But I didn't really know him. I'm teaching a two-and-a-half-week course, which only started last Wednesday.'

Charley's beeper went off. He looked at it and went out into the hall to the phone. He was pretty familiar with the parsonage.

Lorraine Kennedy took advantage of the chief's absence to be even more direct, if that was possible.

'Look, I know you think you're some kind of Nancy Drew, and you've gotten in the way of a number of Dunne's investigations, but you're not going to mess up mine. Is that clear?'

Faith felt her face flush. 'Very clear. And what is it you're doing in my house exactly?' She could make herself clear, too.

'I want to know what the Buxton kid said to you Friday night, where the two of you were, and which way he was going when he left. I've heard what you told Harcourt, but I want to hear it straight from you.'

Obediently, Faith went through the whole thing again. Detective Kennedy took notes, seemed satisfied, and stood up. Charley appeared in the doorway.

'It was Buxton all right, and we have a suspect.'

Lorraine smiled at Faith as she left. 'I know something you don't know' could have been written in a balloon coming out of her mouth. Faith closed the door, and as she called next door to tell Pix she was coming to get the kids, she addressed the absent officer: 'I wouldn't be so sure about that.'

She was no sooner back and struggling to get Amy out of her Rugged Bear snowsuit than the phone rang. She was tempted to let the machine pick it up, but it could have something to do with what was going on at Mansfield. Hastily, she'd whispered to Pix what had happened – it would be, or already was, all over town – and promised to call. So it couldn't be her neighbor.

It was Daryl. A very frightened Daryl.

'I'm in the headmaster's office. The police are here. I can't reach Mrs Avery. They think I killed Sloane!'

Faith reacted swiftly. 'Don't say another word until Patsy gets there. You have the right to remain silent and have your lawyer with you. I'll call my husband and we'll stay with you until she gets there. Don't worry. You know you didn't do it.'

'I do and you do, but they need somebody to pin this on.' He was almost hysterical. 'Somebody told them what I said in class on Friday ...'

'Daryl, shut up! I mean it! Tell them you'll be happy to coop-erate as soon as your lawyer arrives to advise you. Tell them Tom and I will be with you in the meantime. Have you called your parents?'

'No way!'

'Never mind. Just try to stay calm. We're coming.'

Faith called Tom, who arrived immediately and helped

repackage the kids in their outdoor clothes. It had snowed again during the night and it was bitter cold outside. Somewhat bewildered at returning to play with the beloved Miller dogs – Artie, Dusty, and Henry – so soon, the kids scampered through Pix's back door, and Faith returned to her driveway, where Tom had the car waiting.

'I left the Harcourts' number on Patsy's beeper. I don't think Daryl has that number. He must have been trying her at work and home. Pray she's not in court today.'

'Why do they suspect Daryl?' Tom asked.

'Remember I told you about the incident in class Friday? The Aunt Jemima ad in Daryl's bag and Sloane's racist comment? What I didn't tell you is what I – and the whole class – overheard Daryl say to Sloane, something about how Sloane better watch his back, because Daryl was going to kill him.'

'Great. The kind of thing kids say all the time in anger. And this is enough to hang a murder rap on the boy?'

'Apparently.'

Neither of them said what they were thinking – that a lot of people might think it was enough to hang the rap on a black boy.

No one was talking when Connie Reed ushered the Fairchilds into the headmaster's office and left. Daryl was standing with his back to the group, staring out the window. Harcourt was behind his desk and the police were in the two chairs in front of it. Faith went over to Daryl and put her arms around him. The boy had been crying. There were long lines on either cheek, like the first spring rain on the slopes of a dusty creek.

'Is Daryl under arrest?' Tom asked.

Lorraine Kennedy answered. Charley had stood up; she hadn't. Clearly, Faith Fairchild was the last person she wanted around. 'We just want to take him in for questioning. He was heard to threaten the victim's life on Friday, which was shortly before he disappeared, and we are investigating the nature of those threats.'

Faith held her finger to his lips as Daryl was about to burst into an angry denial. 'Wait,' she said softly.

Tom turned to Robert Harcourt. 'This is a horrible business, and I don't have to tell you how it's going to affect your students and their families. Please call on me for any help. And I know my fellow clergy in Aleford will also want to be involved.'

'Thank you. I appreciate it. I'm meeting with the faculty shortly to activate our crisis-management plan. Then we'll be gathering in the chapel with the boys before dinner tonight to announce Sloane's death officially and hold a brief prayer service. The news is out, though, and everyone is shaken. My assistant, Ms Reed, has already been handling calls from parents and the media. How could something like this happen here? It's the act of a madman.' He looked over at Daryl in disbelief. Faith saw the look and hoped it was because Harcourt couldn't possibly imagine Daryl doing something like this, not because the student wasn't who Harcourt had thought he was.

The door burst open. Patsy Avery hadn't waited to be shown in by Harcourt's faithful watchdog. The lawyer was by Daryl's side in a flash and a bayou Valkyrie addressed the group in a booming, extremely precise voice.

'Could somebody tell me why you have dragged an innocent seventeen-year-old boy in front of a kangaroo court on the basis of a few angry words that kids say to one another, their parents, even their teachers' – heavy sarcasm – 'every day of the year?'

Now Lorraine Kennedy stood up. She looked tired, or bored. 'I take it you are Patricia Avery, the boy's lawyer?'

'I am Patricia Avery, the boy's friend, and his lawyer now,' Patsy spat back.

'We just want to know what went on between your client and Sloane Buxton on Friday. The kid was very much alive then, and now he's ash, some teeth, and a bone or two in a cardboard box. We're trying to find out what happened in between. Nobody's arresting anybody. Nobody's accusing anybody.'

'Was Sloane at dinner Friday night?' Faith interjected.

Lorraine ignored the question and looked at Patsy to continue, but Patsy wasn't about to say anything.

After a short pause, the detective answered, 'No, he wasn't.'

'And he wasn't eating pizza in his room with his friends or anything like that?'

Harcourt answered now. 'No. They looked for him in his room before going to the dining hall, and he wasn't there. They assumed he'd gone on ahead, but they were surprised he wasn't there, either. They always eat together.'

Faith knew all about cafeteria segregation – the popular kids' table, the jocks' table, the nerds' table, the druggies' table, the bottom-feeders' table.

'So, he was most probably killed shortly after I saw him. Dinner is at six, right?'

'Right,' Harcourt replied, looking puzzled. Obviously, he was wondering where Faith was going with this. Patsy picked up on it right away. She pulled Daryl closer to the window, and after exchanging a few words with him that the others couldn't hear, she announced triumphantly that if it was all right with everybody, she'd be taking Daryl to her house for dinner.

'Because there is no way he could have killed the boy, put the body in whatever got burned up in the bonfire, *and* been at chorus rehearsal until five minutes before six, then dinner, where any number of students and faculty saw him, followed by attendance at a viewing of *Monty Python and the Holy Grail* and *Johnny Mnemonic* videos in his dorm lounge.'

Daryl looked like he'd just heard he'd won the lottery. Dazed, but happily so.

Lorraine Kennedy wasn't about to give up so easily.

'A boy has been murdered. We need to know as much as possible about what appears to have been his last day on this earth.'

'Then you do that, but my client has nothing to say that could help you.'

'Why don't you let me be the judge of that?'

'Because you are *not* a judge and Daryl Martin is not being charged with anything. I think you'd better let this go.'

The two were very evenly matched. Detective Kennedy turned to Daryl. 'Go have a good dinner, Daryl. If you decide to cooperate with us, here's my card. We'll be in touch.'

Daryl took it silently.

Patsy looked at the headmaster. 'Then with your permission, we're out of here. Depending on what Daryl wants, I'd like to keep him overnight at our house. He's had quite a shock.'

'Certainly. Of course. We have his parents' approval form on file, but I'm sure he'll want to call them. See you in the morning, Daryl,' the headmaster replied, some of his former vigor restored. Protocol. A form filed, a rule followed. These were things he understood – things that were not murder.

Tom and Faith prepared to follow them out, but Connie Reed walked in, temporarily blocking their exit. Faith put her hand on Tom's arm. She wanted to find out what was going on.

'The Beverly police have finally reached the Buxtons and they are on their way. Yesterday, they went from here straight to Foxwoods – you know, that gambling casino in Connecticut.' The woman did not even attempt to hide the contempt she felt for such places and the people who frequented them. 'They were sure Sloane had a good reason for being wherever he was, they told the authorities, so they weren't worried.'

Faith didn't find this unreasonable. Sloane had always seemed like someone who knew what he was doing. Until the end, that is.

'In light of their arrival, I've rescheduled the faculty meeting until after dinner and mobilized the various teams to go into each dorm and talk with the boys immediately. The police are keeping the media at bay and I have informed them you will be issuing a statement tomorrow. Here are the calls you will need to answer personally, although I've told these parents that our top priority at this time is the student body and that you will be with them, of course. These are the calls I've taken care of.' She waved another sheath of pink memo slips. 'These parents simply needed a little reassurance.'

A tour de force, and there wasn't a person in the room who wasn't impressed.

'The main point I've been stressing is that this was a random act of violence' – the old itinerant-tramp theory again, Faith thought – 'and that there is absolutely no cause for any concern regarding their children's safety.' Connie stood up straighter, if that was possible, locked eyes with the headmaster, and declared, 'There is absolutely no cause for any alarm whatsoever at Mansfield Academy.' Her voice rang with truth and her cup ranneth over.

Seven

'But darling, you have it the wrong way round. I didn't seduce *him*; he seduced *me*.' Zoë Harcourt sounded amused – and proud.

'You must have been mad.'

The Harcourts were on the path that led from the parking lot to the chapel and main campus, concealed from Faith's sight by the rhododendrons. It was the next morning and she was late. The students were waiting, but she stayed where she was. Robert Harcourt's voice had been resigned. Zoë's wasn't.

'Oh, grow up, Robert. Sloane fancied himself quite the cocksman – unlike you – and he wasn't half-bad. Nobody got hurt. What was the harm?'

There was a momentary pause; then Robert said softly, 'What about the harm to me?'

Zoë laughed. 'You shouldn't have brought it up; then you wouldn't have known anything about it.'

There was no trace of her sultry Slavic accent. Her matter-of-fact delivery was straight from New York.

She continued: 'This place is beginning to seriously bore me. I'm ready for a new chapter, and if you want to stay, that's your decision, but I can't keep bailing you out.'

'I thought we'd settled all this. Are you threatening me again?'

The words were white-hot with anger. The change was startling.

'Be good for you to do something else. You're in a rut. And there's no need to be so dramatic.'

'I asked you a question. Are you threatening to pull your money out of the school?'

'Figure it out for yourself, darling. Must run now. I have to be in town.'

Faith jumped behind a thicket of bushes as Zoë walked past, her head high and her lips curved in a smile. The sky was overcast and snow was predicted, but apparently everything was sunny and bright for Mrs Harcourt.

'Sorry I'm late, guys,' Faith apologized. It was going to be a challenge turning her thoughts to how to chop onions and make meat loaf when she wanted to think about what she'd just overheard. Zoë and Sloane. Zoë and a whole lot of others. Who had been in the car with Zoë the night of the faculty sherry party? Had it been Sloane? Zoë's answer to her husband's accusation implied that it wasn't her custom to go after students, but when opportunity knocked …

Brian Perkins and the other ninth graders had their notebooks out. Everyone was sitting or standing, displaying varying degrees of uneasiness. There was none of the nonchalance, or even amusement, that had been apparent after the chapel meeting on the Harcourt theft. And what was going on with that? Were the trinkets still among the missing? But Sloane had been found – found dead – and every single boy in Faith's class was frightened.

She couldn't ignore it.

'Let's take a break before we start. I made brownies. Get some glasses and milk.'

Her suggestion met with neither approval nor disapproval. The boys poured milk and grabbed a brownie. Everyone except Zach.

'Not hungry,' he said tersely.

Faith nodded. She hadn't been hungry since she'd heard about the murder, either.

'I know you were his closest friends.' She nodded toward Sinclair and James. 'This must be terrible for you. It's hard enough to lose someone your own age, but in this particular way …' Her voice trailed off. She really didn't know what to say.

Daryl had a wary look on his face. It had been there when Faith walked through the door and hadn't altered in the slightest.

'Dan Miller says you've solved a lot of crimes. That you help the police. And you're here, I mean, obviously you're here, but are you trying to solve this one?' Brian asked.

Some of the boys looked skeptical. The cooking lady, a detective? Not likely.

Without detailing the number of times corpses had turned up on her watch, Faith simply said, 'I have worked with the police on some cases that involved my firm, for example. But no, I'm not trying to solve this one.' She paused. 'If I were, though, what would your hunches be?'

Zach shut down completely. It was astonishing. His body telescoped into itself, as if he were trying to disappear.

'Some kind of weirdo pyromaniac,' John MacKenzie offered. 'Maybe he didn't know Sloane was in the piano case. Maybe Sloane had climbed in there to sleep one off and when the bonfire got lighted, it was Sloane of Arc.'

Nobody laughed and John blushed. 'It was just an idea.'

'Asshole,' Sinclair said angrily. 'Don't you think he'd have woken up when they moved the case? You were there when we built the bonfire. The cases went on the bottom.'

'Wouldn't someone have noticed that one case was heavier than the others?' Faith asked.

'Not necessarily. The maintenance guys had been chucking all sorts of stuff in them. So the fire would have a good base,' James answered.

Faith remembered the broken chairs and other things piled to the side the day she had toured the campus with Daryl. It wouldn't have been too difficult to take a lot of the material out, place the body inside, and cover it with newspapers or something else combustible.

'Do you think it's a serial killer?' Brian asked. He appeared to have the utmost faith in her. 'Some of the kids' parents have taken them home.'

Faith didn't think it was this type of murderer. This wasn't a random strike for kicks or the kind of crime that someone could duplicate again and again, getting off on the victim's pain, the bloodshed, the snuffing out of a life. It was actually a very tidy murder. She presumed Sloane was dead before he was placed in the box that served as his coffin. A quick death, she hoped, and, since it was committed on campus, she was sure she was right. The killer couldn't have chanced someone's happening along – or hearing a scream for help.

'No,' she said firmly. 'I don't think so. I think whoever killed Sloane Buxton intended him as the victim and the only victim.'

'And that person would be who?'

Paul Boothe wandered in and picked up a brownie. He seemed to have had a liquid breakfast and his clothes looked as if he'd slept in them.

He straddled a chair, turning it around, and repeated his question to the room at large.

'So, who did it? And why? Elliot, Smith. You were his buddies. Spill your guts. You've *got* to have thought about this.'

The boys looked at each other. Sinclair cleared his throat. When he answered, his voice was shaking.

'We have no idea, Mr Boothe. The police asked us, too. Sloane didn't have an enemy in the world.'

The teacher stood up. 'Somehow, I find that very hard to believe. The problem here is figuring out which one had the strongest motive.'

He left, leaving confusion and even more fear in his wake. So much for crisis-team intervention, Faith thought. Maybe Boothe had missed the training sessions – or perhaps he was simply sadistic. But he was right. Motive. That's what it came down to at this point. Means had been gruesomely established. Opportunity abounded. But motive? So far, the only one Faith had come up with was jealousy. Sloane was screwing his head-master's wife. A crime of passion?

The rest of the class was a blur. She gave Daryl what she hoped was a reassuring smile as he left. When she turned around, she was surprised to find Zach still sitting in the kitchen, in the same position he'd been in for most of the morning.

'The police questioned me.'

'Because of the bullying?'

Zach nodded. 'Somebody told them about it. I told them I stayed as far away from Sloane as possible. I wouldn't have taken this class if I'd known he was in it, but Mrs Fairchild ...'

'Yes?'

'I didn't tell them about being here on Sunday night – or that you were here.'

What was the boy driving at? Sloane was very, very dead by that time.

'What were you doing here anyway?' he asked, focusing a sharp gaze, very different from the lack of affect she'd seen up until now.

'What were *you* doing here?' It was another cop trick. Answer a question with a question.

It didn't work.

'I asked you first.'

'Look, we're not in third grade here. Everybody was at the bonfire. You were supposed to be there, too – even if there wasn't a rule about it. You certainly weren't supposed to be sneaking around a dorm that wasn't even yours.'

'And you weren't supposed to be sneaking around, either. We didn't have a night class and don't tell me you needed a spatula or something.'

It was a stalemate and they eyed each other warily.

Finally, Zach sighed and looked at his watch. Faith had the advantage when it came to tardy slips.

'Look, Mrs Fairchild. I like you. I don't know what you think of me, but I should tell you that I'm out the door in a very few minutes and I can leave with both of us in the dark, so to speak, or not. But you have to go first. I know something's going on. Clue me in and maybe – no, make that probably – I'll tell you why I was here.'

Faith made one of her typical snap judgments and decided to reveal Sloane's persecution of Daryl Martin.

'I knew he was a shit, but not that much of a one.' Zach's mouth was wide open.

'We never got any hard evidence though. He had a Hotmail account, which couldn't be traced and I searched his room, and his friends' rooms, without coming up with anything.'

'Ah, but I have his laptop. That's what I was doing here. He'd sold it to me a week ago and I'd given him the money. He said he needed it in a hurry, but had to keep the laptop until exams were over. You didn't say no to Sloane; besides, I had a customer for his computer. I don't know why he was selling it. It's a G three, very nice. Not a G four, but maybe that's what he was trading up to. Very sexy, very expensive.' Zach wrenched himself away from Macintosh land and continued. 'Anyway, when I heard he'd split, I decided to go get it. It would be just like him to keep stringing me along and not deliver the goods. When I told you I wasn't stealing anything, I wasn't lying. I even have the agreement he signed.'

'But I don't see how that helps us.'

'He didn't know I was going to take it, so he wouldn't have erased anything, and if there's anything to find, I will.'

A man with a mission.

The police had sealed Sloane's room. Faith knew she really ought to take the laptop to Lorraine Kennedy. On the other hand, there was no harm in waiting. Evidence of Sloane's racist vendetta against Daryl might make the police turn to Daryl as a suspect again. She'd talk to Patsy. This wasn't suppressing evidence. The computer belonged to Zach now.

'Hold on to it, but don't do anything until I tell you. You have to promise that. I want to be with you when you open his files.'

'No problem. You tell me when.'

The Uppity Women's luncheon was Friday and she'd planned to do the preparations on Thursday, but she'd have to shop. She was taking Amy down to Norwell to see Marian today, so she'd have to put off exploring Sloane's laptop until tomorrow.

'Late tomorrow afternoon?'

'Okay. Here is as good a place as any. You can't come to my room' – Faith didn't think it necessary to mention she was already intimately familiar with it – 'but you can always invent some excuse for being here and so can I most days.'

Faith nodded.

'If there's anything on Buxton's laptop, we can get at it,' Zach said again. He smiled at her sweetly, one hacker to another.

Faith had just finished tying the sash on Amy's dress when the phone rang. She sat Amy carefully in a chair, told her to think about a nice story to tell Granny, and raced to answer it. It was Charley MacIsaac.

'You certainly made a great impression on Lorraine Kennedy. It's seldom that you get the chance to hear the rich vocabulary that was coming out of the woman's mouth after we left Harcourt's office. She's not crazy about Patsy Avery, either.'

'And you called me to tell me this, because ...'

'It's not why I called you. It was just the first thing I thought of. You never want to think that a kid has killed anyone, especially another kid, so I wasn't unhappy with the way things went. But you guys were wrong. She's a good cop and she wasn't jumping to any conclusions. She just wanted to talk to the boy. We still want to talk to him and a whole lot more Mansfield students. It makes you sick. This kind of case.' Charley's sentences were running pell-mell into one another.

'I know how you feel. Her cremation remark was crude, but it's how I feel. That I was standing right there a few feet away while a seventeen-year-old's life was being totally obliterated. Or at least that's what the murderer hoped.'

'They want to meet you. The parents.'

'Sloane's parents?' As soon as Faith said the words, she felt stupid. Of course Sloane's parents. 'Because I was probably the last one to see him alive?'

'Yeah. They haven't been taking it well. I mean, how could you? He was their only child. They can't even have a wake yet, let alone the funeral. Could you go and talk with them? They live in Beverly, up on the North Shore.'

It was possibly the last thing Faith wanted to do, yet she knew she had to go. If – and it would never happen – but if she were in this situation, she'd want the same thing. Impossible to see the loved one you'd lost, but you could see the last person he was with, the last person he spoke to – except for the person who killed him, that is.

She sighed. 'I imagine they want me to come as soon as possible.'

'Sooner,' Charley said. 'I knew you had the Mansfield class this morning, or I'd have called earlier. They know their son was in it, and they want to hear about that, too.'

Amy had her hands folded in her lap. She looked like a Hallmark card. The dress had been a bitch to iron.

'I'll go this afternoon. Tell me how to get there.'

Marian had no problem putting the visit off for a day, and when Tom heard the circumstances, he offered to work at home. Amy was puzzled at the change of clothes, but not overly so. So much of her life seemed to be made up of grown-ups moving her along from one quixotic thing to the next at varying rates of speed.

Charley's directions were good and Faith had no trouble finding Route 62 after turning off 128. She'd tried listening to 'Talk of the Nation', yet soon realized her mind wasn't simply wandering, but on an extremely long journey. She popped a tape in and contented herself with not listening to Vivaldi instead.

She checked the address, looked at the house, then checked the address again. There had to be some mistake. This wasn't the solid brick center entrance Colonial abode or sprawling cedar-shingled Victorian with wraparound porch – typical dwellings for the area's elite. Come to think of it, shouldn't the likes of Sloane be in Beverly Farms, Manchester-by-the-Sea, or Prides Crossing?

She got out of the car and approached the small Cape. The concrete path leading to the front door was well shoveled and a heavy coating of Halite discouraged any ice formation. The Buxtons were careful people. Their Christmas wreath still hung limply on the aluminum storm door. New Englanders got their trees down fast, but exterior ornaments lingered on until Easter in many cases. Faith had never been sure whether it was to add some cheer to a dismal season or to match it. She rang the bell and the door opened instantly. They must have been watching from the window.

The two parents stood side by side. Mr Buxton put out his hand and said, 'Norm Buxton. Good of you to drive up here, Mrs Fairchild. This is my wife, Irene.' His voice faltered. 'Please, come in and sit down.'

Irene couldn't speak at all and the tears that she must have been shedding steadily since yesterday streamed down her cheeks, filling the tiny powdery lines of her face. She dabbed at them ineffectually with a handkerchief and motioned toward the adjoining dining area. The table was laden with platters of sandwiches, cookies, bundt cakes, pastries, fruit – the offerings of friends and relatives, when nothing offered can possibly help.

Faith shook her head and sat down.

For an instant, her mind flashed on the Harcourts' living room – the intense colors, the exquisite furniture, the fire crackling in the marble-faced fireplace. Fire. She pushed the thought away. This living room was similar in name only – colorless and truly lifeless. Decor by Levitz and all of it beige. There was a fireplace with fake bricks and a fake fire. It had not been turned on. There was a large TV in an inexpertly stained pine cabinet. The walls were off-white and adorned with two seascapes, probably purchased at one of the open-air art exhibits on a sunny summer's day in Rockport. Faith recognized Pigeon Cove. It wasn't a bad painting, but it wasn't a good one, either. She looked about the room. There wasn't a single item that Sloane could have approved of – except the photographs. Every surface was covered with framed shots of Sloane from birth to his graduation portrait on the mantel, larger than an eight-by-ten, dominating all the others.

It was heartbreaking.

Irene Buxton found her voice.

'Tell us about Friday. Tell us how Joey was.'

'Joey?'

'I mean Sloane. We always called him "Joey" at home. He's Joseph Sloane Buxton, but he decided he liked his middle name better when he went off to private school. He was ten, wasn't he?' She looked at her husband.

He nodded. 'We wanted the best for our son. Because he was the best.' His throat closed over the last words.

Faith told them everything she could think of, embellishing the encounter on the path, emphasizing his good manners, the way he'd helped her retrieve her fallen bag. She waxed enthusiastic about his culinary skills and enjoyment of the class. She dragged in his popularity, his obvious close friendship with James and Sinclair.

Norm and Irene Buxton sat in rapt attention, nodding every once in a while. But eventually, Faith had no more to say. No more she could tell the devastated parents. No talk of bigotry, of bullying, of sex.

'I'm sorry I don't have more to tell you. I met your son only last Wednesday.' It seemed much longer.

'That's all right. You've made us very happy, coming up here. We just wanted to see you, had to see you.'

'I'm sorry,' Faith repeated. 'I'm so sorry.'

'We can't figure out how it happened is all,' Norm said in a dull voice. 'A lunatic. It has to be a lunatic.'

Irene began to sob. Faith stood up to go.

'You'll want to see his room.' It wasn't a question. Norm and Irene led the way upstairs. The top floor of the Cape had been converted into one large open bedroom and bath for Sloane – Joey. Here were all the things Faith had expected to see in his dorm room and more. Stereo, TV, athletic trophies, model cars, a Mansfield banner on one wall, one from Harvard on another. Irene followed Faith's eye. 'He was so excited about going to Harvard. It was what he'd wanted since he was a very little boy.'

'I didn't realize that he'd gotten in,' Faith said. 'I didn't know he was early decision.'

'Oh, it wasn't early decision. He found out two weeks ago. That's why we stopped by on Sunday. To surprise him and take him out to celebrate. Harvard and my birthday.'

Norm's arm, which had been around his wife's shoulders, tightened. 'There, there, now, Mother.' He closed the door and they went back down the stairs.

'He never forgot,' Irene said. 'The package arrived on Saturday and I decided to wait and open it when we were all together.'

Faith realized there was a large 'Happy Birthday, Mom' card on the mantel next to Sloane's picture. What she had also missed seeing was Sloane's gift. Irene picked it up and held it reverently in her hand. It caught the light and sent tiny rainbows across the dull walls.

'He wrote on the card that he'd found it in a flea market last summer when he was in Maine visiting one of his school friends and saved it for now He was always so thoughtful. It's beautiful, isn't it?' Irene's fingers closed tightly around the object.

It *was* beautiful.

It was also Zoë Harcourt's missing diamond-studded enamel powder case.

Faith sped down Route 128 as fast as she dared. She wanted to get home before the Mansfield students went to dinner. Sloane had stolen Zoë's treasures, and there was only one place the rest of them could be. Only one place that made sense. Sense. Things were beginning to make sense. At least she was beginning to get a sense of how and when. The theft had been well planned. Sloane knew the house, knew what to take, and dropped a button to frame Daryl. He knew the first thing the Harcourts would do was order a room-by-room inspection of student blazers. It was pure chance that Daryl got there first. And the murder. After she saw him, Sloane must have gone to his room and dropped off his laptop before dinner. His bed hadn't been slept in, although the murderer could have made it up if in fact Sloane had been killed on Saturday morning. It was important that it appear Sloane had been gone for as long as possible. If the maintenance workers hadn't been so diligent, it might have been some days before the school or the Buxtons raised an alarm. But Saturday morning didn't feel right. Nighttime, not daylight. Faith was certain Sloane had been killed on his way to the dining hall. Killed shortly after she'd seen him. And killed after he'd sent her that E-mail. He hadn't liked being questioned about what had happened with Daryl in class, hadn't liked Mrs Fairchild suggesting he, Sloane Buxton, could be up to anything wrong. Sent a last message through cyberspace, went down the stairs, out the door to his death.

She passed the Burlington Mall. She had yet to enter the place.

Just the size of the parking lots was discouragement enough. If she had taught the class on Saturday, she'd have marked Sloane absent and the sheet would have gone to the headmaster's office. Connie Reed would have known and certainly would have hunted the boy down to issue whatever the punishment was for cutting classes. But Mrs Mallory took the class, and it was a fair assumption that she wouldn't take attendance. Who knew about the substitution? Sloane, and possibly he'd mentioned it to James and Sinclair, but no. They were saving his place at dinner. They hadn't seen him since sometime that afternoon, she recalled. Mrs Mallory knew, of course, and Mabel, and anyone going to the kitchen for information the way Daryl did. Then there was Connie Reed and possibly Robert Harcourt, who might have heard about it from her. And one more person. He'd come to prepare his frugal repast Friday evening. Paul Boothe. Paul Boothe knew she wouldn't be teaching Cooking for Idiots the next day. And Paul Boothe hadn't been in the dining hall, either.

As soon as she entered the house, Faith said a hasty hello and 'Won't be a minute' to her family, then headed to her computer and went on-line. 'Be there, Daryl. Be there,' she prayed as she went to instant messaging. He was there.

'Whazzup?'

'I know this sounds weird, but go to your bookshelf and open up Janson and Brinton. Don't touch what you find there, if you do find something,' Faith typed.

'Will do.'

She could see him crossing the room and lifting the other books that had been piled on top of his art history text and the one for History of Western Civilization. It wouldn't take long.

'Holy shit! What am I going to do?' The words flew on to her screen.

'Absolutely nothing. The only other person who knows what's in them is dead. Put the books in your knapsack and bring it to the Carleton House kitchen before chapel and class tomorrow. I'll take care of everything.'

'I am not going to sleep well tonight. I can tell you.'

'Sorry. It's the only safe way to handle it. I can't come on campus now. It's too risky. Delete all this and don't worry!'

'Okay. By the way, you are one smart lady.'

'Thanks. See you tomorrow.'

Faith hit delete, closed down, and went to join her family.

Sloane had created a win-win situation for himself. He must have cut the hiding places in the thick books well before the theft, then stashed the three objects inside and switched his books with Daryl's when he cut the button from Daryl's blazer. If the room searches had been more thorough, Daryl would have been exposed as the thief and that would have been okay for Sloane. Since they weren't, he had the goods safely stashed to retrieve sometime during Project Term, before the Western Civ course started again. It was highly unlikely that Daryl would decide to bone up on Masaccio or Donatello during this down-time.

As soon as Faith had seen the birthday gift, she knew the rest of the Russian treasure trove had to be in Daryl's room. She – and the police – had searched Sloane's and she had also gone over his friends' rooms, assuming they were in on it. That left Daryl, and it was all about Daryl. Hollowed-out books make nifty hiding places, and there weren't really any other places Sloane could have used in Daryl's sparse room.

Zoë would get her trinkets back. But not all of them. There was no way Faith was going to expose Sloane as a thief to his grieving parents. Irene could keep her flea-market find, a last gift from a devoted son – and he did seem to have been devoted to his parents, his worshipers. Faith would put on gloves tomorrow, take Grandmother's pillbox and the other things from the gutted books, wrap them in something, and put them in the mailbox in front of the Harcourts' house. A pleasant alternative to junk mail. The only prints they'd find, if they dusted for them, would be Sloane's, and there was no way to compare them now.

She couldn't wait to tell Tom.

With an apology to make it up to them another time, Faith ended the Wednesday class early so she could get Amy and make it down to her mother-in-law's in time for lunch. She also had to leave a little parcel for Zoë. Being in possession of stolen goods, even briefly, was making her nervous. And when she saw how tired Daryl looked, she knew he'd meant it when he said he wouldn't sleep. He had left his knapsack under the table by the window and she had taken it upstairs to Sloane's room to make the exchange. The police had unsealed it and his parents had not yet come to pack up his belongings. Once again, she'd been struck by its impersonality. It was like a department store room. For a moment, she'd toyed with the idea of removing the portable bar, then decided to leave it alone. Nothing Sloane had done would have upset his parents. Boys will be boys. Especially their boy. Unconditional love.

But what about a boy who puts a noose on another boy's bed, who sends obscene messages over the Internet, who tries to frame him for a felony? She'd read that teenagers rarely commit crimes alone, especially murder. When a teen kills, or pursues the kind of hate campaign Sloane had, it's almost always in partnership, or with a group. If you want to find out the why, you have to look at the who – friendships, relationships. Hate feeds upon hate. That she knew. Was Sloane an exception, a loner – or, the thought that had plagued her from the beginning, was someone else involved?

She'd taken the two books from Sloane's bookcase and opened them. Daryl's name was in the front of each. When had she searched Sloane's room? Last Thursday. The theft had been discovered Wednesday morning or late Tuesday night. If she had examined the books more carefully and seen Daryl's name, it

might have triggered a train of thought that would have identi-
fied the real thief. Would it have saved Sloane Buxton's life? Were
the thefts and the murder connected? She'd put Sloane's books –
no name on the flyleaves – back in place. Let the Buxtons make
of them what they would. She'd done what she had to do.

It was raining. So much for a nice walk down by the North
River with Granny. She hastened along the path to the parking
lot, umbrella up, head down. Smack – once again, she bumped
straight into someone. Someone as polite as Sloane, but definitely not Sloane. It was Winston Freer, the English professor,
and he was hastily making amends, bending down to retrieve
both his briefcase and one of the bags Faith had dropped. Not
her pocketbook with those fragile objects, thank goodness. She'd
wrapped them in many layers of paper toweling and put them in
a brown paper bag, but as soon as she felt her grip loosening, in
her mind she heard the splintering of enamel and tightened her
grip on her precious cargo.

'Nasty weather, so sorry. Didn't see you.' Winston was
rambling on. Faith hadn't seen him since the bonfire and she was
shocked at the change in the man. Granted, he was elderly to
begin with, but he seemed to have aged even more in a very short
time. She remembered he had been tutoring Sloane. Had they
become close? Yet simply the loss of a young life, one of your
own students, was cause enough. On impulse, she reached out
for his arm.

'I'm so sorry about Sloane Buxton. I know you must be
terribly upset about it.'

He looked at her with something like gratitude.

'Yes, yes, I am. "Beauty, truth, and rarity, Grace in all
simplicity, Here enclosed in cinders lie". The Bard, again. A fine
specimen that boy. Credit to his kind. Damned fine.'

The rain threatened to drown out the old man's words. Faith
had to leave.

'I'll come by for tea soon,' she promised.

'Today?' His face brightened.

'I'm afraid I can't make it today....'

'Then we'll say tomorrow.'

Faith thought of everything she had to do, looked at his face again, and agreed.

'It's a toasted cheese kind of day,' Marian said, taking their rain-coats. 'And soup. I made pea soup.'

Faith felt all the stress of the last few days begin to seep away. Comfort food and comfortable Marian. Amy would fall asleep after lunch. Her eyelids were heavy now. Maybe Marian could shed some light on the whole Mansfield business. She'd called as soon as she'd heard about the murder on the news, and Faith had been grateful for her concern.

While Marian put the food on the table, Faith peeked into the living and dining rooms. From Tom's report, she'd been expecting glass and chrome. She should have known better. It was a big change, but the only drastic part was the light and airy feeling, apparent even on a rainy, gloomy day like today. The walls in the dining room remained the same – dark wainscoting. The house was one of the oldest in Norwell, if not the oldest. But Marian had found a simple Shaker-style dining room table and chairs. A trimmer cherry sideboard, which Faith suspected might be the work of Thomas Mosher, made the room seem larger. The heavy drapes were gone, replaced by sheers and William Morris Willow Bough valences – fronds of pale green leaves on a blue-green background. The wallpaper in the living room was gone and the walls had been painted a warm buttery yellow that picked up the color of the flowers in the chintz covering a large overstuffed couch, piled with extra cushions for even more comfort. The same chintz hung at the windows. An armoire contained the TV and a stereo system. The den had always served as Dick's home office, and the TV there, placed squarely in front of the La-Z-Boy, was his alone. Faith noted that Marian had had cable installed. She must be watching the Discovery Channel. The old wall-to-wall carpeting was gone and the floors had been refinished.

'What do you think?' Marian called from the kitchen. 'I'm not done yet. I still have to get a rug or two, a few more things to hang on the walls, and a new coffee table. I'm sure I'll find something on my travels.'

'It's fantastic,' Faith enthused, returning to the kitchen. And what was even more fantastic was that Marian had whipped most of it up on her own. The notion was daunting.

'I got the idea for the valences from that show house we went to in Aleford. Remember?'

It would have been hard to forget. That was the place where Faith had spied some of the silver that had been burglarized from her house.

They sat down to eat and Marian said, 'Dick will get used to it. He's already admitted the new sofa is more comfortable than the old one. A major concession.'

The two women smiled.

'Men are not good with change,' Marian continued. 'I'm not sure why that is. But I can imagine the hunters returning to the women they left behind and complaining that the cave was different.'

'I have a friend whose husband keeps adding on to their house because he can't stand the thought of moving. They have two kids now, and she swears if there's a third, she's calling the Realtor herself rather than undergo yet another remodeling job.'

Faith remembered why she was here – supposedly.

'Do you think that's why Dick doesn't like to travel?' she asked.

The question of what to call her in-laws had come up shortly before the wedding. Dick had cheerfully suggested she call him 'Dad', but Faith already had a dad, and while she was trying to figure out how to tell her future father-in-law kindly how uncomfortable this made her feel, Marian had weighed in. 'I don't want to be called "Mother Fairchild". That sounds like somebody's pies or a patent medicine. Why can't she call us by our first names? She already has two perfectly good parents'. Faith fell in love with her at that moment and forever more.

'Let's put Amy in the guest room and I'll make coffee,' Marian suggested.

Soon they were sitting in the new living room. Marian had her glossy travel brochures spread out on the old coffee table, which did look pretty forlorn.

'I've always wanted to go to the Galápagos. I was a bio major, you know.'

Faith hadn't known.

'And this particular cruise is perfect. Wonderful lectures, and we also visit Peru. I wish Dick would come, of course, but not if he doesn't want to, and he doesn't. He'd complain the whole time. It's not so much that he doesn't like to travel. He just wants to know where he's going. After this, I plan to go to Italy next fall – Tuscany. But I've suggested Scotland – all those golf courses – in June for us. He hasn't actually read the brochures I've piled next to his bed, but he hasn't thrown them away, either.' She drank some coffee and put the cup down. 'I would no sooner leave Richard Fairchild for good than cut off my own head, and deep down he knows this.'

'Still, it doesn't hurt to shake things up a little after all these years.'

'Exactly. Consider your mission accomplished. You've done your duty and are a perfect daughter-in-law. Now, tell me what's going on at that school? Those poor parents. I can't conceive of how they must feel. To lose a child is the worst thing that can happen. It's against the natural order.'

As usual, Marian had put her finger on the problem. The natural order was completely awry. Sloane and Daryl. Sloane and Zoë. Sloane and the kids he bullied. Sloane and his murderer.

It took a while to tell Marian everything, but it sorted things out in Faith's own mind.

'This Zoë must really be something. Do you think she was telling the truth – that it was the boy who went after *her*? Or was she just saying that to appease her husband?'

'I don't think she's ever tried to appease anyone, particularly her husband.' There had been so much contempt in Zoë's voice. 'The headmaster's wife. That's a major conquest. And, of course, that explains Harvard. Oh my God, Marian. Thank you. Another penny's dropped.'

'What do you mean?'

'I've been wondering how Sloane could have been accepted by Harvard, early, late, or whatever. He's not a good student, and even though he had extracurricular activities a mile long – not that they're all suitable for listing on an application – competition for college, especially the Ivies, has never been fiercer. But Sloane wanted to go to Harvard, had all his life. So he seduced Harcourt's wife, then blackmailed the headmaster. He was a juvenile. He could have threatened that he'd go to the police and have Mrs Harcourt arrested. Maybe Harcourt altered his GPA. Certainly he would have pull with the admissions head; all the private schools do.'

'He was a very evil boy.' Marian looked aghast.

'I'm afraid he was.' Faith drank the rest of her coffee. It was still warm, and she needed some warmth.

'I would love to stay for the rest of the afternoon,' she said, meaning it. She'd like to stay for even longer. Marian could feed her more soup and toasted cheese sandwiches. They could watch old movies on cable. 'But I have an appointment with a geek.'

'If Amy wants to stay, why don't you leave her for the night? I have to go to town tomorrow afternoon and I'll drop her off then. Dick will be thrilled, and I won't see her for a while when I'm on my trip.'

'But don't you have a lot to do to get ready?' Faith knew Amy loved to sleep over at her grandparents', but Marian had to be busy.

'Nonsense. I've been packed for days.'

Zach was where Faith expected him to be – in Carleton House's former dining room. She was, however, surprised to see Dan and Brian with him. This time, she didn't call out, but crept silently over to the computer terminal. They were so engrossed that even if she had made a noise, they wouldn't have noticed.

She had to find out what they were up to, especially Dan. What was it that was obsessing the boy, causing him to fail at school, drop off the hockey team, and establish an armed camp at home?

When she saw what they were looking at, she couldn't help herself. She burst out laughing, and whether it was from humor or relief, she laughed so hard, tears came into her eyes.

It wasn't *Kitten with a Whip, All-Nude College Girls, The Sopornos,* or a chat room where everyone talked dirty.

It was eBay.

Eight

'What do you mean sneaking up on us like this!' Dan Miller was livid.

She couldn't very well deny the accusation. She *had* been sneaking up on them. With teenagers, it was almost always best to tell the truth.

'The other day when you saw me, you blocked the screen and turned the power off. I've been wondering what it was you didn't want me to see.'

'Well, now you know.' His voice was surly.

'No, I don't actually. Why wouldn't you want me to see that you were checking out something on eBay?' The screen was in full view and she could see the list. '*Star Trek* collectibles. I know you're a Trekkie. What's the big secret?'

Dan's mouth was clamped shut.

Zach sighed and looked at Faith. She knew he was thinking what she was – that this was no big deal compared to the very big deal the two of them needed to get working on.

'Dan,' he said, 'I told you and Brian that Mrs Fairchild was coming and I had to help her with some computer stuff. She's here. She knows. Tell her everything or I will.'

Faith didn't put her hand on Dan's shoulder – teenagers did not like to be touched when they were angry – but she let it hover. 'I know things haven't been going well at home, and at school. And *you* know how much I – and the whole family – care about you. Talk to Tom, if you don't want to tell me, but you have to do something.' She played her last card. 'I know where your stereo is – and no, I haven't told anyone except Tom, because I haven't figured out what to do about it.'

More anger, then fear, then relief passed across Dan's face at roughly the speed of lightning.

'They don't understand. They keep saying they're toys, but they're not. That's what my mom keeps saying. She even brought me a carton to pack up my "space toys" to put in the attic.'

'You mean the *Star Trek* models you have in your room?'

He nodded. 'I've been buying and selling them on eBay.'

'He has an awesome collection,' Brian piped up. 'Most in mint condition and in the original boxes.'

Faith was looking for the *but* in all this and found it.

'But how can you do this without a credit card?'

'I used money orders until I met Zach.'

Zach smiled. 'I'm the kid with everything, remember? A credit card from each parent, so I can get exactly what I want for my birthday and Christmas, they said. Not because they didn't want to have to go to the trouble of picking something out themselves. Oh no, not that.' He raised his hands in mock horror.

'So where does the stereo come in?'

'I had a cash-flow problem,' Dan confessed. 'I had a chance to buy an Enterprise NCC-one seven oh one-B for next to nothing. Only that's what I had. Nothing. I can't take money out of my savings account because Mom checks my statements. To see how much interest I'm getting she says, but I know it's to check up on me. To make sure I'm not taking any money out,' he added bitterly. 'They don't trust me at all.'

'Would you have been taking money out to add to your collection?'

'Probably. But it's not just a collection. It's an investment.'

Brian spoke earnestly. 'He could already sell it for more than twice what he's paid for it, and it's going to be worth more and more as time goes on.'

'So, you come over here after school to go on-line with Brian and also to do your homework. So far, this doesn't sound like a capital offense.' Faith was amused and was sure it would all get sorted out. Pix would be so relieved that Dan wasn't doing anything worse, she might consider loosening the reins a bit.

But it wasn't everything. Brian was blushing and having a hard time looking at Faith. *Star Trek* chat rooms. Was that it? And Dan had sworn he didn't go into any. Dan himself had shut down again and Zach looked impatient. It was time to get to Sloane's laptop.

'Yes, they go on-line. Yes, they do homework, but – how can I put this? – it's a *very* collaborative effort with Brian here, who is a math wizard, doing more than his share.'

Of course. Faith felt stupid. Dan couldn't have been doing his own homework so brilliantly and then failing every math test.

'Okay, here's what's going to happen. I want you, Dan, to go to the parsonage and tell Tom everything, starting from the beginning of the year. I know he's home now. No more cheating on homework, or anything else.' Faith thought she should throw this in. 'No more pawning. I don't care if Spock's ears show up for ninety-nine cents. If you don't have it, you can't buy them. You'll thank me when you're an adult with no maxed-out credit cards.'

'None of this would have happened if my parents hadn't made me come here,' Brian complained. 'No offense, Zach.'

'Hey, it's not exactly the Garden of Eden for me, either. Don't worry about it.'

'Have you told your parents how unhappy you are here?' Faith asked. She wasn't sure of his logic, yet his conviction was painfully real.

'They wouldn't listen. They put a decal on the car the day I got accepted.'

'Decals can be removed with a razor blade.' Faith felt full of solutions. 'Your mother and father should know how you feel.'

'I live in Aleford. I always went to Aleford schools. They did, too.' He sounded as if he was rehearsing.

'Go home. Spill your guts. But go. *Now*. Oh, and Miller – get your sound system out of my room. You can owe me. I know where you live.' Zach was turning off the computer in front of them. Faith had time to see that currently eBay had 13,579 *Star Trek*-related items for sale. Maybe Brian was right and Dan would astound them all by selling his 'toys' at Skinner's in ten years or so for some astronomical amount of money. Like those lunch boxes from the fifties or the original Barbie dolls pristine in unopened boxes. Faith herself would prefer collectibles like Zoë's, but they were way out of the Fairchilds' price range. Well, she had her cookbook collection, and Ben was saving the new state quarters. The two together should bring enough for train fare to Boston.

Zach waited until Brian and Dan left before opening the laptop case. He placed the computer reverently on the table and pulled up two chairs.

'Kids.' He smiled at Faith. 'What will they think of next?'

He cracked his knuckles and wiggled his fingers over the keyboard.

'Now let's see what Mr Buxton has in here. Yes, yes. There's something here. He didn't erase the hard drive.' He was clearly enjoying himself.

Faith moved her chair closer. 'What is it?'

'Nothing – yet. He locked all his files; ergo, there's got to be stuff there he didn't want people to see.'

'Ergo?'

'I take Latin. Believe it or not, it's my favorite course.'

Faith could believe it. There was something reassuring, and

engrossing, about translating such an orderly language. Ergo, it was perfect for Zach, a boy in need of such things.

'*Love, sex, secret,* and *God* – the most popular passwords, and Sloane has, or I should say had, very little imagination. Nope. Well, let's try his name, birthday – I looked it up for this very reason.'

'Mansfield lists everyone's birth dates?' Faith thought it was a homey touch.

'Not exactly, but I've been able to check certain things out in the school records. Ms Reed is not into protecting files.'

He was so intent on what he was doing that he wasn't thinking about the implications of what he was saying. Faith decided to bring it up with him another time. Right now, she wanted him to find out what was buried in Sloane's files, and it might help find out what buried him. She was thinking like a teenager again, she realized with a start.

They struck out again, and again, and again – trying variations on all the possibilities. Faith had a brainstorm.

'Try "Joey".'

'Joey?'

'It's his first name. Joseph Sloane Buxton.'

Zach raised an eyebrow.

But Joey didn't work, either.

'I really wasn't expecting that we'd be able to get in using a password. It's probably something like "Magic Eight Ball" or even "paper clip" – whatever was on his desk at the time.'

'Sloane didn't have a Magic Eight Ball.'

'No, but I do. Oops, guess I'll have to change mine now?' He gave her a roguish grin. It was amazing the effect computers had on these kids. She had never seen the boy so happy.

'This may take a little time.' He was intent on the screen in front of him. 'First we'll run Disk First Aid and see what that tells us.'

'Absolutely. Why didn't I think of this?'

'Aha,' he said after a while. 'Misplaced file. Now this is interesting.'

Her 'Why?' went unanswered as Zach's fingers flew across the keyboard. He hadn't even heard her. A sonic boom perhaps, not much less. Zach was in the zone.

'I didn't think the kid knew this much. Clever. Very clever. But definitely not Sloane's work. He had to have had help.'

'What did he do?' Faith asked.

'He took a regular file, marked it as an application, stripped it of its resource fork, and put it at the end of the file-system catalog, so it wouldn't be immediately available. It is also scrambled by seventy-two-bit encryption, which has to be correlated with a hundred-digit PGP key. All we have to do is reconstruct the resource fork, run our own copy of PGP, decipher his key, reconstruct the file, open it in ClarisWorks, and read it.'

'And I thought it would be complicated,' Faith said.

The results were extremely satisfying – and extremely disturbing.

Sloane kept meticulous records. Lists of names, addresses. Lists of money in, money out, money owed. Sloane was dealing drugs at Mansfield and Cabot big-time.

'I heard you could get anything you wanted from him, but I don't do that stuff – despite what the world thinks – so I never paid much attention. He must have started dealing in junior high. A few of these names have addresses on the North Shore, so they're either his suppliers or customers.'

'Suppliers. How would he deliver to customers from here?' Faith reasoned.

Zach was staring at the list. 'A lot of self-medication going on. Shit! What are we going to do?'

Faith had been thinking exactly the same thing.

'We have to turn it over to the police and they'll work with Dr Harcourt. Are you surprised by some of the kids on here?'

'Yes – and no.'

Faith was looking at the list. There was one entry that was only initials, 'P.B.' She hoped Zach wouldn't pick up on it, but he was too smart. He looked at her. 'P.B.? Do you think ...' He didn't have to finish the sentence.

Paul Boothe wouldn't be that stupid. He couldn't take this kind of chance. But if he had and then Sloane began blackmailing him, what would he do? His whole career on the line. People killed for less, far less. She remembered what he'd said when Sinclair had protested that Sloane didn't have an enemy in the world. Boothe had said he didn't believe it and it was a question of finding out which one had the strongest motive.

She decided to change the subject – quickly.

'Let's see if there's any evidence of the stuff he was doing to Daryl.' That was what they were looking for, after all.

And there was – plenty. Articles and a whole list of racial epithets, some of which Faith recognized as components of the E-mails Daryl had received.

'This is beyond sick! The bastard!' Zach looked like he was either going to cry or punch a hole in a wall. He stood up and walked to the window. It was beginning to get dark, but they hadn't put on any lights. Only the monitor glowed.

Faith opened another list. Female names with stars. It wasn't hard to guess what it was – cyber belt notching. She hastened to close it, but Zach was peering over her shoulder.

'Susan Beach – she's at Cabot. Three stars. Omigod, it's everyone he's laid. Mr Stud Buxton.'

'We don't need to keep this. We should delete it immediately.'

'Mrs Harcourt? He was sleeping with Mrs Harcourt? I mean, she's older than my mother. Four stars! Mrs Harcourt!' Zach was in shock.

'Zach, you can't repeat this to anyone. We have to delete these names.'

'Can't. Not without getting rid of the whole file.'

'All right, then. Shut down and show me how to bring it all up again. I'm going to take it to someone who will know what to do with it.'

As soon as the first list had appeared, Faith had decided to drive straight to Patsy's.

'I want Harcourt – and the rest of the teachers here – to know I'm not on Sloane's customer list. Just because I dress the way I do and my hair isn't Joe the Prep, they think I'm a druggie.'

Appearances. Daryl had talked about the same thing to Faith. Except with him, it was the reverse. 'No matter what I'm wearing, what people see is Mr Hip-Hop – baggy jeans, crotch at my knees, Tommy Hilfiger shirt, and lots of gold chains.' Appearances. Real or imagined. It's the way kids are judged.

'One good thing.' Zach was still staring at the screen.

'What's that?' Faith asked.

'Maybe he got in over his head with his suppliers. Maybe he stiffed one of them. Maybe he just pissed them off. The police have got a whole list to choose from now, and somebody he may have bullied a little too much looks pretty feeble as a suspect in comparison.'

'You've been worried?' Faith asked.

'Yes and no.' This appeared to be a stock answer for Zach. 'Let's just say I wasn't comfortable with their line of questioning.'

'You would have had to have an accomplice. You could never have lifted him into that piano box alone.'

'Accomplices wouldn't have been hard to find, but thank you for your reassuring words. I guess I should be lifting weights or something.'

'You're fine just as you are. Don't worry about it. Now show me what to do. I have to get going.'

His words had reminded her of the line of questioning the police might pursue with Daryl once they saw the kind of provocation on the laptop. And Daryl would definitely have been able to put Sloane's body in the packing crate. She was fervently grateful for Daryl's alibi. The racist attacks – it would all have to come out now, though, and give Robert Harcourt one more nasty shock.

Zach whirled around suddenly. They had been sitting with their backs to the kitchen door. He ran into the next room and came back slowly.

'Nobody there. Not in the hall, either. It must have been my imagination. All this has me spooked.'

Faith hadn't heard anything.

It wasn't long before she knew exactly how to get to the material.

'Technically, this is my property,' Zach said. He'd shown her the bill of sale Sloane had signed.

'I have a feeling you won't be seeing it for a while.'

'That's okay, so long as I get it eventually.' Priorities. And this *was* a G3.

They walked out into the darkness. He'd missed dinner, but he said Mrs Mallory would give him something to eat in the kitchen. They were old friends, apparently. Go figure, Faith thought.

Sleet was falling and the wind was beginning to pick up. An unforgiving climate. They parted where the path divided, and for a moment Faith felt unwilling to leave the boy. She wished she could take him home for the night. There was a bond between them now: shared secrets and genuine friendship. She knew she'd keep in touch with him.

'Don't worry about Miller and Perkins,' he said as he strode off. 'Little geeks tend to get obsessed, but they'll grow out of it, and that *Star Trek* stuff is worth investing in. He knows what he's doing.'

'I'll try to talk to his mother. She's a good friend. Good night. And thanks.'

'My pleasure.'

Faith walked on toward her car. She wished there were a few

more of the quaint gaslights the school used to illuminate the paths. And the wind was blowing the sand that had been scattered on the icy paths into her face. She pulled her hat from her pocket and put it on to keep the grit out of her hair. Think warm, she told herself. Think – well, in New England you couldn't say May – think June. She hurried on, head down. Once again, she didn't see a figure coming from the opposite direction until they crashed into each other. This was getting to be an occupational hazard at Mansfield. First Sloane, then Winston Freer, now who? Her hat had slipped down over her eyes, and as she pulled it up, she was astonished to see a figure racing into the bushes. No apology. No 'Are you all right?' She was, but she'd have a hell of a black-and-blue mark on her right knee. She grabbed her purse and reached for the laptop.

It was gone.

'Damn, damn, damn!' was all Faith could say at first. She'd driven to Patsy's, called Tom to say where she was, accepted the drink Will Avery poured, then poured out her own tale.

'Regrettable,' said Will. 'But not your fault and maybe not all that important.'

'I'm not sure Lorraine Kennedy would agree with you,' Faith mused. The scotch was working.

'Look, you remembered a couple of the names from the North Shore. We've got them down. The other stuff isn't that relevant. Except now we know for sure Sloane Buxton was the one and probably the only one doing the number on Daryl. Kid strikes me as a loner,' Patsy said. 'He had his buddies, but he was in charge. Just look at those lists! A control freak. I'm sure – what were their names, Sinclair and somebody? – would be surprised to know about his lists, and maybe by what he was doing to Daryl. Their names were on his customer list, right?'

'Yes, and Sinclair owed him two hundred dollars.'

'But why was Sloane going after Daryl?' Will asked. 'I mean, aside from his extremely Neanderthal view of black people. Why go to so much trouble? Tying a noose, cutting out pictures, articles. The Aunt Jemima ad was Xeroxed from a book, probably one about racism in advertising.'

Faith had been wondering the same thing.

'I suppose he got off thinking about Daryl's reactions. And he did plant the stolen goods in his room. Maybe he was on some weird campaign to systematically rid Mansfield of all people of color, starting with Daryl,' Patsy offered.

Faith nodded and added, 'I think he must have been jealous of Daryl's success, academically and socially.'

'But I thought this Buxton kid was a big man on campus,' Will said.

'He is – was – but he wasn't the scholar he may have wanted to be, and he was more feared than liked, from what I've been hearing,' Faith told him.

'So, where are we?' Patsy splashed a bit more of the amber liquid into their glasses.

'My job is done,' Faith answered. 'I mean what we set out to do – find the person behind the mask. Things just got complicated, that's all and now I feel I have to find out—'

Will raised his glass to her. 'Who knocked you down and stole the computer.'

'Do we tell the police?' Faith asked, acknowledging Will's unspoken toast with her own glass.

Patsy answered. 'Oh yes, we do, baby. Together. Right away.'

Lorraine Kennedy was *not* happy. It was written all over her face.

'Withholding evidence. Pretty serious.'

'She wasn't withholding evidence. She was bringing it to you when someone assaulted her and stole it. Can we focus on what's important here?' On the way to Kennedy's office, Patsy had told Faith the line she intended to take. 'Always better to go to their turf when you want to make a good impression,' she'd added when Faith had voiced the notion that maybe the police would like to come to her. She was tired.

'I have the names from Salem and Danvers, the North Shore.' She'd stared at the screen long enough. Zach might recall them, too. She didn't intend to mention his involvement. She merely said that one of the students in her class had told her in confidence that he had a computer that had belonged to Sloane and asked what he should do with it. She'd told him to give it to her and said she'd make sure it got to the proper authorities. All of which was true.

She described most of what else had been on the computer. Detective Kennedy took notes and had Faith sign them.

'If you come across anything else, say a murder weapon or a confession, you will let me know, won't you?' Kennedy said sarcastically.

No need to be so snippy, Faith thought, missing her old friend John Dunne. John was never snippy. Pissed off, furious, but never, ever snippy.

Faith went back to the Averys' to get her car. Lunch with her mother-in-law had been eons ago, and Faith was hungry. It was highly unlikely that Tom had whipped up anything, but it wouldn't take her long to throw something together. The egg. Your best friend in the kitchen. A puffy golden omelette. Food was good.

Ben was enjoying his temporary 'only child' status to the hilt. He'd convinced Tom to get steak and cheese subs, then listened to his dad read several chapters of Jane Langton's fantasy *The Diamond in the Window*. Life doesn't get much better than this was written all over his face when Faith walked in. They let him stay up later than usual and Faith made omelettes for everyone. Fairchild males could always eat. Then when Ben went to bed, she told Tom everything that had happened, the unedited version – the one that included Zoë Harcourt's name.

'Rabbit, rabbit,' Faith had said to Tom. It was the first day of February. Not a single person she'd encountered since her move to Aleford had ever been able to explain the derivation of this old custom – that you'd have good luck all month if you said, 'Rabbit, rabbit' upon awakening on the first day. Lucky rabbit's foot taken a few hops further? Some months, she forgot. Not this month.

And the sun was shining. The rain had stopped. She was teaching the boys how to make a couple of easy main dishes. Daryl had given her his grandmother's smothered pork chop recipe and Faith planned to get Zoë's for Stroganoff, even if she could not get the woman herself to demonstrate it. Today Faith had brought the ingredients for a quick and easy coq au vin with a nonalcoholic red wine that didn't taste half-bad.

She let herself in at Carleton House. Light streamed in through the fanlight over the front door, falling upon what looked like a pile of blankets or coats at the bottom of the stairs. She'd put the food away and then pick up the stuff before the boys arrived. She was early. But as she walked into the dining room, it became clear that this wasn't something she could tidy up. What she'd mistaken for a blanket was a voluminous dark gray hooded woolen cloak. She dropped everything, walked over, and pulled the material back from the head it was covering.

It was Zoë and she was dead.

Faith felt for the pulse she knew wasn't there, stood up, and gazed down at the back of Zoë's head, at the mass of Zoë's tumbled curls. The beautiful animated face – Faith saw it clearly in her mind, saw it the way it had been that night at the Harcourts' house. So vibrant – so very much alive. Now it would be still. The whole house was still. She couldn't even hear a clock ticking, and on this windless, bright day with its false promises of spring, not even a branch tapped at the window. She took her phone from her purse, called the police, and continued to stand there rooted in the hall, keeping watch. The wine bottle had broken when she dropped her bags and the red liquid was seeping out into a pool, making its way across the hardwood floor toward the body.

Two motionless, silent women. A few minutes passed, passed slowly in a stately manner, like royalty, like a czarina – then pandemonium broke out. Everyone came at once – the local and state police, Robert Harcourt, Connie Reed, Paul Boothe, and some other teachers. Faith was dimly aware of the boys being turned away from the door. She was dimly aware of it all – Robert's face distorted in grief, Connie's in horror – until Lorraine Kennedy's voice brought the entire scene into sharp focus.

'You're in shock. Come with me. We have to get you some coffee with plenty of sugar. Your husband's on his way.'

Kennedy seemed to be familiar with the campus, and she led Faith out the front door, past the small crowd gathered there, and took her to the kitchen, the warm kitchen. Mabel was crying. So was Mrs Mallory.

'Who could have wanted to hurt her? Maybe she was a little too colorful for this place, but everybody liked her. She livened things up. Loved to cook. Came here and we'd do it together. God knows, I'll miss her.' More words than Faith had ever imagined hearing kept issuing from the woman's mouth. Mabel, meanwhile, was getting coffee, piling a plate with doughnut muffins and butter. Then she put an arm around the cook, no easy task, and took her away.

Lorraine Kennedy was heaping sugar into Faith's cup and urging her to drink. It tasted terrible, but Faith drank it anyway.

'Why are you being so nice to me?' she asked. This kinder, gentler Lorraine was giving Faith a Jekyll and Hyde feeling.

When was the other Detective Kennedy going to take up residence in the body of the pleasant woman sitting next to her?

'Maybe because January is over. Maybe because it's nice out. Maybe because it's like you can't get a break here and I feel sorry for you. Finding a corpse is no picnic.'

'Very true.' Faith took a muffin. It was still warm. 'Although around here lately, there doesn't seem to be any shortage.'

'Except this one is different. The guys are going over everything, but her heel was caught in the hem of the cape she was wearing. Boots with very high heels. That's all it would have taken to send her down those stairs, and she landed wrong. Very wrong.'

'She liked high heels.' Faith felt relief flood her body, or maybe it was all the sugar she was consuming. An accident. A terrible accident and one of those cosmic coincidences – two deaths at Mansfield in one week.

'You're feeling better. Could you tell me what happened this morning? You didn't see her fall?'

'No. I didn't even think it was a person at first, but when I got closer, I knew – and knew it was Zoë. Her hair.'

'I'm not an expert, but I'd say it must have happened shortly before you came. And she must have died immediately.' Lorraine took a muffin. 'These are great.' She slathered it with butter. Clearly, she wasn't on the white diet or the grapefruit diet or any other one. She finished the muffin and took another.

'Metabolism. My whole family – I'm one of seven – all skinny, which is good, because in my work it's hard to keep track of the basic food groups.'

Faith was familiar with the machines at headquarters that dispensed bags of chips, candy, and sandwiches that the forensics lab would certainly declare unfit for human consumption.

It was pleasant sitting in the kitchen shooting the breeze with the detective. Lorraine's lipstick was wrong again. Maybe Faith could tactfully work it into the conversation. Tom would come soon. The three of them could chat. If she kept talking, maybe she wouldn't keep seeing Zoë's lifeless body in front of her eyes.

'There's still the Buxton case.' Lorraine poured more coffee. 'And that business with the laptop.'

So that was what all this was about. Lull Mrs Fairchild into a good mood, then hit her with what? An accusation? Indictment?

But it wasn't. Lorraine sat down again and mused, 'Whoever knocked you down knew what was on the computer. You said his friends were listed as drug users. If they'd known he was keeping a list like that, they would have done something about it sooner – and not continued their glorious friendship. So who? The names you gave us are well known to the police on the North Shore and they're checking out where they were during the time Buxton was killed. Again, they wouldn't have been happy to know about his lists, but how would they have known? Which leaves?'

Faith remembered the noise Zach had heard. The one she, intent on the screen, hadn't.

'There may have been someone in the kitchen of Carleton House when we were looking at the computer. Whoever it was couldn't have seen the lists, but we were talking about them.'

Lorraine looked interested. 'So it could have been a student, specifically James Elliot or Sinclair Smith, or both.'

'Yes, they would have been the right height, but the person was bent over, so whoever it was could have been taller than I remember.'

She hadn't mentioned P.B. before, but now was the time, and she told Lorraine about the teacher.

'He lives in the house, too, right?'

'Yes.' It was all so unbelievable.

'Daryl Martin seems pretty much in the clear on everything. He would have wanted the laptop with all that information about Sloane Buxton's other activities to get to us.'

'That's what I thought, too,' Faith said.

'Although, as we know all too tragically, kids who are victimized can turn against the perpetrator, with terrifying consequences. But Daryl doesn't fit the profile, except for that one remark he made in your class. These kids usually talk about getting even to other kids and unless this school is extremely tight-lipped, there was none of that from Martin or anybody else.'

Faith was aware that each dorm had had meetings with faculty and someone from the police after Sloane's body was discovered. She realized now it was not simply to help the Mansfield students deal with the situation but to get information, too.

'Piece of work – Buxton,' Lorraine said.

'An understatement,' Faith said ruefully. She told the detective about how Sloane had tried to frame Daryl for the Harcourt theft. For a moment, there was a flash of the old Detective Kennedy.

'And there was a reason you didn't tell the police this?'

Faith thought of Sloane's parents. How pathetically happy his mother had been with her birthday gift, her flea-market find.

'Yes, there was a reason.'

Lorraine sighed. 'I'm beginning to understand why you make Dunne so crazy – and maybe why he doesn't hate you.'

She could have said 'why he likes you', Faith thought in annoyance, but she'd take what she could get.

'I have to get back, and I'll bet your husband is there by now. Let's go.'

They put their dishes in the sink and rinsed them. They were women – and besides, Faith was still afraid of Mrs Mallory.

'Poor Dr Harcourt. This is devastating for him,' Detective Kennedy said as they walked back to Carleton House.

Faith remembered the conversation she'd overheard. No need to speak ill of the dead. But devastating as it might be, his wife's death had solved a major problem for the headmaster.

*

Only the police were at the scene – and Tom, who immediately rushed over to his wife and hugged her hard.

'Are you all right?'

'Yes and no.' Zach's answer. He was on to a good thing.

'I understand. Let's go home. Obviously, your class, and all classes, have been canceled. Once again, the teachers are meeting with the kids, and I imagine the efficient Ms Reed is at her phone. But Charley says this was clearly an accident. She tripped.'

Charley himself walked over, and after also asking Faith how she was, he said, 'Ridiculous shoes. Boots, whatever. Heels a mile high and as thin as spaghetti.'

Faith thought of the L.L. Bean boots that were standard winter footwear for the ladies of Aleford and said, 'Zoë liked to dress fashionably.'

'Well, it killed her,' Charley said bluntly.

On that note, the Fairchilds left, walking out into the cool sunshine.

'Harcourt was here when I arrived,' Tom said. 'He's a mess. I told him to call me, and I think he might. He just kept saying over and over, "What am I going to do without her?" Connie Reed was trying to console him – you still have the school sort of thing – but I don't think he even heard her. She was looking pretty bad herself.'

But Faith wasn't listening, either. She was thinking of Zoë's dark cape. Her assailant had been dressed in something dark, something woolen from head to toe. It could have been a cape. Had it been Zoë listening in the kitchen? Or someone else? Someone who could have borrowed his wife's cape easily? And – the thought that had been hovering just beneath all the others since she'd discovered the body rose to the surface – what was Zoë doing at Carleton House this morning?

'Faith, Faith!' someone called as the Fairchilds were getting into their car. It was Winston Freer. He rushed over.

'I was going to call you. You poor dear. How ghastly for you!' His eyes were round with concern. For once, he didn't seem to have an appropriate quotation.

'Thank you, but I'm all right now. It was a shock at first ...' Faith's voice trailed off.

'Glad to hear it. Then we'll say three o'clock, shall we? I bought some sinful cookies from the Lakota Bakery in Arlington and we'll have cucumber sandwiches. So very Oscar Wilde.'

For a moment, Faith had no idea what the man was talking about; then she realized he still expected her to come for tea that afternoon.

She opened her mouth to speak, to put it off, yet she couldn't disappoint him. Marian was bringing Amy back at four and Ben was going to a friend's house straight from school, which Faith had arranged in order to have tea with the professor. She reluctantly pushed the thought of a house empty of children and the possibility that Tom might have an hour or two to spare to the back of her mind and said, 'See you at three.'

He gave her directions and bustled off.

'You are a very, very good person,' Tom said.

By three o'clock, Faith was feeling better. She'd had lunch with Pix and they'd talked mostly about Dan. Dan *had* gone to Tom, and then, at Tom's urging, he had told his parents everything. Apparently, the Millers had talked long into the night, and while Pix was still inclined to throw all the electronic devices in the house on to the recycle heap at the landfill, she had given in to both her husband and her son. The computer could stay, but the time Dan could use it and for what would be regulated until his parents felt he could regulate himself.

'The eBay thing is hard for me,' Pix had told Faith. 'It seems like such a waste of his money, but Sam pointed out that he had collected stamps when he was Dan's age and that if there had been an eBay in those dark ages, he would have traded on it.'

'Two against one?' Faith had asked. 'Were you feeling out-numbered?'

'A little, but that's not unusual when you live with two males. I really miss Samantha. She's coming home this weekend.' Samantha Miller was a sophomore at Wellesley.

They talked about what had been going on at Mansfield and Faith realized with a start that she hadn't filled Pix in on the racist attacks on Daryl. She gave her a lightning-fast version of recent events and was rewarded by her friend's look of total astonishment.

'What do you think Zoë Harcourt was doing at the dorm this morning?' Pix asked finally.

'I think she must have thought Sloane had something incrimi-nating in his room that the police had overlooked. The room isn't sealed anymore. Or, maybe she'd spent the night – or early morning – with Paul Boothe. He definitely had a thing for her, and it's my impression that that was enough for Zoë to recipro-cate.'

'But what a chance to take! The students could have seen her.'

'I would imagine that added spice to the whole thing – and it wasn't that great a chance. She simply had to wait until they left for chapel.'

'It's really very sad. I met her a few times when the library was raising money for the endowment. The Harcourts attended some of the events. This was before your time. She was very pretty and very funny. Such a pointless way to die. Not that there's a way that has a point, but you know what I mean. Accidental death. It wasn't meant to be.' She stared at Faith. 'Don't tell me you think—'

'That it might have been? Well, yes, I do.'

Winston Freer lived in what had been a gatehouse, a Victorian dollhouse. Inside, it was more like a hunting lodge crossed with the Folger Library. The living room was paneled in walnut, a bust of the Bard stood on the mantel of a fieldstone fireplace, and the walls were hung with more Shakespeariana – a copy of the Chandos portrait, a nice oil of the Hathaway cottage – and English hunting prints. Prints like Sloane's, Faith realized. Could the boy's have been a gift from his teacher, or had Sloane sought to emulate the master? Tea was laid in front of a blazing fire. Faith would just as soon have dispensed with the flames, but the Darjeeling with lovely comestibles soon blunted any bonfire images. And Winston was a delightful host. They talked about living in a microcosm, a parish and campus having much in common. Faith told him about her resolve not to marry a minister and how it had given way almost at once when she'd met Tom.

'I don't think my wife minded living here. We didn't have children of our own, so the boys were a welcome substitute. I lost her fifteen years ago. We met when we were students. Our whole lives were academic. Heidelberg. In the spring. I'll never forget it.'

Faith was surprised. She'd assumed any study abroad would have taken the man to that 'blessed plot, this earth, this realm, this England'. She was about to say as much, but Winston rambled on.

'She was studying German – which she taught here for years, very well, too. I was doing research on Heine.' His eyes got a bit misty, Faith patted his hand. She couldn't imagine what it would be like to have Tom gone and didn't intend to try.

'Our parents were both from Bavaria. We had that in common – and so much else.'

Winston was younger than he looked, Faith thought. His parents had probably come just before the war. Lucky to get out. Winston must have been named after Churchill. She looked at her watch. It was getting late. She had studiously avoided any mention of the recent deaths at Mansfield. She didn't want to think about them, and Winston hadn't brought them up. Perhaps it was the memory of his wife, but his next remark was definitely an allusion to Zoë and Sloane.

'Who would have thought that two of the best and the brightest would be cut down in one week? "What a piece of work is a man!" The boy, especially the boy – so perfect.'

'Maybe not all that perfect,' Faith ventured. Winston had been a source of campus gossip before.

His reaction startled her. He clapped his hands over his ears and said shrilly, 'I don't want to hear any of that. I know people are saying he was involved with drugs, but it's a lie. He would never sully himself that way.'

Faith changed the subject. 'Only February to get through. Somehow, even if the weather is terrible, March is easier.'

'February? Oh yes, today's the first. I put in mounds of bulbs last fall. If the squirrels, deer, and other fauna haven't eaten them all, you must come and see my garden when the daffodils are in bloom.'

'I'd love to,' Faith said. 'But I'm afraid I have to leave now. My mother-in-law is arriving at four and I don't want to keep her waiting.'

'Mustn't keep a mother-in-law waiting.' Winston's humor was restored.

'Would you mind if I freshened up before I left?' Why didn't she say 'bathroom' or 'toilet'? 'Freshened up' was such a euphemism. The fact was that she had to pee – all that Darjeeling. But Winston was so refined.

'Of course not. Down the hall on your right.' He took a Florentine from the cookie plate and bit into it with obvious satisfaction.

Faith walked down the hall, passed a door on her left, and went farther, opening the next one to her right. It wasn't a bathroom. It was Winston's study, and two things dominated it: a large portrait of a woman Faith assumed had been his wife – and a Nazi flag.

She shut the door quietly behind her. She'd been a fool. Winston and Sloane. Soul mates. Or the boy a willing acolyte. She could hear the filth Winston must have poured into young Buxton's ears. How he was the flower of Aryan youth and the Daryls of the world had to be exterminated like the vermin they were. And Zach. Zachary Cohen, a Jew There was no Shakespeare here. The books were mostly in German – one exception, *The Hitler We Loved and Why* by Ernst Zündel, jumped out at her. It was a White Power Publication. She knew all this existed, but at the same time, she really *didn't* know, or hadn't wanted to believe it did. She believed it now. There were also several shelves of Mansfield yearbooks, neatly arranged by year. Freer had been one of the holdovers – and his wife, the German teacher. The yearbooks stretched back to the early sixties. She found last year's quickly, and Daryl's picture had indeed been neatly incised. So neatly, the boy on the next page peered through, and until you turned the page, the hole was not apparent. She went to the desk and opened the drawers. Coils of rope were in the largest one at the bottom.

Why had Freer used Sloane? A test, or simply logistics? A bit hard to get into the dorms, and perhaps the man was not computer-literate enough to figure out how to hide his tracks in E-mails, although a computer sat on his desk. Those E-mails to Sloane from Freer. She had assumed they were about tutoring or other school-related work, but of course they were commands – 'Repeat the exercise', one had read. And Sloane had followed the professor's orders, not blindly, but with his eyes wide open. Attacking his victim with newspaper clippings, E-mails, the noose – bayonets plunged into Daryl's body over and over again.

She'd seen enough. She took out her phone, blessing technology, and rapidly called Chief MacIsaac and Patsy Avery. She didn't want to tackle this one alone. She told Patsy to call Harcourt's office. He wouldn't be in shape to deal with this, but Connie would.

She put the yearbook back and started for the door. She'd have to wait to go to the bathroom. It opened just as she put her hand on the knob.

'I see you've discovered my little secret.'

It was Winston Freer, and she realized with a rush of fear that he was completely insane.

Nine

Help would arrive soon, but would it be soon enough? Faith smiled brightly, 'I see you're a World War Two buff. A collector,' she said, stepping back into the room.

It was quite possibly the worst thing she could have said.

'A collector!' he exploded, closing the door firmly behind him. 'Do you think this is some sort of idle pursuit?' He glanced in apology at a silver-framed photograph of Hitler with several young men that occupied a prominent position on his desk.

'I only meant that you seem to have accumulated a great deal from that time,' Faith said, backtracking.

Freer picked up the photo and sat down on a corner of his desk. 'My father and his two brothers. What a day that was for them. Five minutes with the Führer. A very misunderstood man. A very misunderstood philosophy.'

These were not the words Faith would have chosen, to put it mildly, and 'Five Minutes with the Führer' sounded like a production number from Mel Brooks's *The Producers*. She decided not to choose any more words in this particular minefield. They would either antagonize the professor further or make her sick trying to placate him. It was time to steer him back into the living room. They could talk about the weather again, about daffodils. He could gobble up more cookies. Then the people she'd called would arrive and Winston Freer would go away for a long, long rest. He hadn't killed Sloane. That was clear. And despite his catty remarks about Zoë Harcourt in the past, he seemed genuinely grieved by her death. No, Freer wasn't a killer. He just worshiped one.

'The boy understood. And he wasn't the first. What times we had when Gretchen was alive! She'd make schnitzel and strudel; we'd sing and talk until the wee hours of the morning. I must confess' – he gave her a conspiratorial grin – 'I occasionally served the students some good German beer!'

Was it seeing themselves as the incarnation of Hitler Youth or the beer that attracted the boys? Faith wondered. She hoped it was the beer.

'We went underground when Harcourt came. Gave me quite a dressing-down – I thought we'd have to leave – yet in the end, he let us stay. It wasn't easy getting teachers of our caliber.'

Faith took a step forward, the smile on her face still pasted in place and beginning to ache. 'We can sit and have another cup of tea, but I really do have to go soon. My mother-in-law will be wondering where I am.'

'But what to do? What to do?' Winston shook his head and his hair puffed out in a small cloud before settling down, the carefully brushed strands untidily rearranged. 'It's a matter of trust, you see. Do I trust you? Now, Sloane was the soul of integrity. I even loaned him my car. Always returned it with a full tank of gas. But you. I don't really know you.'

Faith hastened to reassure him. This she could do without lying – or gagging. 'Daughter, granddaughter, and wife of clergymen, remember. Surely that convinces you.'

He rubbed his chin. 'I suppose so. It's my own fault, of course. Always had this right, left problem. Said "right" when I meant "left." The first door on the left. That's the bathroom.'

'Well then, I'll just stop there and be on my way.'

He wasn't showing any inclination to move from his perch on the desk, nestled close to his treasured photo. She walked purposefully toward the door, passing him, hoping he wouldn't change his mind. Unless he suddenly pulled a Luger, or some other Gestapo souvenir, from his pocket, she didn't feel in any physical danger. She had to stay until the police arrived, and Patsy, so she could explain the situation. But every bone in her body was shrinking from further contact with the man. Simply being in the same room was causing her palms to sweat and her heart to beat faster with fear. The kind of fear being in the presence of madness induces. The kind of fear that should send her running away as fast as possible.

He jumped up, startling her, and followed closely behind. He smelled like 4711 – Kölnisch Wasser – and pipe tobacco. They were in the hall when the front door burst open and Connie Reed, looking quite Wagnerian, strode up to them, shook her finger in their faces, and said sternly, 'I do not want Dr Harcourt bothered with any of this nonsense. The man has had enough to deal with this week.'

Faith had had enough.

'Hate crimes are scarcely nonsense. Professor Freer, Sloane Buxton, and perhaps others at Mansfield have been waging a scurrilous racist campaign against Daryl Martin since last fall.'

Ms Reed stepped in front of Winston. 'You and your wife were told to stop all that. I was there when Robert spoke to you!' She was furious, taking Freer's actions as an affront to her beloved school, her beloved headmaster – and totally missing the point. Fortunately, Charley and Patsy arrived to make it.

Faith left. As fast as she could.

It had been a relief yesterday to bake cookies, marinate the game hens, and put together the meal she was now serving. Standing in Sandra Katz's kitchen, Faith could hear the Uppity Women luncheon group's steady buzz of conversation, punctuated by frequent peals of laughter. When she'd put out the soup, a rich wild mushroom broth with translucent strands of Chinese vermicelli, the women had been discussing a new Declaration of the

Rights of Women. Toilet seats down was first on the list. Someone suggested guaranteed time alone, preferably somewhere with room service; another called out, 'Equal opportunity for men to clean up vomit!' Sandra added, 'Permitted to drive with member of the opposite sex in the passenger seat.' Almost at once, someone exclaimed, 'Permitted to abrogate household duties and go to bed when sick!'

Faith wished Marian had a group like this, people with whom she could laugh about the foibles and frailties of men, women, and children. The Uppities laughed at themselves, which was perhaps their most endearing quality.

Faith hadn't stuffed the game hens, in deference to the diets all or some of the women were on, accompanying the birds with roasted winter vegetables instead and walnut raisin rolls for those who wished. For dessert, she offered them a choice of raspberries au naturel or the fruit piled on top of a meringue. The group split fifty-fifty, with much discussion about the body-image baggage they all carried around. 'I'm a perfectly respectable size, arteries as clean as a whistle,' an attractive woman with rounded curves said, 'but every ad tells me I'm fat. And I believe it.' Faith was pouring coffee. They were right, and it was scary. She worried about what it would be like when Amy was a teenager. Pix had related a number of cautionary tales about Samantha's friends, who couldn't believe what they saw in the mirror and almost starved themselves to death.

'That whole "You can't be too rich or too thin" stuff is a crock on both points,' a tall woman with graying hair said. 'And consider the source. Other than the duke – and he was no prize – the only love the Duchess of Windsor had was her pug dogs.'

Lonely women and dogs. Faith thought of Connie Reed with her corgis. Why hadn't the woman married or had a partner?

Sandra told Faith to pull up a chair and join them.

'So Niki's in Australia,' one woman said. Niki usually grabbed this job for herself and was a favorite with the group. 'Any chance she'll stay there?'

'Bite your tongue,' Faith said. She was missing Niki terribly. 'I'd be lost without her. She's due back in a week. The postcard we got yesterday said she wasn't homesick yet, but that she planned to be so she could leave. It has been pretty spectacular – the card was from the Ningaloo Reef, where she'd been snorkeling – and reentry will be tough.' The card had also said, 'No worries,' which sounded like an interesting concept. The Aussie philosophical version of their delectable dessert, pavlova.

They talked about travel, favorite destinations, yet all the while, Faith was aware of an undercurrent, a subject studiously and courteously being avoided. She owed it to them and raised it herself. Or part of it. Not Winston Freer, not the way he'd ranted at her as she was leaving: 'I knew I couldn't trust you!' He'd gone from that to Daryl and what was happening to the school and society by encouraging 'those people', people who should be 'eliminated' to keep the race pure, to save mankind. She wished she could blot out his voice – and knew she never would.

Patsy had gone straight to Daryl, and, although conflicted about not wanting to make the school look bad, he was going to press charges against Winston Freer. The name Winston had been an attempt by his parents to mask their leanings. Apparently, his near and dear had always called him 'Hansie'. When she phoned Faith last night, Patsy had commented that considering the way the school looked at the moment, taking action against this kind of bigotry would, on the contrary, serve to make Mansfield look good. And they needed it.

Harcourt was still sequestered in grief, and Connie had been slightly accusatory, asking why Daryl hadn't reported it all sooner. But Patsy said she had dealt with her. Faith was sure she had.

Now it was the murder and Zoë's death that the women wanted to talk about, Faith was sure.

'You know I've been teaching a cooking course at Mansfield during their Project Term?' She'd told Sandra when they'd finalized the menu and was sure Sandra had passed the news on.

'Could you repeat it for my family?' one woman begged.

Momentarily diverted by the thought of running some cooking classes with Niki at the catering kitchen, Faith tuned out of the conversation. When she quickly shifted her attention back, Sandra was talking.

'Remember when Zoë came to lunch with us? You invited her, didn't you, Sally?'

'Yes, I met her in New York, not here, and the coincidence of our both being from such a small place seemed enough to start a friendship. I was very fond of her, even though she could be totally self-absorbed and outrageous. She was also generous to a fault and never, never boring.'

Not a bad tribute, Faith thought.

'A tragic accident and somehow typical. Zoë wasn't the type to have gone quietly in her sleep,' Sally continued.

'But the student. That's something else. Do the police have any leads?' Sandra asked, her face filled with a fear reflected on the faces around the table. If it could happen to that boy, it could happen to …

Everyone looked at Faith, her past activities well known.

'If they have, they're not telling me, and I'm puzzled myself.' Noting their expressions, she added, 'I do know they're considering it an isolated incident and not the work of a serial killer, or anyone who might strike again, even once.'

The only thing that made sense at the moment was that Sloane's death was related to his drug trafficking. She wasn't about to reveal this, though. She and Lorraine Kennedy had just started what Faith hoped would be a long and beautiful friendship. Leaking privileged information to a group of women who could cover the town in minutes with a few well-placed calls would not be to Faith's advantage.

Talk drifted to other topics as Faith brought more hot coffee and then started back into the kitchen to clean up.

The woman who wanted to be able to go to bed when she was sick was telling everyone that her husband was proposing to start a group of his own.

'He says it's only fair, and I told him I had no problem with it at all. Guys talking to guys except in front of a TV set watching a game sounds like a major breakthrough to me, and I don't mean the Iron John stuff. Just lunch. Like what we do, no real point.'

'I like that,' Sandra said in mock indignation.

'You know what I mean. Anyway, he even has a name – It's Always the Husband.'

The women applauded and Faith got busy packing up.

It's always the husband.

As she drove back to Have Faith, she repeated the words over and over. Yes, Zoë's heel had been caught in the hem of her cloak, but it would have been easy enough to tear out the stitches and push her foot in place. Zoë had been going to pull the plug on his school. Maybe Mansfield could have limped along for a while without her money, but not for long. Robert Harcourt might be a superb fund-raiser, but he wasn't a magician, and even schools with healthy endowments were scrambling these days. And Sloane. Sloane Buxton was a blackmailer. He'd used his affair with his headmaster's wife to get himself into Harvard, if what the Buxtons had said about his acceptance was true. Blackmailers never stopped. Sloane would have continued hitting Robert up for false recommendation letters, ways to get financial aid for years. It was Robert Harcourt who had been in the kitchen. Robert Harcourt who had heard what was on Sloane's laptop. The list with his wife's name *and* the list of drug users at Mansfield. It was Robert Harcourt who had knocked Faith down. The last thing he would have wanted was for the police to get either list. Not when he'd killed his persecutor and was planning to kill his wife. Without the lists, there was nothing to tie him to Sloane, or a motive for getting rid of Zoë. Acts of passion, both of them. Faith had little doubt that it was the knowledge that his wife was having sex with his nemesis that pushed Harcourt over the edge.

The only problem was that the laptop was gone. Unless Harcourt had transferred the files to his own computer. Even if he hadn't, there could be a glowing recommendation letter to Harvard about Sloane. Confronted by the obvious falsehood – GPAs and SATs don't lie, and Sloane's would have been mediocre – the headmaster might be sufficiently thrown to make some fatal errors: Where had he been when Sloane was killed, for instance?

Faith put everything away quickly from the luncheon and left for home. There was nothing she could do today, but tomorrow morning she planned to be at Mansfield Academy bright and early, slipping into the headmaster's office when everyone was at chapel. She hadn't wanted to ask Mrs Mallory, or anyone else, to take the Saturday class after seeing the boys this morning. They had all been in varying degrees of shock. The death of their head-master's wife would have been enough, but the news of Freer's arrest and why topped everything.

Daryl had rushed in before the others arrived and had thrown his arms around her.

'I can't believe it! Buxton, yes. Kids do things like this to other kids, but an adult? A teacher! Mrs Avery is going to try to keep the whole thing as low-key as possible. I know what the school is and what it stands for – the kind of race and class privilege – but it's still my school and I don't want to see it in the headlines, or me, either. I guess – as they say – I have some "issues". I called my parents last night to let them know what had happened, and the first thing my mama is going to do when I go home on Sunday is whack me upside the head for not telling her, then cry. My dad was cool, as usual. Just said he figured I knew how to handle myself.'

The class had prepared the chicken dish, but when they sat down to eat, no one had seemed very hungry. It had been distressing to watch a roomful of teenage boys pick at their food. After his initial good humor – and relief – Daryl had been subdued, too. The only one chowing down and smiling was little Brian Perkins. He didn't seem to have a care in the world. When he'd left, Faith had found out why. 'My parents said I can go to Aleford High next fall if I still want to transfer.'

'I guess they didn't know how unhappy you were,' Faith had said.

'Not really.' Brian had squirmed. 'I think it's more because of … well, the bad stuff that's been happening here.' And he was out the door.

Duh, Faith had told herself.

Surprisingly, Sloane's friends, Sinclair and James, were the ones who'd broken the silence earlier at the table, turning to Daryl.

'Man, you have to believe that we didn't know he was doing any of that shit,' Sinclair said, then glanced at Faith, 'Excuse my language.'

'Go ahead,' she'd encouraged. 'You're doing fine.'

James had blushed. 'I mean, we know he wasn't your best friend and made some remarks – to you, too, Cohen – but we didn't know what a sick bastard he was.'

Daryl nodded, but Zach was someplace else. Had been someplace else since he'd arrived at class. And Faith knew where. He was thinking of the lists – and his lost laptop. She'd called him and he'd given her as much as he remembered of the relevant information. The irrelevant information – the stars next to Zoë's name – was traveling into deep memory.

Mrs Harcourt. Dead. The boys hadn't wanted to talk about that. Several of them had come in Carleton House's back door, avoiding the front hall altogether – the front hall, with its faint chalk outline still visible.

No, thinking about the kids, she knew she couldn't leave them to someone else the next morning. There would be plenty of time to go to Harcourt's office. He made a big thing about his door always being open, so it wouldn't be locked. His philosophy was intended to assure students and faculty of his accessibility. Faith was interested in accessing something else. She'd have to do it without Zach. Maybe Tom and she should rent the *Hackers* video tonight to watch when Ben and Amy were sound asleep. She might pick up some pointers.

There wasn't a soul around when Faith crept into the head-master's office early the following morning. She'd waited in her car until she'd seen everyone go into the stone chapel. Now she carefully closed the door to the outer office and checked the other door – behind Harcourt's big desk – which led to a back staircase. If necessary, she could dart down it. Pleased at the way things were going so far, she turned to his computer. It was on, and as soon as she clicked, the screen sprang to life. A neat row of folder icons were arranged from top to bottom on the right side. She clicked on 'Personal', almost giddy with anticipation. It opened right away. No password. Not even *Sesame*. She looked at the files: 'Mother', 'Sis', 'Zoë', and one entitled 'Hgt./Wgt.' She checked them rapidly. Letters to his mother and sister, the 'Zoë' file proved to be a list of presents he'd bought her over the years for Christmas, anniversaries, and birthdays. She'd done all right. 'Hgt./Wgt.' was exactly what it said – his height and weight by year. Definitely anal-retentive. Mother's fault?

She closed the folder and looked down the list of remaining ones: 'Chapel Talks', 'Teacher Evs.', 'Correspondence', 'Misc.' What she was looking for could be hidden anywhere. She went to 'Find File' and typed in various possibilities, but nothing came up. Not until she typed 'Rec Letters', and there it was, a five-star endorsement of Sloane Buxton's application to Harvard, addressed personally to Harcourt's old friend, the dean of admissions. 'Seldom have I had the opportunity to recommend a student so highly', the headmaster had written. And there was no 'Call me if you want to talk about this further' at the end to give the game away. That phrase was code for 'Everything I've written is bullshit; call me to find out what I really think'.

She printed the letter and tucked it into her pocket, then turned to 'Misc.' It would have been madness for Harcourt to transfer information from Sloane's laptop on to this office computer. If he had copied anything before getting rid of the computer, he would have put it on his own laptop or another computer at home – or even his Palm Pilot. There was nothing in 'Misc.' Faith thought she'd have a quick look at his E-mail before she left, when a folder marked 'Firmness' caught her eye. It must have something to do with discipline, or, knowing Harcourt, New Year's resolutions for the past twenty years and whether he'd stuck to them. She opened it and was stunned to see only one item fill the screen, a studio portrait of Connie Reed, a portrait taken some years ago, probably about the time Harcourt bought the school.

'Firmness. Constancy, Constance, Connie.'

They were in it together. In love with each other and in love with the school. And they'd do anything for Mansfield, even kill.

Feeling sick, Faith started to shut down. She'd found what she was looking for.

'He didn't put it there; I did.'

The door behind the desk closed softly. It was Connie.

'I told him it was a joke. When he needed me, all he had to do was click. I labeled the folder "Firmness" because that was another of our little jokes. That I was the one who kept his backbone firm. Not that he needed it. Not when it came to the school, that is.'

'Except it wasn't a joke,' Faith said.

Connie didn't answer; then, lowering her eyes, she muttered, 'He doesn't know.'

'That you killed Sloane Buxton?'

The woman's head jerked up.

'He deserved it! He was blackmailing Robert and selling drugs to some of our weaker boys! I knew he wasn't good enough for us from the moment he came to be interviewed, but Robert wanted to increase our diversity. Sloane's family wasn't like most of our families. Robert thought the boy deserved a chance. A chance to do what? Have sex with the headmaster's wife and God knows who else, degrading our campus with his perverted behavior!'

Connie took a deep breath.

'He had to be stopped. He would have plagued Robert for the rest of his life in one way or another.'

She was strong and fit enough to have murdered Buxton, then lifted his body into the crate, Faith realized, at the same time noting that Connie wasn't mentioning Sloane's hate campaign as one of his sins.

'I'm not sorry. I'll never be sorry. It was easy really. He met me down by the lake. I told him I had something to tell him I didn't want overheard. He was so stupid.' Her voice was filled with contempt. 'Why would I meet him there?'

Why indeed? Faith thought. Because Sloane thought Connie Reed a pathetic old maid, one who could no longer control her desire for him. Another notch.

'There was almost no blood,' Connie continued in a slightly wondering tone. 'I had thought there would be a lot of blood, but there wasn't. I stabbed him; he gave a little cry and died. I'd left a sled in the woods, and it was easy to move him to the old piano packing boxes on it, then lift him up and drop him in one. I covered him with a thick layer of old rags and linens that I'd taken from housekeeping. They're so lax, they never know what they have. Then I put some of the cartons lying by the bonfire on the very top. I dropped my gloves down one of the holes the ice fishermen have made and went to dinner. It didn't take long.'

And then all Constance Reed had to do was wait until someone struck a match.

Well planned and well executed by the trim figure standing before Faith in her camel-hair coat, woolen muffler in the school's colors, and sensible boots. Boots. Connie had killed Zoë too.

There was no need to ask questions. The woman was obviously dying to talk to someone about her accomplishments. And Faith was glad to listen – in between wondering how she could get to the phone in her purse on the floor and once again call the police.

'And then, of course, I had to get rid of that woman. We all knew she slept with members of the faculty. That was no concern to me. But a Mansfield boy! I heard it all, heard it from the kitchen in Carleton House when you and that misfit Zachary Cohen were using Sloane's computer. Computers! Sometimes I think they're more of a curse than a blessing, although they do make scheduling easier.'

Connie's mind was wandering far afield. Well, at least Faith now knew there was no hope of retrieving the laptop. It was no doubt at the bottom of the lake with the gloves – possibly also Sloane's watch and signet ring – its battery shorted out and all those names obliterated forever.

'So you told Zoë to meet you the next morning at Carleton House?'

'Another ignorant one. Oh, my poor Robert, how he's suffered with her. She was threatening to stop funding the school! "We may have to pursue some alternative funding sources, Connie", he said. I knew what that meant. Selfish woman! I told her to meet me in Sloane's room after the students went to chapel, said I'd found his laptop with the list. She turned up all right, but when I confronted her, she just laughed and said she would be leaving the school for good soon and didn't really care what happened to it. She only wanted to look at the list to see who else was on it! Her wantonness knew no bounds. I simply pushed her, and down the stairs she went. The funny thing was that her heel did catch in her hem. I didn't have to do a thing. Now Robert is free and the school is safe.'

And all's right with the world, Faith was tempted to add. But it wasn't. She bent down to pick up her bag.

'Don't do that,' Connie said sharply.

Faith straightened up.

'Everyone will be leaving chapel soon. We have to hurry,' Connie added.

Faith was afraid to ask where they were going. But she had to stall, for suddenly another stumbling block had appeared on Ms Reed's road to happiness, and she wasn't about to let it get in her way. Faith was not underestimating the lengths to which this efficient killer would go, and Faith's only ally was time.

'Hurry? Why? Where are we going?'

'To the lake. That way, when your body is discovered at the same place, the police will assume it's a serial killer.'

How many bodies did it take to categorize someone as a serial killer? Faith had never thought about this before, but closing in on three could well qualify a person as such. The woman was larger than Faith, but she figured she could put up a good fight and make enough noise to attract attention as they walked across campus. There had to be someone about. Then she felt the blade. It passed through the bulky layers of Faith's winter clothing like a butter knife through a stick that had been left out on a summer's day. It wasn't a deep wound, but it hurt like hell.

Connie's voice hissed sibilantly in Faith's ear: 'I left chapel early. There's been so much to do with Mrs Harcourt and then this Winston Freer trouble – your fault completely. I saw you through the door and slipped around to the back, Miss Nosy Parker. I had to find out what you were up to now. None of this was any of your concern. That's why I followed you to Carleton House, too.' She made it all sound like an egregious breach of manners. 'You should have stayed out of everything and stuck to your cooking. Now, move!' She pushed the knife in farther.

'Please,' Faith pleaded. 'You're right. You needed to do what you did. You *don't* need to kill me. I have nothing to do with all this. Please, I have two small children....' She was begging for her life.

'No, Connie.' Robert Harcourt strode into the center of the room. Without letting go of her weapon, Connie threw herself at his feet, a dog come to heel.

'No, Connie,' he repeated loudly. 'I've been in your office for the last few minutes, not believing what I've been hearing.'

Faith wished he had thought to step in a little sooner. She could feel blood oozing from her wound, and aside from the fact that several articles of designer clothing, including a silk Lejaby camisole, were irreparably ruined, she knew she needed stitches – immediately.

'I think we should call the—' she started to say when Connie's paroxysm of sobs drowned out all else.

'You can't say you don't know that I love you! Have loved you from the beginning! And you love me, too. I've always known it. We can leave right now. Even if she' – she paused, and the distaste in her voice was evident; between Freer and Connie, Faith hadn't been making a whole lot of friends at Mansfield lately – 'calls the police immediately, it will be awhile before they get here. We could tie her up. Yes, that's it. Tie her up and get to the airport. Start another school, where no one will ever find us. I have quite a nest egg saved up, and it's all yours. Ours. We can stop at the bank.'

Robert Harcourt was aghast, and revolted, all six foot one, 180 pounds of him, the latest 'Hgt./Wgt.' entry.

'But I loved my wife. Surely you knew that. Yes, she had some weaknesses. I didn't care. She was so beautiful, so charming; of course men flocked to her. But she was everything to me.'

'You can't mean this,' Connie gasped. 'More than the school?'

'More than the school,' Robert said, and without actually kicking the woman prostrate at his feet, he made the gesture. She stood up. Her face was drained of color and emotion. It was as if Robert had taken an eraser to a blackboard, obliterating all that had been written on it. Only in this case, the blackboard had been Connie Reed's life.

She reached into the depths of her soul and tried one more time. 'I thought Mansfield – and I – stood for something special, that you and I stood for something together. *Veritas et Bonitas.* Remember the day we composed the motto? You told me it was perfect. That I was perfect.'

Faith wished Connie would stop. It was excruciatingly painful to listen to the woman debase herself, detailing years of living a fantasy.

Robert cut her off. 'Please don't make this any more difficult than it already is. I need to call the police now.' He walked behind his desk to the phone.

And Constance 'Firmness' Reed did stop talking. Comprehension dawned and she looked at the man she had loved in vain for so many years – had worshiped – and with great deliberation, slowly plunged the knife she was holding into her own breast before Faith, or Robert Harcourt, could stop her.

The headmaster froze, and Faith grabbed the phone away from him, punching 911 at last. She looked at Harcourt, who was now stooped over the dying woman, and thought in frustration, How clueless could the man have been? He'd worked with the woman for over twenty-five years. She'd put her picture on his computer, and practically bowed and/or had an orgasm whenever he entered the room. Did he need it spelled out more than that?

Apparently so.

Faith had had enough of Carleton House and assumed the boys felt the same way, so she moved the locale for the pièce de résistance student dinner to her own house. In the process, the guest list had grown. Several of the boys had invited girls from Cabot, Brian Perkins had asked Dan Miller, and Faith added Pix and Sam. Then Daryl wanted the Averys. Faith herself extended an invitation to Mrs Mallory and Mabel. Only Mabel had accepted. Mrs Mallory gave work as an excuse, even though Faith had offered to help her get the Saturday lunch ready ahead of time. It was exactly a week since her encounter with Connie Reed. So long as no one clapped her on the back, Faith felt fine. Impulsively, she'd also called Lorraine Kennedy earlier, and the detective had said she'd try to drop by at the very least.

The boys had been hard at work all morning, and now that they'd gone back to school to change, Faith stood in the doorway, surveying the table. It was set perfectly and Zach had made place cards on the computer. For a centerpiece, they'd tucked small pots of bright yellow and deep blue primroses into a basket, covering the tops with Spanish moss.

'Like the egg, Spanish moss is your friend,' Faith had told them. 'Get an all-purpose basket lined with plastic and change the pots of flowers with the seasons, hiding the dirt with the moss.

Tom walked in. Ben had wanted to eat with the big kids and Faith had promised him he could return for dessert, but at the moment he was next door with his sister and Samantha, who had come home from college for this very reason.

'You've taught these boys a lot in a very short time,' Tom said. 'They – and a whole bunch of people in their future – should be very grateful. Dad will be here any minute. Where have you put him?' Marian had left the day before on her cruise and Dick Fairchild was coming for the weekend.

'At my right, and next to Sinclair Smith, because they're both such sailors. Boy/girl isn't exactly working here, but I always thought that was pretty stupid anyway. Like the ark.'

'The ark wasn't stupid, honey. Without it, we wouldn't be having this shindig,' Tom said in mock seriousness. His wife punched him lightly. The boys came back, and for the next few hours, the parsonage would be filled with food, conversation, and laughter.

'Mrs Mallory sent these, and a note,' Mabel said, thrusting a large box into Faith's hands. It was filled with cookies, which the boys greeted with delight. Faith had taught them to make delectable flourless chocolate cakes for dessert, but the cookies would fill in any corners.

'You'd better read the note,' Mabel advised. 'And I'll go see if I can lend a hand.'

James Elliot came through the door carrying one of the bread baskets. 'Oh no you don't. *We're* cooking today! And we're really cooking.'

With Harcourt's support, Patsy Avery and Tom had made themselves available to any students who wanted to talk about Winston Freer, and any of the other recent events at the school. Tom had commented on the sensitive way Patsy handled the kids and how he'd enjoyed the way they'd worked together. He was hoping to set something up permanently – there and at Aleford High. No more Freer disciples had surfaced – or perhaps were not admitting it – but a number of other kids had come to talk to them, among them James. He'd been powerfully affected by the events of the last weeks and had decided to defer admission to whatever school accepted him in order to participate in Boston's City Year, a post-high school community service program where he'd live and work with people very different from himself.

Settling Mabel in the living room with Tom, his father, who'd just arrived, and a 'tetch' of sherry, Faith opened the note from Mansfield's cook.

Dear Mrs Fairchild,
I owe you an apology. I'm the one who's been spoiling your ingredients. I guess I just didn't like having another cook

around, even for a little while. I'm deeply ashamed of myself and anytime you want to come to Mansfield to teach the boys, I hope you will and not let the actions of a foolish old woman stand in your way. Come and have some coffee in the kitchen soon.

Sincerely,

Evangeline Elizabeth Mallory

P.S. If you took the olive oil from the cabinet next to the sink at Carleton House, don't use it.

Faith tucked the note in her apron pocket. She was definitely going to save it. And she would go over and have coffee.

The meal started with carrot ginger soup, 'very easy but elegant', Faith had told the boys during the class on soups. Almost any vegetable with an onion or some other seasoning thrown in could be heated in chicken broth – canned for these cooks – until the vegetable was soft enough to puree in a blender. They'd added some light cream and powdered Jamaican ginger to produce today's soup. The main course was also simple. They had made Daryl's grandmother's smothered pork chops with her secret spices, which she had revealed to her beloved grandson. While the pork chops had smothered – producing a delectable gravy – the boys had made mounds of mashed potatoes and steamed green beans with a hint of garlic. Patsy had insisted on bringing corn bread and there were some rolls from Boston's wonder baker, Iggy. It was a feast, and even the slender Cabot student Zach had invited asked for seconds. He'd introduced her to Faith with more than a hint of mischief in his eye. 'Mrs Fairchild, this is Susan Beach. Susan, Mrs Fairchild.' Zach had been a quick study when it came to *that* list of Sloane's.

Plates were cleared and everyone stood up to stretch before dessert was served. The boys and their friends disappeared to pop the chocolate cakes into the oven.

'I feel like taking a walk around the block. Maybe several blocks,' Sam Miller said. 'I hope Brian passes on some of what he learned to Dan.'

It hadn't taken the Millers long to get used to calling their son this, and the name Danny seemed to belong to the distant past. In a way, it all did.

'Speaking of walking, someone walking across your grave?' Will Avery asked, only partly in jest. 'You look so serious, Faith.'

'I was just thinking about what's happened, how it seems like a long time ago already. But it wasn't – isn't.'

'You don't betray the dead you loved by not grieving hard every minute,' Mabel said. The woman had intuited what was really bothering her, Faith realized – that three people had died and here she was eating pork chops. She couldn't say she had loved them, but she did mourn them. And they had been loved by others, even Connie. The faculty and students had been the most upset by her death. She was a fixture at Mansfield, a kind of matriarch. One of the boys had summed it up this morning when they were all together getting ready. 'Who's going to take care of everyone at school now?' he'd asked.

And Sloane Buxton. Dead before his eighteenth birthday. She thought about his parents, his room, his dreams of the Ivy League since childhood – escape into a world that measured success by the right brands and the right genes. He'd been fertile ground for the seeds Winston Freer had to sow, and the two had become inextricably entwined in one noxious growth. But dead before his eighteenth birthday. Sloane was just a kid.

Faith had been deep in her thoughts and hadn't realized there was someone at the door until Tom escorted Lorraine Kennedy into the living room. She was wearing black woolen pants and an attractive turquoise sweater. Her hair was loose – and her makeup was still wrong.

'You're just in time for dessert,' Faith said.

'Then I'm a lucky girl,' the detective said. 'I talked to John this morning and he told me whatever else I had to do today, forget it and get over here if you were serving food.'

'Cake,' John MacKenzie said succinctly from the doorway, and they all returned to the table.

Faith and Lorraine trailed the others.

'He also said to try not to find any more bodies until he got back,' Lorraine said. Then she added, 'But I'm getting out of line here. What you went through, are going through, is nothing to joke about.'

The woman's Boston accent sounded stronger.

'It's all right,' Faith said. Today was making it all right. She was glad Detective Kennedy had joined them. Here's my chance, Faith thought. 'Maybe we could get together for lunch sometime. A fun thing to do is go to Bloomingdale's and get a makeover at one of the cosmetics counters.'

'You don't like my makeup.' It wasn't a question.

Faith linked her arm in Lorraine's. 'I don't like your makeup.'

'Well, why didn't you just come out and say so, for Gawd's sake?' Lorraine laughed. 'Now, I want some of that cake and everything else I missed. I'll work backward.'

The kids were in high spirits. In the kitchen, they'd put some Jimmy Cliff on Dan's sound system – his well and truly. He'd taken money out of his bank account after telling his parents how much he owed. Faith started to tell Zach to go turn it off, but then 'Many Rivers to Cross' started playing. Her favorite. She looked around the table and thought of all the rivers they'd crossed and all the ones to come. Dick Fairchild had been talking about sailing with Sinclair, but Sinclair had turned to Patsy on his other side and Dick was looking wistful. Maybe he was imagining Marian with a stud muffin, binoculars looped about a muscular bronzed neck; maybe he wanted more cake; or maybe he was thinking he would never, ever again let his wife go on a trip alone and leave him behind.

John MacKenzie was talking with the girl he'd brought, who

was similarly serious-looking, but she was one of those girls with glasses straight out of an old movie where someone says, 'Why Miss so-and-so, I never dreamed you were so pretty!' when her spectacles are removed. Faith had been afraid John would want to invite Paul Boothe and had debated telling the boys no faculty guests. She'd mentioned it to Zach, who had hastened to reassure her that some of the bloom was off the rose, Boothe's feet having developed definite clay-like properties. 'Maybe John's just pissed at not getting into the class, but it's more seeing the guy stoned or loaded a lot. I don't think you have to worry about Paul Boothe coming to our party,' Zach had said.

Then there was Daryl. Daryl looking like a kid again. Daryl – where it had all started. He would carry the searing memory of the noose on his bed, the hate mail, and the clippings forever. She hoped it wouldn't make him bitter, then chided herself. How could it not? And it should. Make us all bitter. Not poisoned, but very, very bitter.

Ben came running into the room. Faith saw a look of annoyance cross his face as he realized they had already started dessert without him. She opened her mouth to head him off at the pass. Instead, she heard Dan, who was sitting next to her, say, 'Hey, little buddy, come over here. Your cake is waiting.'

He pulled Ben on to his lap.

Faith saw Pix beaming at the two boys, maternal pride on her face. Dan's latest math test had been a very respectable C+. For the moment, the lid was on next door.

All these boys. What kind of men would they be? She'd learned more than she wanted to know about what it meant to be an adolescent in these times, but what she had learned had been an affirmation in the end. These were fine boys, crossing rivers deep and shallow, each in his own way, each with courage – and dumb luck. Still, she wished she could slow life down and give both her children more years of childhood, a buffer against learning names for things Faith hadn't known existed until she was so much older than the teenagers here at the table. She suddenly realized she'd heard Marian say the very same thing about Tom and her other children – it all went too fast. Whistler's mother, Adam and Eve's – well, forget that, they didn't have a mother – all mothers back to the beginning had probably said or thought the very same thing. She smiled to herself; she'd tell Tom later.

Dan and Brian Perkins were talking about computers. It sounded as if they were speaking in code. Ben was demolishing his cake. Some was above his right eyebrow, but she knew enough to resist the urge to reach over with her napkin and wipe it off. Now they were talking about sonic games they wanted. Ben piped up with his own opinions. She listened in surprise. He seemed extremely knowledgeable.

She listened in surprise – and more than a little alarm.

The pulse of the reggae music was continuing to drift out from the kitchen – 'You Can Get It If You Really Want'. She felt herself relax, and took the words to heart: 'Try and try. You'll succeed at last'.

She'd keep trying.